A Week in
BRIGHTON

TIMELESS *Regency* COLLECTION

A Week in
BRIGHTON

Jennifer Moore

Annette Lyon

Donna Hatch

Copyright © 2020 Mirror Press
Print edition
All rights reserved

No part of this book may be reproduced or distributed in any form whatsoever without prior written permission of the publisher, except in the case of brief passages embodied in critical reviews and articles. These novels are works of fiction. The characters, names, incidents, places, and dialog are products of the authors' imaginations and are not to be construed as real.

Interior Design by Cora Johnson
Edited by Kelsey Down, and Lisa Shepherd
Cover design by Rachael Anderson
Cover Photo Credit: Martha Keyes
Cover background: Deposit Photos #30255627

Published by Mirror Press, LLC

A Week in Brighton is a Timeless Romance Anthology® book

Timeless Romance Anthology® is a registered trademark of Mirror Press, LLC

ISBN: 978-1-952611-10-0

TIMELESS REGENCY COLLECTIONS:

Autumn Masquerade
A Midwinter Ball
Spring in Hyde Park
Summer House Party
A Country Christmas
A Season in London
A Holiday in Bath
A Night in Grosvenor Square
Road to Gretna Green
Wedding Wagers
An Evening at Almack's
A Week in Brighton
To Love a Governess
Widows of Somerset
A Christmas Promise

Table of Contents

The Grande Hotel by the Sea
by Jennifer Moore _____ 1

Signs of Love
by Annette Lyon _____ 97

The Reluctant Heir
by Donna Hatch _____ 187

The Grande Hotel by the Sea

Jennifer Moore

1

ARTHUR GRANDE WAS PLEASED to find his hotel suite was less than satisfactory. The rugs were faded, the rooms drafty, and the view from the windows marred by a warehouse in desperate need of paint. He rolled up a stack of schematics and architectural drawings and slid them into his satchel, then double-checked that the contracts, lease agreements, titles, and other documents were in order—not that he doubted the competency of his solicitor, Mr. Fawcett, in the least—but today's meeting was extremely important, and arriving at the site unprepared would not do at all. First impressions were everything.

He checked his presentation once more in the mirror, straightened his cravat, locked the door, and started down to the dining room, noting with a pleased nod the musty smell of the staircase—yet another aspect in his favor. Brighton was in need of a luxury hotel, and as luck would have it, that endeavor was precisely what had brought Arthur Grande to Sussex in the first place.

Mr. Fawcett stood when Arthur entered the room, and Arthur was not surprised to see that the man's collar was freshly starched and his cravat tied in a splendid knot. The solicitor was always immaculately attired. "Good morning, sir. I know you're likely too overwrought with nerves to have an appetite"—Mr. Fawcett motioned to the breakfast table—"but a meal will do you good. And you'll need your energy today."

The man was correct. The sight of eggs and sausage turned Arthur's anxious stomach, but he obediently put a piece of toast onto his plate and poured a cup of tea. "Thank you."

Mr. Fawcett settled back into his seat, opened the newspaper, and tucked into his breakfast. The solicitor was past his sixtieth year, but one would hardly know it based on the man's energy—and his appetite. He had served the Grande family for thirty years, since before Arthur was born, and knew both the man and his finances better than even Arthur.

Arthur buttered the toast and took a reluctant bite.

"You have everything?" Mr. Fawcett pointed with his fork at the satchel.

"Yes." Arthur handed the bag across the table, knowing the detail-oriented solicitor wouldn't be satisfied unless he inspected the documents with his own eyes.

Mr. Fawcett looked through the papers. "All in order." He gave a nod, flipped over the satchel's flap, and fastened the buckle. He set it on the floor beside his chair and returned to his breakfast, mopping up a drip of yolk with his toast as he read the *Times*.

Arthur took a sip of tea and tapped a finger on the table, wishing the older man would eat faster. He'd planned and worked and waited years for this day.

The final titles and contracts had been signed over six months earlier, loans had been negotiated and plans had been drawn, and at last today the real work would begin. He glanced at his pocket watch. They were not expected at the site for another hour, but they had arrived in town late last evening, and Arthur was eager to see the property again.

He'd first come to Brighton years earlier in search of a location for his hotel. Mr. Pickering, the land broker, had shown him various sites. They'd visited the hills of the downs and properties throughout the town, but when Arthur saw the block of the mismatched cluster of warehouses, shops, and tenement buildings directly facing the beach, he knew it was the perfect spot for The Grande Hotel by the Sea. Purchasing the properties had been a test in patience. While some of the shops were leased or rented from the same owner, many were independently owned, and negotiating various loans and transactions had been complicated and time-consuming—not that Mr. Fawcett was the least bit incapable of such an undertaking.

But now the final lease was expired, the initial plans were drawn, and Arthur would begin working in earnest with the builders, engineers, and craftsmen. His dream was becoming a reality.

Arthur patted his coat pocket, ensuring his pocketbook was inside. Supplies and materials had already been purchased, and others were on order. Thank goodness Mr. Fawcett was such a fastidious bookkeeper. Arthur's mind spun with the immensity of the project, and a thrill of anticipation moved through him. He stood, unable to sit still a moment longer. "I'll meet you at the site." Arthur put on his hat, grabbed his walking stick, and pushed in his chair.

Mr. Fawcett nodded. "The clean air will do you good, sir. I'll be along presently." He lifted the satchel. "And I'll bring the documents."

Arthur stepped outside as an ocean breeze rushed past. He grabbed hold of his hat lest it blow away. The street where he was staying was narrow, with high buildings on either side funneling the wind from the ocean. He set off at a quick pace. This early in the morning, the roadway was nearly empty. But that would change in just a few months as soon as the Season ended and high society turned its attention to the coast and the latest health craze: the sea-water cure. Bathing machines would line the beach, and vendors and pleasure seekers would crowd the walkways. Each year the city became more popular for both recreation and health-improvement purposes. And when the prince regent had begun renovating his pleasure pavilion, making it into an Oriental-style palace, Brighton had fairly exploded with tourists.

Arthur emerged from the street and stepped onto the smaller road that followed the rocky shoreline. The sea spread out before him. He slowed his pace and breathed in deeply. Overhead, seagulls glided, their calls distant beneath the sound of the waves. Further down the beach, fishermen spread out their nets on the rocks. The water was a light-grey color, broken by the frothy white crests of waves. Arthur thought he could never tire of the view. Only a few other people were out for a morning seaside stroll, and the air felt crisp and the day full of possibilities.

Arthur put his hands on his hips, closing his eyes, and inhaled a deep breath, enjoying the feel of the cool air on his skin.

A breeze blew past, followed by a sudden gust that lifted his hat from his head.

He whipped around, grasping for it as it flew off. When it landed on the rocks, another gust picked it up, rolling it down the beach.

The hat blew past a young woman walking up the path toward him. She snatched at it but missed. She glanced toward him, then turned around and hurried after it.

Arthur ran to catch up to her.

The hat landed on a patch of prickly grass but blew away before the woman reached it.

She smiled at Arthur when he drew near. "I suppose we'd better give chase." Her eyes were bright and filled with amusement.

Arthur couldn't help but grin in return. "Surely it will tire before we do." He chuckled and swept his arm in an exaggerated invitation for her to precede him. "Tallyho, then, miss."

As if in answer, a swirl of wind blew the hat up and away, and the two broke into a run. The hat landed, bouncing along the rocks ahead of them, and seemed to jump away when one of the pair reached for it. They scampered across the beach, climbing over driftwood, scooting around large rocks, and no doubt looking extremely comical to anyone who might be watching. The hat evaded them again and again, and each time, their laughter grew with the absurdity of the situation.

Finally, the hat settled on a flat rocky area. Arthur sprinted forward. He kicked out with his foot to trap it, but unfortunately his step was too well placed, and the hat was crushed beneath his boot.

He and the woman stopped and stared first at the hat, then at each other. They were both panting. Her hair was in shambles beneath her bonnet, honey-colored locks falling around her flushed face.

"Oh, what a pity." She burst into laughter, bending down and lifting the remains of the headpiece. The hat's crown was smashed and split apart from the brim on one side. The woman peered at Arthur through the opening. "I think it is quite done for."

Arthur bent at the waist, catching his breath with hands on his knees. "Poor chap." He took the hat from her. "It put up a good fight."

She brushed the hair from her face. "I'm sorry, sir. This is not the outcome you'd hoped for."

He squeezed the hat's crown, pushing from the inside, trying to reshape it, but the hat was well and truly finished.

"You might as well have allowed it to fly out to sea," she said.

"I think that's what it wanted, the sly devil." Arthur scowled at the offending headpiece.

The woman nodded, putting on a serious expression, though her eyes still sparkled and her mouth fought against a smirk. "Top hats can be very crafty."

The smile broke through, and it was utterly fetching. The expression was not restrained like those cultivated by proper ladies in London, but an honest grin. Seeing it muddled his thoughts for a moment. Arthur cleared his throat and shook his head. "Have you an idea where I might find a hatter in this town? Or a men's clothier?"

"You're a visitor." She nodded. "I wondered why I hadn't seen you before. Not a very nice welcome, I'm afraid." She glanced at the hat and then toward the town. "Brambles and Guff Haberdashery is on Broad Street, there." She pointed to a side street that was directly in front of them. "Your hat almost led you right to it."

"Thank you, miss . . ." He stepped back up from the beach to the roadway and offered a hand to assist her, realizing he'd not introduced himself. "I—"

"Sir!" Mr. Fawcett strode toward them, the satchel banging against his leg as he hurried down the pathway. "I've been looking for you."

"I had a bit of a mishap." Arthur released her hand and turned. He held up the hat. "We'll need to make a brief stop at . . ." He turned back to the young woman, raising his brows.

"Brambles and Guff," she repeated.

"Yes. It is just down Broad Street," Arthur pointed with his walking stick.

"Then we've no time to waste," Mr. Fawcett consulted his pocket watch, then his eyes widened and his expression took on a tinge of panic. Few things were more important to the solicitor than punctuality. He inclined his head, lifting his hat in a farewell. "Pardon us, young lady." He started toward Broad Street.

"Thank you for your assistance, miss. If you'll excuse us." Arthur held the remains of his hat over his head, tipping it forward in farewell. The top flopped over, eliciting a smile from his companion.

She dipped in a curtsey.

Arthur started away after Mr. Fawcett, but he stopped and turned back toward the woman. "I wonder ... do you walk here often?"

"Every morning."

"Good. I mean, very well." He winced at his awkward reply and out of habit moved to put his hat onto his head, but he caught himself and tucked it under his arm instead, giving another bow. "Good day to you." He walked quickly to catch up to his solicitor. "A very good day indeed," he muttered to himself as he stepped onto the paving stones of Broad Street.

DAPHNE DAYLEY TAPPED THE top of a raisin bun and, satisfied that it was sufficiently cool, took the batch from the pan, placing them one by one on a tray and sliding it beneath the glass display counter.

She glanced at the other trays of baked goods, taking a mental inventory. The shelf of rye buns was still full, but the sweet breads had all sold earlier today than usual. Perhaps she'd send Mary to fetch some gooseberries, and they could fill the space with tarts.

Daphne stepped through the doorway into the kitchen just as Ruth pulled the first pan of meat pies from the oven. "We should have some very pleased customers." Daphne nodded at the golden-brown pastries and inhaled the savory aroma. "The pies smell divine."

Ruth set down the hot pan on the preparation table and went back for another. "You appear very happy today, Miss Dayley."

"Do I?" Daphne grasped the side of the pie pan with a towel, sliding it over the table to make room for the next.

Ruth paused. She leaned her head back to scrutinize Daphne through the spectacles resting low on her nose. "You've been smiling, humming even." She set down the pan and wiped her forehead with the back of her hand. "Ever since you came in from your morning walk to the bank."

"I can't imagine why." Daphne shrugged and used a spatula to take the warm pastries from the pan and slide them onto a tray. She made certain to keep her face turned downward so her countenance didn't give away more than it already had.

"Neither can I." Ruth slid two more pans into the oven, then pulled a ball of pie pastry from the cooler and used a pin to roll it flat. "Not with ..." She motioned with her chin toward the west wall of the shop.

Daphne's stomach went hard at the reminder of the construction that was due to begin any day, and a tinge of dread threatened the happy feeling. But she maintained a pleasant expression. "Perhaps it's the fine weather." She hadn't told either Ruth or the woman's daughter, Mary, about the encounter with the handsome gentleman and his hat.

Typically she would have recounted the meeting with her two employees, and the three would have happily laughed and speculated about the stranger for days. But today, gossip didn't feel right. Although it would have been a pleasant change from the tension, Daphne just couldn't bring herself to talk about anything but their daily tasks. Doing more would involve feelings and worry, and she just couldn't deal with the realities of the situation. If she allowed herself to wallow, she wasn't certain she'd recover. The reality was so overwhelming that Daphne put it out of her mind completely. When it was time to worry, she'd worry. But until then, she had a business to manage. And an amusing encounter with a handsome gentleman was just the thing to distract her mind.

The bell over the bakery door rang, and Daphne hurried through the doorway from the kitchen.

Mary's arms were filled with groceries. She stepped around the door and closed it with her hip. Mary was much curvier than her mother, and her face was soft and rounded where Ruth's features were sharp and stern. The two women, Ruth and Mary Coombs, had worked in Our Dayley Bread since Daphne was a young girl, and she considered them the perfect team. Ruth kept the kitchen tidy and orderly. Her recipes were exact, and she measured each ingredient carefully. Mary, on the other hand, chatted and laughed with the customers. She cooked with messy abandon, adding a pinch of this and a dash of that, and never kept a record of exactly how her recipes were made, but each baked item came out delicious all the same.

Daphne stepped between the chairs and tables of the dining area and took a bag of flour from under her employee's arm.

"I noticed the sweet breads were sold." Mary shifted one of the parcels to her other arm. "So I purchased some berries to make . . ."

"Tarts." The two said the word at the same time.

"Excellent idea." Daphne grinned as she hefted the flour onto her hip and started toward the kitchen.

Mary pulled aside a curtain and looked through the front window. "They're out there, you know."

"Who is out there?" Daphne lowered the flour sack onto the floor and joined her.

"Builders," Mary said. "Recognized Bob Simper and his crew."

Daphne saw movement among the buildings beside the bakery. "Some gentlemen as well," she said, seeing a few of the men wore coats and top hats.

"Suppose those are the ones with the blunt," Mary said. "Bankers and what have you. They were signing papers and looking at sheets of plans when I walked past."

Daphne scowled. "They should find a proper office for their business instead of making such a display." She picked up the flour and took it into the kitchen, letting it drop onto the floor by the side table. She tugged apart the strings on the top of the sack and scooped out cupsful of flour into a bowl for the tart crust. She worked a bit too forcefully, and a cloud of white puffed over her face and hair.

Mary had followed her into the kitchen and was helping her mother prepare the next batches of meat pies. The silence in the room was strained, and Daphne could feel the other women's unspoken conversation behind her back. She snatched a towel and brushed the flour off her face, then started pulling off the stems and ends from the berries.

She dropped the berries into a pot as she worked. Typically the repetitive motions would have soothed her nerves, but not today. Not with the reminder that this was all to come to an end, and soon.

Ruth carried the trays of cooled pies through the doorway to load the display trays.

"Move the rye buns to the top shelf, Ruth." Daphne set the bowl of flour onto the preparation table and took the crock of butter from the cooling chest. "Mary, please finish the crust for the tarts. The midday rush will begin any minute." Of course neither of the women needed to be told—they'd spent more hours in the bakery than Daphne—but the silence was too much.

Daphne checked that the oven fire was burning steadily, then left the kitchen to help Ruth behind the counter. The pair worked quickly, transferring the pies and arranging the trays in the display case.

When the bell over the door rang, Daphne smoothed her apron and turned.

In a delightful surprise, the gentleman from the beach entered the bakery. The older man she'd seen him with earlier accompanied him.

She smiled, wiping the grease on her fingers onto a towel as pleasant warmth replaced the unease in the shop.

"It smells marvelous." The gentleman closed the door behind him.

"Very nice." His older companion patted his belly. "I shouldn't mind a meat pie and perhaps a bun or two."

Daphne came around the counter into the dining area.

When the younger man's gaze met hers, his eyes widened, then his brows pulled together. He was obviously taken off guard, seeing her so soon after their first meeting.

"Hello again," Daphne said. "I see you found a new hat. I do hope it behaves better than the last."

The man glanced at his friend, then back at her. He looked slightly uneasy.

She wondered again if he was taken by surprise.

"Yes." He blinked and his smile returned, but it appeared to be rather strained. After a moment's hesitation, he removed the hat and showed it to her, displaying it this way and that with a flourish so that she might see it from every angle. "I do as well. I particularly asked Mr. Brambles for a hat that did not possess a predisposition for sea bathing."

"A wise precaution." She nodded sagely and couldn't help but smile at the silly banter. "Now, what can I do for you?"

He glanced around the bakery. "You ... work here, miss?"

She raised a brow and smirked, giving him a flat stare and indicating the flour covered apron she wore. "I do." She curtseyed. "Daphne Dayley."

The man winced, and his friend glanced up at him.

A sliver of unease moved through her. The men were certainly acting strange.

"Miss Dayley," the older man said. "How do you do?" He lifted his hat. "Donald Fawcett."

The other man cleared his throat and twisted around the hat in his hand. "And I'm Arthur Grande." He enunciated the name, grimacing.

Cold hit Daphne's core. She stepped back. "*You're Arthur Grande?*" She forced out the words, feeling like they choked her throat. She had cursed that very name for months. She'd fantasized about what she would say if she ever met the man, and now here he was, standing in her bakery holding his blasted hat and *flirting* with her.

A surge of anger made her skin hot and her sight redden. Every thought flew from her mind as she stared at this man who'd *pretended*... while... She shook her head, fighting to keep her breathing calm and took another step back, every muscle tightening as her mind grappled with the realization. She had been taken in... deceived by none other than... *him*.

Mr. Fawcett looked between the two. He cleared his throat, looking supremely unconcerned with the tension that hung in the air like a wet curtain. "Ah yes, Miss Dayley. We do have a matter of business that should come as no surprise..." He clasped his hands in front of him. "Just before Christmas of last year, you were sent an eviction notice..."

She folded her arms and scowled at both Mr. Fawcett and Mr. Grande. *Thank you for the reminder. What a delightful Christmas gift it was.* If she'd been capable of shooting daggers from her eyes, she would have done it gladly.

Both men pulled back, giving her a small amount of pleasure that her glare had been sufficiently potent.

"And...?" she asked, daring him to continue.

Mr. Fawcett blinked as if confused by her question, or more likely her tone.

"And, you are... ah... still... here." Mr. Grande motioned around the room.

Daphne clenched her jaw. "One moment, if you please."

She went behind the counter and through the kitchen to the small box where she kept papers and legal documents. After a quick search, she fetched the letter as well as her lease agreement and land-tax receipt. The sight of her mother's handwriting on the contract made her throat tight, which just added to her fury.

She returned to the dining room, glancing at the family picture that hung on the wall beside the door to the kitchen. Her parents and grandmother looked at her with painted eyes. Her own much younger eyes watched, her painted figure sitting on her father's lap, and Daphne felt extremely aware of her own failure.

The bell over the door rang, and a group of fishermen came inside.

"Good afternoon to you, gentlemen." Daphne gave a wide smile. "Chicken pies today." She knew the men, of course. Until the last few years, when so many people had moved to Brighton, she'd known every person in the town. "Mr. Taylor, how are Sarah and the baby?"

The fisherman smiled, crinkling his weathered skin. "Happy and healthy, both. Though I wouldn't mind if that little one slept a bit more."

Daphne returned behind the counter. She set down the papers and wrapped a loaf of bread and two raisin muffins, handing the parcel to Mr. Taylor. "Tell Sarah I'll be by to call on her soon."

He tipped his head forward. "Much thanks. She'll be pleased to hear you asked after her."

She chatted for a moment with the customers in an extra cheery voice to make certain there was no question as to the extent of her displeasure when she returned to speaking to the other men.

Mr. Grande and Mr. Fawcett had taken a small table in

the corner. They stood when Daphne joined them and then returned to their seats.

She sat tall in her chair and turned through the pages of the lease agreement until she found what she was looking for. "If you read the second paragraph of section four carefully, gentlemen, you will see the agreement clearly states that notice to quit must be given half a year before the expiration of the lease. If land taxes are paid and rent is maintained"—she slid the other papers forward without looking up, though she could feel Mr. Grande studying her—"which they clearly are, the tenant is guaranteed possession for six months once acquainted in writing." She handed the eviction letter across the table. "As you can see by the messenger's receipt, this letter was received December 5th, 1814."

Mr. Fawcett took his spectacles from his pocket, adjusting them on his nose as he studied the letter, then handed it to Mr. Grande.

He glanced at it, then returned to watching her.

Daphne gave the lease agreement to the solicitor. "Today's date, as I'm certain you are aware, is May 29th. So you see, gentlemen, these premises are mine for one week more."

Mr. Fawcett read the paragraph she'd indicated. "It appears you are right, Miss Dayley. You are indeed entitled to retain occupancy until June 5th."

"Thank you." Daphne took the papers and stood. "If that is all, I bid you good day."

The men rose as well.

"Miss Dayley," Mr. Grande said. "If I may . . ."

She tapped her foot. "Yes?"

"It doesn't seem . . ." He motioned to the bakery. "You don't appear to be . . . preparing to vacate."

She straightened the papers, tapping them once on the

table. "Mr. Grande, right now, my concern is preparing for luncheon customers. If you've no other business to discuss..."

"Luncheon sounds delightful," Mr. Fawcett said, apparently oblivious to the tension.

"Mary will serve you." She lifted her chin to indicate the woman behind the counter. "And Mr. Grande, there is a special price for the building's owner." Daphne gave a sweet smile.

He raised his brows. "Oh?"

"We will charge you double." She spun on her heel and marched away.

The effect of her exit was somewhat dampened by the sound of Mr. Grande chuckling behind her.

3

ARTHUR ARRIVED AT THE building site just as dawn broke, and he was pleasantly surprised to find the work crews had arrived even earlier. The buildings that had been silent and dark were now a bustle of activity and noise. Lantern light glowed in the windows, and voices and hammering echoed in the empty buildings.

He looked toward the sea, watching the emerging daylight play on the waves and enjoying the long anticipated satisfaction of his dream finally becoming a reality.

Turning back toward the buildings, he glanced at Our Dayley Bread. Light shone in those windows as well, and he imagined the three women were inside rolling and kneading, and Miss Dayley was expressly ignoring the chaos surrounding them.

The aroma of baking reached him, and his stomach growled in response. He'd taken his midday meal at the bakery again the day before and had found the food—in spite of its exorbitant price—to be exceptional. And the baker—he smirked, thinking of Miss Dayley's parting shot two days earlier—strong-willed didn't begin to describe the woman. But he was certain hurt was beneath her anger, and for that, he intended to make amends.

Bob Simper waved as he came up the road with another man.

Although Arthur didn't recognize the builder's companion, he knew him by reputation, and a thrill moved through him. Today he was to meet in person the gas plumber, Lewis Wells. Interior gas lighting would set The Grande Hotel by the Sea apart, not only in Brighton but in all of England. He knew of only a very few buildings with such a modern feature, the most famous, of course, being the prince regent's own palace. And Lewis Wells was the man responsible for such a marvelous innovation.

The men were introduced and joined by the architect and engineer as they escorted the gas plumber into the old furniture warehouse.

"According to the plans, the reception desk will be located . . . near here?" Mr. Wells looked up from the roll of paper and pointed.

"Yes," Mr. Simper said. "This wall is coming down, and a row of pillars will line both this side of the lobby, and the other." He motioned toward the far side of the room.

"We hoped to have sconces on each of the pillars." Arthur pointed to the circles representing the pillars on the plans.

Mr. Wells nodded and made a note. "What is this area here?" he pointed to the far corner.

"Kitchens here." Arthur pointed. "With laundry facilities beneath. And here are the business offices."

"Some of the buildings are still separated, and we need to break down walls, set up a support system—arches and beams—and join them all together." Mr. Simper explained.

Mr. Wells nodded again. "I see. Somewhere . . . here"—he tapped near the offices—"we will need a closet for the gas valves and coal burner."

"Mr. Grande allocated this area for both gas pipes and water pipes." Mr. Miller, the architect, pointed. "Will that be sufficient?"

Mr. Wells muttered to himself as he ran his finger along the imaginary pipelines. After a moment, he looked up. "You are to have indoor water closets in every room?"

"Yes," Arthur said.

Mr. Wells nodded his approval. "Yes, this space will be sufficient. And I expect you intend to have gas lights outside as well?"

"Of course."

Mr. Wells looked back at the plans. "A separate gas source would be wise. Perhaps here..."

The tour lasted another hour, and by the time Mr. Wells took his leave, Arthur was extremely impressed by the gas plumber. He was very attentive to details, a quality that Arthur prized. He'd offered ideas, seen places where extra lighting would be beneficial, and come up with ways to be more cost-efficient. Arthur was confident the job was in the best hands.

Mr. Miller laid a sheet of plans out onto a wide board that rested between two barrels. The area near the door gave good light but was still sheltered, and it had become the project's unofficial office. He and Arthur set rocks on the corners of the paper and discussed the addition to the garden shed.

Hearing raised voices, Arthur excused himself and returned back inside to find the source.

The barrel-chested builder, Mr. Simper, was standing with a group of workers. He pointed toward one of the small stoves used for heating varnish. Next to the stove was a pile of oil-covered rags. "This cloth is filled with fumes." He kicked the rags away. "One spark, and this entire place would burn down. How many times do I have to tell you to keep used rags outside?"

One of the workers hurried to move the cloths away.

"I'm sorry, sir," another of the workers said. "I thought Garrick knew better."

"He does know." Mr. Simper said. "I reminded him yesterday. And the day before." He looked around at the group. "Where is Garrick?"

"Believe he's out back, sanding the new beams," one of the men said.

Simper stormed off, presumably to have a word with Mr. Garrick.

The idea of a fire destroying the building was terrifying. Arthur walked through the entire worksite, ensuring that none of the other stoves was near to rags or buckets of varnish or anything flammable. He spoke briefly to the head engineer and watched for a moment as supports were fixed into place in preparation for a wall to come down.

When Arthur returned to check on the architect's plans, he found two worried-looking workers at the makeshift table with Mr. Miller.

" . . . sent us away, sir, 'fore we could get the measurements," one of the men said.

"I'm not going back there," the other added.

Mr. Miller shook his head. "Miss Dayley is a small woman. I hardly think she warrants this level of fear."

"She threatened to call a constable."

"What is happening?" Arthur asked.

The architect hooked a thumb over his shoulder toward the bakery. "I sent these two to take measurements for your smoking lounge, sir. Per Mr. Wells's recommendation, the east wall will need to be adjusted for extra piping."

"And Miss Dayley . . . ?" Arthur prompted the workers.

"She yelled at us, sir. Threatened us. Said we're not to disturb her customers."

"She had a rolling pin, sir." The other man looked at the bakery with a frightened gaze. "Think she'd have pommeled us if we'd been slower."

Arthur quickly covered his mouth and looked toward the bakery as if contemplating what they'd said. After a moment he thought he had control enough to talk without laughing. "Shall I speak to her?" he asked with a voice that came out choked.

"Don't know if that's wise, sir, you bein' a dandy and all."

He tipped his head, thinking it was the first time he'd ever been considered in that light. Perhaps he should look into joining the local gentleman's pugilist club. "I think I shall be safe. Thank you for your concern."

"Good luck, sir." One of the workers removed his hat as if giving a solemn farewell.

Arthur took up his walking stick and strode toward the bakery, chuckling at the thought of Daphne Dayley frightening the dickens out of the workers. He felt very pleased for an opportunity—or an excuse—to see the young lady again. Throughout the past days he'd thought of her often. He had walked along the beach yesterday morning hoping to see her and had eaten a meat pie for luncheon, but he had yet to see her since their encounter at the bakery.

He pondered why it was that he wished to find someone who so obviously wished to avoid him. Perhaps it was guilt at the situation he'd unknowingly put her and her business in. While that may be part of it, the majority of the reason was something deeper. He'd felt a connection at their first meeting. And he thought she'd felt it too. For those few moments on the beach, she'd been unguarded and happy. The image of disheveled hair blowing about her flushed face while she laughed at his broken hat had entered his thoughts often over the past days.

Rather than guilt, he thought it was knowing that if he were not the man forcing her from her place of business, she might *like* him. But was a friendship with Miss Daphne Dayley even possible when he was Mr. Arthur Grande?

The bell rang when he opened the door, and the aromas of baking surrounded him. Arthur's stomach reacted as it had each time he'd entered the shop—with a loud growl.

He closed the door, and when he turned back around, his path was blocked by a very angry Daphne Dayley. And she was indeed holding a rolling pin.

Arthur let out a dramatic sigh. He removed his hat and hung it on a hook by the door. "I'd hoped it wouldn't come to this, Miss Dayley."

Her forehead wrinkled. "Come to what?"

"It appears we shall have to duel." He grasped the walking stick in the middle and tipped the end toward her. "Very well then; *en garde*."

She rolled her eyes, blowing out her breath in a huff, and turned back toward the kitchen.

Arthur caught her arm. "I am only teasing, miss."

"Well, it is not at all funny." She pulled away her arm and watched as he lowered his walking stick back down to the floor. "I suppose you're here on behalf of those ... witless clods?"

He fought back a smile, pressing a finger against his lips. "Well, that is rather harsh." He cleared his throat. "Apparently you ... ah ... threatened Mr. Simper's workers?"

She raised her chin and shrugged. "This business is still mine for four days. I will run it as I see fit."

"They were just doing their job."

Miss Dayley's gaze shifted to the side. "I did not want them disturbing my customers." The challenge in her voice lessened a bit.

"I don't see any—"

Her eyes flashed, but their anger seemed to fade. "If you are not here to purchase baked goods, then I'll ask you to leave. I am very busy."

Arthur glanced past her to a glass-domed cake stand. "Are those éclairs?"

Miss Dayley kept her gaze fixed steadily on him. "Yes."

"They look delicious." He stepped past her, looking closer at the pastries.

Miss Dayley walked behind the counter and lifted the lid.

"And the usual price?" Arthur asked. "Double for the owner?"

She put an éclair into a paper sack and handed it to him. "You may just take it."

Every bit of defiance was gone, and she looked exhausted—defeated.

"Miss Dayley." Arthur spoke seriously. "All of this—these business dealings . . . None of it is personal."

"When it affects a person, it is personal. And what you are doing affects a lot of persons."

Hearing the despair in her quiet voice caused a twinge of discomfort. She was partially right. But there was more to the story. And he needed her to understand. "But it does not affect every person negatively. The hotel will be a benefit to Brighton. It provides jobs and—"

"Not for Jim Garrick. You dismissed him today." She folded her arms, scowling. "He has a wife and two children. Will you tell *them* it is not personal?"

"I did not dismiss him, Miss Dayley. Mr. Simper did. And he did so because Mr. Garrick refused to follow safety procedures."

Miss Dayley glanced to the side. "I did not know the whole of it. But I do worry for his children."

Arthur leaned his forearms on the counter. "If I convince Mr. Simper to give Mr. Garrick a second chance, would that make you happy?"

"I don't think that is something you could ever do," she said.

"One conversation is all—" he began, as if he'd not understood her meaning.

She shook her head. "That is not what I meant, and you know it."

Arthur pretended to look startled. "Are you issuing me a challenge, miss? Questioning my ability to make you happy? Because you must know, when I put my mind to something, I do not fail."

"I am doing no such thing. I am simply telling you that you are the last person who would ever . . ." She shook her head. "You are the most . . . *infuriating* man I have ever met. You have the audacity to *flirt* with me—*you.*" She jabbed her finger toward him. "The same man who sent me an eviction notice less than a year after my mother died. This place"—she swept an arm around—"I grew up here. Made hot cross buns with my grandmother, learned to take orders and give change—this bakery is nothing but a plot of land to you, Mr. Grande, a chance to make money. But to me, to me, it . . . this is my heart."

Her outburst left her red-faced and trembling. A heaviness settled into Arthur's chest. "I did not do this to hurt you."

"Well, you did." She crossed her arms, deliberately not looking at him, and he suspected she was holding back tears.

"For that, I am sorry, Miss Dayley. I—"

The bell over the door rang, and they both turned to see Mr. Miller enter. He unrolled the schematic paper onto a table and looked around the room, his gaze coming to rest on the west wall of the bakery. "The problem's easy enough to fix, Mr. Grande." He took the pencil from behind his ear and made a note on the paper, then walked to the center of the room. "If we shift the entrance to the gentlemen's smoking lounge just two feet this way"—he moved his arms as if physically pulling the entrance to the side—"there will be enough room for the extra piping behind this wall here."

"You're making my grandmother's bakery into a smoking lounge?"

Her voice held no anger, only disbelief. Arthur carefully slid the rolling pin to the far side of the counter, out of her reach.

"Indeed, miss," Mr. Miller said. "With a tobacco bar and standing ashtrays. It will be quite popular with the gentlemen, I assure you."

Miss Dayley's jaw went tight, and her eyes narrowed. "Get out."

Arthur recognized the warning in her voice and snatched up his éclair before she could take it away. "Farewell, Miss Dayley." He hurried across the room, grabbing the paper from the table and turning the architect toward the exit. "Come along, Mr. Miller. Let us discuss this outside."

He lifted his hat from the hook, crammed it on his head, and practically shoved the man through the door, pulling it closed and feeling a wave of relief as though he'd escaped certain death by rolling pin. Not daring to even give a backward glance, he hurried Mr. Miller away from the bakery and back to the makeshift table to look over the plans.

The interaction with Miss Dayley had not gone at all how he wanted. Especially the end, when he'd feared for his life—but he still felt encouraged. He'd seen a crack in her battlements, and he knew that beneath the anger and hurt was the woman he'd met at the beach. Arthur had a plan, a purpose. He could make this woman happy. Fix the hurt he'd caused. And he hadn't exaggerated his claim. In this, he did not intend to fail.

4

AFTER SUNDAY'S CHURCH SERVICE, Daphne followed the congregation outside, but instead of continuing along to where people gathered on the grassy slopes near the road, she went around the side of the building. She walked the familiar paths through the gravestones until she came to the marker with her mother's name carved on its smooth face.

Margaret Bellingham Dayley
1766–1813

"Mother, what am I to do now?" she whispered, running her fingers over the words.

But just as it had each time over the past six months, the grave remained silent. And what did she expect? A ghost to appear and give her advice? A letter to fall from the heavens telling her exactly which way to turn? Either would be nice, she thought.

Daphne was exhausted, and though she would not admit it aloud, she was frightened. Following her parents' wishes had been easy enough. Go to school. Work at the bakery. But now, the direction she was to take was her choice alone, and she was terrified. *What if I fail?*

She rolled her eyes at that thought. She'd already failed. She hadn't completed her education; she hadn't kept the bakery running. How was she expected to develop a new plan when she couldn't manage to keep afloat the things that had been planned for her?

She walked slowly toward the road, considering her options, but she had very few. Mr. Cawston of Cawston's Baked Goods had offered to purchase her ovens and kitchen equipment. He'd even agreed to employ Ruth and Mary, which was an enormous relief. The money from the sale would be enough to live on for a while ... but what then? Should she purchase property for a new bakery? Go to Cornwall to care for her cousin's children? Join a gypsy caravan and read palms?

She gave a frustrated sigh.

"Daphne!"

Hearing the voice, she turned to see Sarah Taylor coming toward her, pushing a pram.

She waved at her friend and walked in her direction, meeting her at the road. "I've yet to see this little one," Daphne said. She peered into the pram and smiled at the sleeping baby. "He is beautiful," she whispered, touching the small fist.

Sarah beamed at the infant. "He is at that." She groaned. "But lud, I'm tired. If only Little Ronald would sleep so well at night."

Daphne chuckled.

Sarah turned the pram, and the pair walked toward the crowd of parishioners who gathered to visit in the churchyard. "Thank you for the bread and muffins, Daphne. Such a treat. I'll miss Our Dayley Bread."

"You're very welcome."

"What will you do now? Mr. Cawston mentioned you might come to work for him."

"I haven't decided yet," Daphne said. "But I suppose I must make a decision. And soon."

"Perhaps the bakery closing is a blessing," Sarah said. "Now you have the opportunity to do whatever you please."

A feeling of panic made Daphne's breath come fast, and she pushed it away quickly before it overcame her. "You're quite right." She forced a smile.

Seeing a feathered hat moving through the crowd toward her, Daphne glanced around for an escape. Before she could hide, Mrs. Libby, the vicar's wife, emerged from the gathering and made a beeline toward Daphne.

"Daphne Dayley, there you are." Mrs. Libby's short, round figure and her love of ruffles, ribbons, and pastel colors always reminded Daphne of an elaborately frosted cake. She took Daphne's arm. "How do you do, Mrs. Taylor? I hope you don't mind if I steal away your companion. There is someone I am simply *dying* to introduce Daphne to."

"Then you must do so immediately." Sarah's lips twitched as she tried to maintain a straight face. "It was nice visiting with you, Daphne."

As Mrs. Libby pulled her away, Daphne turned so only Sarah could see her horrified expression. "Traitor," she mouthed.

Sarah smiled cheerily and wiggled her fingers in a wave. And Daphne resigned herself to her fate. Mrs. Libby was ever trying to play matchmaker, and lately she'd set her sights squarely on Daphne. Much to Daphne's dismay.

The vicar's wife led her through the crowd to where Mr. Libby was speaking with a small group of gentlemen.

The vicar was tall and very slender with a long hooked nose. Daphne could not imagine a stranger-looking couple than the Libbys existed anywhere. He smiled when his wife arrived with Daphne. "There she is now." He patted the man beside him on the shoulder and motioned to the ladies.

Daphne froze. The man with the vicar was Arthur Grande. *Oh heavens, no.* Was fate playing a cruel joke on her?

"Mr. Arthur Grande, allow me to introduce Daphne Dayley. Isn't she lovely?"

Mr. Grande gave an overly bright smile. "Extremely." He lifted his hat and gave a deep bow. "How do you do, Miss Dayley?"

Daphne opened her mouth to explain that she was already acquainted with the man and that he was in fact the very person ruining her life, but seeing Mrs. Libby's hopeful smile, she could not do it. "A pleasure, sir."

"Mr. Grande is the newest member of the parish choir," the vicar said. "And he donated a very tidy sum to the building of new pews—we shall need them in the summer with all of the out-of-towners crowded into our small church."

Mrs. Libby nudged Daphne with her elbow. "He has also agreed to attend the Bible study on Wednesday nights."

Perhaps the town should throw Mr. Grande a parade.

"Has he?" Daphne said. She put on an exaggerated smile of her own and opened her eyes innocently wide. "I imagine Mr. Grande plans to volunteer at the orphan school as well?"

Mr. Grande watched Daphne with an infuriatingly amused expression.

"And assist the Ladies' Auxiliary League with their annual picnic tomorrow?" Daphne added, her brow ticking.

Mrs. Libby pressed a hand to her bosom. "Oh, Mr. Grande, you really are a godsend to our town," she gushed. "Isn't he, Daphne?"

"What did we ever do without him?" she asked, shaking her head as if Mr. Grande's presence in Brighton was more than she could have ever hoped for.

Another of the gathered gentlemen, Mr. Brambles, the haberdasher, cleared his throat. "So tell me, how did you get into the hotel business, Mr. Grande?"

Mr. Grande winked at Daphne, turning toward Mr. Brambles. "It is a rather dull story, sir."

"I think we should all like to hear it," Mrs. Libby piped up. "Shouldn't we, Daphne?"

"I should like nothing more," Daphne said.

His lips pulled in a small smirk that disappeared as he turned back to Mr. Brambles. "My father and uncle worked in the hotel business," he said. "As ... investors of a sort, purchasing lodging houses or inns that were in financial hardship. They would make repairs or update the décor—whatever it took to add value to the property—and sell." He glanced around at the group—perhaps judging whether he still had their attention.

"My uncle died, and when my father became ill, he asked what I wished to do with the company's funds. Would I continue with the same business? Or use the inheritance for a new venture?

"I wanted to make something amazing, instead of just passable. A hotel that was beautiful and grand." He smiled at the appreciative chuckles at the pun on his name. "And together we came up with the idea for The Grande Hotel by the Sea."

He looked in the direction of the hotel, though of course he couldn't see it through the town. "The project took years of preparation and planning. My solicitor, Mr. Fawcett, and I moved to London. We invested and researched and finally found the perfect town, and later just the right location. And my dream is finally becoming a reality." He spread his hands.

The group applauded.

"A wonderful story," Mr. Brambles said.

Mrs. Libby wiped her eyes. She clasped his hand. "And we are so very happy to have you here, Mr. Grande."

Daphne had heard enough. She pulled away her arm from Mrs. Libby's, ready to make an exit.

But the vicar's wife looped her arm back through Daphne's elbow. "Miss Dayley used to live in London as well—for school. Didn't you, dear?"

"Yes, I did."

Miss Libby still had a hold on Mr. Grande's hand. She tugged it to ensure she had his full attention. "Her father insisted Daphne needed an education, you see. A pity she had to leave it all and return home to manage the bakery when her mother died."

Mr. Grande studied Daphne.

Mrs. Libby held her arm tighter as if she were hugging it. "But we are so happy you did, aren't we, gentlemen?"

The other men agreed that they were very pleased Daphne had returned without finishing her schooling. What did a woman need schooling for anyway, and Daphne was much more suited to baking.

Daphne pulled at her arm again, anxious to leave.

Mrs. Libby held on tight. "And what will you do now that the bakery is closing, dear? Will you move Our Dayley Bread to a new location?"

"You could work as a cook in a manor house or a restaurant," Mr. Bramble offered helpfully.

"Or bake for Mr. Cawston," the vicar suggested.

Daphne gave her arm a strong pull, breaking free from Mrs. Libby's grip. "Thank you all for your suggestions. Please do excuse me." She gave a curtsey and turned before anyone could protest, nearly running down the road in her haste to escape.

Footsteps sounded behind her, and Daphne looked up to find Mr. Grande had joined her.

"Shall I walk you home?" He offered his arm.

She ignored the gesture and quickened her pace, nearly to a trot. "I'm not going home."

"Where are you going?" He walked faster, his longer strides keeping up with her.

She glared at him. "Don't you have a ladies' society meeting to attend or a lost kitten to rescue?"

He laughed. "Of course. But that is all scheduled for later this afternoon. Right now, I should like to see you safely to . . . wherever you are going."

"That is not necessary." Daphne was getting winded, and her breathing was becoming labored. Seeing that he was not planning to relent, she slowed. If he wished to walk beside a person determined to ignore him, well, that was his problem.

"I didn't know you lived in London," Mr. Grande said conversationally.

"Perhaps I forgot to mention it when I told you the entirety of my life story," she said.

"You did leave out quite a few key elements."

His walking stick tapped on the paving stones as they strolled. "And now, what? Do you intend to return to London? Will you open another bakery? Work for Mr. Cawston?"

"Why the sudden interest in my welfare?" Daphne asked.

"It is not sudden at all," he said. "I take a great deal of interest. For example, what if my hat should fly away again? Or what if the workers become unruly and I need a person who knows how to wield a firm rolling pin? In either case, I should like to know where to find you."

Daphne opened her mouth, but the witty retort didn't come. "I don't know," she said quietly.

He looked toward her. "You really have no plans? Or just none you wish to tell me?" Disbelief chased all humor from his voice.

Daphne kept her eyes on the road ahead. "Both."

The pair walked in silence, coming to the end of the road and turning to walk along the beach.

Daphne let the sound of the waves soothe her strained nerves. If there was one thing she could count on it was the steadiness of the sea. If only her future were so predictable.

She glanced to the side. Mr. Grande seemed completely

content to walk beside her without any idea of their destination. She tried to rally the anger she'd felt toward him but found it had weakened, and that left her feeling exposed.

"Your father seems to have been very supportive. An admirable trait."

"He was that," Mr. Grande agreed. "I only wish he could have lived to see . . ." He motioned up the beach toward the hotel site.

"He would have been proud," Daphne said, then felt instantly embarrassed. Did she just compliment him?

Mr. Grande looked at her for a moment, then turned his gaze back to the sea. "Miss Dayley, I am very envious of you."

She blinked, stopping and turning fully toward him. "You are . . . envious? Of *me*?"

He nodded, motioning at the town with a sweep of his arm. "You have what I always wished for. A community. A town. A place you belong." He sighed. "The first place I ever lived for more than a few months was Eton. Many of the boys there knew each other; some had grown up together. Their families were established in their communities . . . They spoke about neighbors and distant relatives and long-standing holiday traditions . . . and I envied it more than I can say."

"Your mother . . ."

"Died when I was born," he said.

"And you have no family at all?"

"None." He played his thumb over the silver handle of the walking stick.

Daphne had never seen him so serious, nor had he spoken so openly. "It can be annoying," she said. "A small town where everyone pokes their nose in your affairs."

"I should love it. To have nosy neighbors bothering about my business is preferable to being alone."

Daphne turned and kept walking. His words had given her a lot to ponder.

"So, where are we going?" he asked.

She looked up at him, confused by the question. "Uh . . ."

"Ah," he said, tapping the side of his nose. "You didn't have a particular destination in mind? You were just trying to avoid me?"

"Yes," she admitted.

His teasing smile returned, and he put a hand over his heart as if wounded. "Well, Miss Dayley. I'm hurt. And I think Mrs. Libby would be very disappointed to hear it. She did think we were quite well suited."

His words, though spoken in jest, brought a flush to her cheeks. She spoke quickly, trying to dispel it. "That could not be further from the truth, sir."

He didn't reply.

When her face felt sufficiently cooled, she glanced to the side to find his gaze on her. "You bring out the worst in me, Mr. Grande." The explanation sounded defensive, but she could not help it.

"This is your worst? I don't believe it." He shook his head. "You haven't yelled at me once today."

"The day is not over, sir," she said. She kept her face turned away as the cursed flush returned.

Daphne stopped at the end of Middle Street and pointed. "My home is that way."

"And I suppose you're planning to invite me in for tea?" he asked with a tease in his voice.

"No." She looked away to hide her smile.

"Ah well, one cannot have everything." He offered his arm. "Shall we?"

Daphne slid her hand into the crook of his elbow, and as she did, a strange wiggle moved through her middle. "Thank you."

5

EARLY ON MONDAY MORNING, Arthur, Mr. Simper, and Mr. Fawcett stood in front of the old furniture warehouse, staring at the words scrawled in bold letters over the outer wall. Though the spelling was atrocious and the vandal hadn't bothered with punctuation, the meaning was clear. Somebody was unhappy with the building project, and more specifically, with the men in charge.

"Who could have done this?" Mr. Fawcett sputtered. Such an affront was offensive to his sense of decency. "This . . . filth . . . must be punished. And swiftly." He stomped toward the building and rubbed his fingers on the paint, but it had dried.

"I've a few guesses." Mr. Simper scratched his cheek as he spoke. "First one who comes to mind is Jim Garrick."

"The same Jim Garrick I convinced you to rehire?" Arthur asked. He felt sick inside, looking at the words. Vulnerable at the threat.

"Sacked him again the same day," Mr. Simper nodded. "The man couldn't manage to come to work sober." He motioned with his chin further down the beach to the wharf. "Last I heard, he'd taken up with some of the lads down at the docks. A rough lot, if you get my meaning."

"Unacceptable," Mr. Fawcett said. "This is un-ac-cept-a-ble." He punctuated each syllable with a jab of his walking stick into the ground. His face was very red.

"Calm yourself," Arthur said, leading Mr. Fawcett to sit onto an overturned crate. "We'll sort this out." He called over one of the workers and sent the man to the bakery for a cup of tea. With Mr. Fawcett's advanced age, Arthur worried for his heart.

Mr. Simper set a few workers to painting over the words. The result was far from aesthetically pleasing, but it was much nicer than the foul language that had been so prominently on display. The wall would eventually be covered with stone anyway.

"I've sent for a constable," Mr. Simper told Arthur. "Not to worry, sir. This won't happen again."

"Was anything stolen?" Arthur asked. "Tools? Supplies?"

"I don't believe so."

"And what of sabotage? Should we worry that the structure has been rendered unsafe?"

Mr. Simper shook his head. "It is a far leap from scrawlin' profanity on a wall to thievery or property destruction." He motioned toward the drying paint. "This here's the work of a drunk blowing off steam."

"I'll send Mr. Fawcett to inquire after a night watchman," Arthur said. "Give him something to take his mind off the insult."

"Good idea," Mr. Simper said.

The constable arrived and listened to their claim. But with no witnesses, there was little more the man could do than promise to speak to Jim Garrick and to keep an eye on the building site.

"Well, no use fretting about it," Mr. Simper said. "There's work to be done."

Arthur admired the man's work ethic. The threatening words had put a damper on his spirits, and he was determined to shake it.

The incident was still bothering Arthur when he stepped into Our Dayley Bread an hour later.

At the sound of the bell over the door ringing, Mary Coombs came from the kitchen. She smiled widely. "Mr. Grande, how nice to see you this morning!"

Arthur couldn't help but smile in return. He didn't know when he had ever met a woman with such a merry disposition. "Good morning, Miss Coombs."

She wagged a finger at him. "Mary, sir. I insist upon it. Don't care much for formalities."

"Very well. Mary it is, then."

"Now, what'll you have today?" She opened a paper sack and moved to the display case, waiting for his order.

"Actually, I wondered if you'd join me for breakfast this morning." Arthur motioned to the table near the window.

"Oh." Her cheeks went red, and her grin grew. She gave a curtsey. "I would be delighted, sir." She glanced into the kitchen and then to the front window. "Miss Dayley's gone to the bank, and the buns are rising, so I can spare a few moments."

"Very good." Arthur took a plate of scones to the table, and Mary brought a tea tray. He hung his hat by the door.

She poured both cups, offering the milk and sugar. "How is Mr. Fawcett? Ron said the poor man suffered a shock."

"We had a bit of vandalism this morning. Nothing to be worried about."

She stirred sugar into her cup. "He's a dear man, isn't he? A bit persnickety, isn't he? But he's not hurting anyone. He's a right pleasant man." She poured in a bit of milk. "Well, I hope you don't have any more trouble. Not with you being such a nice person and all. You don't deserve it. Not one bit." She put a dollop of clotted cream onto her scone and kept up her steady discourse. "You certainly don't deserve the treatment you've gotten from Miss Dayley either, if you don't mind my saying. But you must excuse the poor dear. Losing the bakery's been difficult for her. Not that I blame you at all, sir. I never would."

Arthur took a sip of tea. "I take no offense to either your or Miss Dayley's words."

Mary smiled. "I'm glad to hear it."

He took a bite of scone and brushed the crumbs from his lip with a napkin, hoping to sound casual as he led into the real reason for his visit. "I heard from Mrs. Libby that Miss Dayley spent time in London."

Mary made a tut-tut sound and shook her head. "Oh that Wilhelmina Libby. She does like to gossip." She blew over the top of her tea. "Vile habit." She sipped her tea and set down the cup, leaning forward. "Well, you see, Miss Dayley went to London to attend a ladies' finishing school. Her father insisted on it, though both she and her mother protested. Thought a lady should be educated, he did."

"I should think he was a wise father," Arthur said.

Mary shrugged. "And her mother thought she should work in the bakery. Poor dear, our Daphne. She spent so much time trying to please everyone that I think she lost a bit of herself, pulled in so many directions."

As Arthur chewed another bite of scone, he considered what Mary said. Her words were surprisingly insightful. "This bakery was her mother's dream for her," he said. "A London ladies' school was her father's. But what is Miss Dayley's dream?"

Mary dabbed her napkin on her lips. "Well, that's the question, isn't it?" She jumped up and motioned with a crooked finger for him follow her to the counter.

Mary tapped the glass dome over the cake stand where he'd seen the éclairs a few days earlier. Today the stand held macarons.

"I'm not sure I understand," Arthur said.

She glanced toward the door to the kitchen and then leaned toward him, keeping her voice low. "A few years ago, I found a brochure for a French culinary academy in the kitchen. And when I asked Mr. Dayley about it, he became extremely cross."

"It was Daphne's," Arthur guessed.

Mary nodded, looking very conspiratorial.

"She made these." He pointed to the macarons.

Mary nodded again.

"And the éclairs."

"The day after I showed him the brochure, I heard Mr. and Mrs. Dayley giving young Daphne what for." She shook her head. "And a few weeks later, she was sent off to London."

Arthur leaned his forearm against the counter, feeling as if he understood Daphne Dayley in an entirely new light. "She wanted to go to school to become a pastry chef."

Mary gave another clandestine nod.

The bell over the door rang, and Miss Dayley entered. She paused, looking surprised at seeing the two of them huddled in deep conversation.

Mary jumped up and hurried around the counter to clean off the table.

Arthur stood up straight. "Good morning, Miss Dayley."

"Good morning, Mr. Grande." She removed her bonnet, hanging it beside the door, then crossed the room to join him at the counter. "To what do I owe the pleasure of your visit?"

He waited for a bite of sarcasm in her tone or a smirk, but none came. "I hoped to place an order, if I may," he said.

"An order?" she asked, looking tired.

Mary took the tray of dishes into the kitchen, giving Arthur a secretive wink as she passed.

Miss Dayley shot Arthur a questioning look, which he chose to ignore.

"I should like to purchase forty loaves of whatever bread you choose," he said.

"Forty?" Miss Dayley moved to the other side of the counter and opened a notebook. "And it doesn't matter the type?"

"I wish to give it to the workers as a thank you."

"That is very nice of you." She made a note in the book. Her pleasant attitude was beginning to worry him. "Today, of course, we are busy baking for the Ladies' Auxiliary League's spring picnic."

"Tomorrow, then?"

She winced and looked down at the notebook. "Well, it will have to be tomorrow, won't it?" she said in a quiet voice.

Arthur mentally reprimanded himself at the reminder that the bakery would be open for only one more day. "You will be at the picnic this evening?" he asked clumsily, desperate for something to change the conversation.

She tipped her head, looking confused at the question. "Yes."

"I look forward to seeing you." He put on his hat and strode through the exit and to the construction site before he said anything else foolish.

He felt a pang of sadness, realizing the bakery would close in two days. He'd come to enjoy the easy proximity to the baked goods and, even more, the baker.

Instead of stopping at the hotel site, he continued up the road toward the Steine, where the fishermen spread out their nets.

Today Daphne had looked utterly defeated. Though she acted strong, the closing of her bakery had taken a toll on her spirits. He found himself wishing she would yell at him or threaten him with a rolling pin. Anything was better than this.

Though he'd been teasing when he'd said it, the goal of

making Daphne Dayley happy had risen to the highest level of importance. He must see her laugh again, and he determined to figure a way to do it.

The things he'd learned from Mary gave him a lot to contemplate. He understood Miss Dayley's comment about his father the day before in a new light. If only her own parents had supported her dream instead of forcing upon her their own vision of what her life should be. They must have acted out of love—he assumed—in what they considered to be the best interest for their daughter. But was it truly? And was he glad they had done it? In spite of his frustration over her situation, he realized that if Daphne had gone to France all those years ago, he may never have met her. And in order to achieve his goal of her happiness, he feared the answer lay in encouraging her to go . . . The thought left an empty feeling inside, and he spent the next hours looking for a different solution—any solution—but always arrived at the same conclusion.

6

Daphne set a basket of lemon buns onto the table among the other baked goods. Mary and Ruth had both delivered a basket from Our Dayley Bread as well. She shooed away a fly and made certain the cloths covering the food were tucked underneath to prevent them from blowing away. The afternoon was sunny and pleasantly warm, but a sea wind was always a possibility.

Seeing Sarah Taylor sitting on a grassy hill overlooking the lawn behind the church, Daphne left the food tables and walked across the grass.

Little Ronald was awake today, and his mother was cooing and making faces at him.

Daphne smiled at the sight. "Good afternoon," she said when she drew near. "Might I join you?"

Sarah scooted to the side of the blanket, leaving a space. "Oh, what a treat you are in for, Daphne." She turned the baby toward her. "Little Ronald has been smiling all day."

Daphne sat onto the blanket and tickled the baby under his chin. "Will you smile for me, then, little one?"

Ronald's chubby face broke into a toothless smile that melted her heart. "Oh, that is precious," Daphne said. "What a handsome little smile you have."

Sarah held the baby toward Daphne. "Would you like to hold him?"

Daphne reached for Ronald and pulled him close, cradling him in one arm. She bounced her leg beneath him. "There you go, dearest," she muttered.

"So tell me," Sarah said. "Who is the latest eligible bachelor Mrs. Libby has her heart set on for you?"

Daphne's cheeks heated. "You would not believe it. She introduced me to Mr. Arthur Grande."

"The hotel builder? The man who evicted you from the bakery?" Sarah put a hand over her mouth. "How could Mrs. Libby possibly be so obtuse?"

"It was rather awkward," Daphne grimaced.

"Yes, I imagine so. If only I had followed along." Sarah sighed. "I can't believe I missed it." She wiped a drip from the baby's chin with a cloth. "So how do you find him?"

"Mr. Grande?" Daphne asked.

"Of course, Mr. Grande. I hear he's very handsome."

Daphne blushed again, which was really becoming a nuisance. "I suppose he is handsome." She tried to keep her voice sounding casual. "He is very nice."

"Nice?" Sarah scrutinized her face. "That is all you have to say about him?"

"I said he was handsome," Daphne said. She turned back to the baby, hoping the line of inquiry would end. "Come, Ronald, let's have another smile."

"I think you fancy him." Sarah spoke the words with a note of triumph. "Now where is Mr. Arthur Grande? I should like to see with my own eyes the man who causes you to act so flustered."

"I am not the least bit flustered." Where did Sarah get such a daft idea? "I imagine he's here somewhere," she said in an offhand voice, gazing around at the gathering. After a moment, she spotted him. "Over there." She pointed. Mr. Grande was kicking a ball with a group of children on the green. His hat, coat, and walking stick had been discarded onto a bench. He laughed when a boy attempted to kick the ball past him, stopping it with his foot.

The other children cheered.

Mr. Grande grinned and kicked the ball back to the boy.

At the sight, Daphne's stomach flopped over. She was glad Sarah couldn't see inside her. Her friend would really have something to say.

She turned back to continue their conversation, but Sarah had other ideas. She waved toward the green, and catching Mr. Grande's eye, she gestured for him to come over.

"What are you doing?" Daphne was aghast at her friend's boldness. What must Mr. Grande think of such behavior?

"Oh, hush." Sarah swatted at her. "I simply wished to meet him."

Mr. Grande said something to the children. He ruffled one boy's hair and grabbed his hat, walking stick, and coat, sliding his arms into the sleeves as he strode up the hill toward them.

Daphne's face burned, and she took deep, calming breaths to try and cool the flush of embarrassment.

When he reached them, Mr. Grande tipped his hat. "Good afternoon, ladies. So nice to see you, Miss Dayley."

"Mr. Grande, allow me to introduce my friend, Mrs. Sarah Taylor."

"How do you do?" Sarah said.

"A pleasure."

Sarah pulled on Daphne's arm, scooting her toward the middle of the blanket to make room. "Won't you join us?"

"Delighted to." Mr. Grande sat beside Daphne, stretching out his legs. "And who is this?" He leaned close to see the baby.

"Ronald." Daphne spoke in a singsong voice, shifting the baby around to face him. "Show Mr. Grande your smile." She tickled him beneath the chin, and the baby opened his mouth in a grin.

"Will you look at that?" Mr. Grande whispered. He watched Little Ronald as if completely fascinated. He reached out a hand toward the baby but pulled it back.

"He won't bite you," Daphne said.

"Doesn't even have teeth," Sarah added.

"I've just never . . ." Mr. Grande began. "I don't know any babies. Are they always so small?" He touched Ronald's little hand with the tip of his finger.

Sarah snorted. "Considering how he came into the world, I shudder to think of the alternative."

Heat exploded on Daphne's cheeks. "Sarah, that was . . ." She didn't dare to look up at Mr. Grande for fear she'd meet his gaze.

"Ah yes." He cleared his throat. "I imagine so . . ."

Daphne prayed for a distraction. Anything at all to save her from the humiliation of this conversation.

A voice behind her immediately made Daphne wish her prayer had been more specific. "Yoo-hoo! Miss Dayley, Mr. Grande!" Daphne braced herself as Mrs. Libby hurried over, lavender ruffles fluttering around her.

Mr. Grande stood. "Lovely to see you again, Mrs. Libby." He helped her to sit in his vacated spot on the blanket.

"Oh, thank you, Mr. Grande. Sarah, Daphne, how do you do this afternoon?" she asked. "Oh, and Little Ronald," Mrs. Libby went on without waiting for the other women to reply. "Isn't he growing so fast?"

Daphne handed the baby into Mrs. Libby's outstretched arms.

"Wonderful day for a picnic, is it not, Mr. Grande?" Mrs. Libby asked.

"It is indeed," he said.

"And where would we be without your help, sir? Mrs. Eddings would still be carrying crates of preserves, and Mrs. Johnson was just thrilled with how you arranged her quilt display." She turned to Daphne. "He has been here all afternoon, assisting with the preparations."

"How thoughtful," she said. She was surprised to find she meant it.

"If you please, ladies"—Mr. Grande reached out a hand—"I was hoping Miss Dayley would join me for a promenade about the green."

"That sounds lovely." She took his hand and allowed him to help her to her feet.

"Oh!" Mrs. Libby clapped her hands, and Sarah snatched away the baby before the vicar's wife could drop him in her excitement. "Don't the two of you look nice together?" She smiled fondly between Daphne and Mr. Grande. "Getting along well, are we?"

"I—" Daphne began. She heard a snort and narrowed her eyes at Sarah's poorly restrained laughter. Sarah pressed her fingers over her mouth.

"I hear there will be dancing at the assembly hall this Saturday. It's been a long time since we had an assembly, but I suppose with summer on the way, and all the tourists who will be joining us, it is time again . . . though I don't care for dancing myself. I do hope the two of you will attend."

"Perhaps," Daphne said. "Excuse us."

Mr. Grande tucked her arm beneath his. "Good day, ladies." He tipped his hat. and they started off toward the road.

"And shan't you make a fine-looking couple?" Mrs. Libby continued, raising her voice so they could hear as they drew further away. "With your figure, Daphne, and Mr. Grande's broad shoulders, I dare say, you will be quite the . . ."

"Do you still long for a community, Mr. Grande?" she asked as Mrs. Libby's voice trailed off behind them.

He threw back his head, laughing heartily. "I shall certainly never worry about life becoming dull." He laughed again. "And she's right, we are a fetching couple."

Daphne slapped his arm, her cheeks heating at the tease in his voice. She needed to do something about all this blushing. She hadn't realized it was a problem until Mr. Grande came along.

"In truth, Daphne, I find every member of this town to be absolutely endearing," he said in a more serious tone.

Daphne started. "What did you say?"

"Well, some of the townsfolk are . . . unconventional, but they mean well. And their quirks are charming."

"No, I . . . I was just surprised that you called me by my Christian name."

"Oh, did I?" he asked. "I beg your pardon. I didn't realize I had taken such a liberty."

"I don't mind." Why did she feel so uncertain? Where had all this shyness come from? And had her cheeks developed an ailment that kept them permanently warm?

"Well, I'm glad you take no offense," he said. "I believe friends should call one another by their names."

"Are we friends, sir?"

He slowed his steps, turning toward her. "Daphne, I consider you to be one of my very dearest friends. I do hope you think of me in the same light."

She tried to think of something witty to say, but her thoughts had become confused by the warmth in his voice. "I—" Hearing men's raised voices, she looked ahead, then pulled on his arm. "Mr. Grande, let's turn around now."

"Arthur," he said.

"What? Oh yes, Arthur." She walked completely around him, turning him in a circle, and started back along the road in the opposite direction. "I should like to avoid those men."

He glanced back over his shoulder. "Oh?"

"Jim Garrick is not a nice person when he's been drinking," she said.

"Garrick?" He looked back again. "Weren't you the one who defended him when Mr. Simper had him dismissed from the hotel?"

"I was extremely angry with you at the time," she said. "And I do worry for his wife, with him out of work." She pointed to where Sally Garrick stood with a group of women. "That is her there, in the tan-colored dress. She's a delicate sort. Very quiet."

Arthur looked in the direction of the woman and then back toward Jim Garrick and his friends. "Young, isn't she?"

"She is. Much younger than her husband."

She felt more relieved the further they got away from the loud men. "Mary told me about the vandalism to your property. She was very worried about Mr. Fawcett." She glanced up at him. "Do you suspect Jim?"

"Well, I rather suspected *you*," he said. "But I imagine your lettering to be much neater, as well as your spelling of profanities."

"If it had been me, I'd have signed my name, leaving you with no doubts."

"Good of you." He nodded, his lips twitching. "In truth, I have no reason to suspect Mr. Garrick, but Mr. Simper believes it could be him. He says Garrick is just the type to do something like that."

A cool feeling of foreboding made Daphne shiver. "He's definitely the type. I hope you'll be careful."

"If I need a bodyguard, I'll send for you."

"Do be serious, Arthur," she said. "A dangerous man threatened you. I hope you do not take it lightly."

A boy ran up to them when they approached the green. "Mr. Grande, we need you to finish our game."

He smiled. "If you'll pardon me, Daphne. This match is very important." He winked and started away after the boy, but he turned back. "And I plan to walk you home tonight, if that is agreeable?"

"Thank you." She hurried away to hide her blush.

Once she was certain Mrs. Libby was otherwise engaged, Daphne returned to the blanket beside Sarah. They watched Arthur and the children play, and she considered how the man had become an important fixture in her life in such a short while.

As much as the townsfolk bothered her at times, she still loved them, and she had worried that once away from Sarah and Mrs. Libby, Arthur would say something insulting about them. It was one thing for her to be frustrated with her people, but quite another for a newcomer to be. But he hadn't been. Even when she'd given him the chance. He really did love Brighton and its people.

She watched him lift a child up onto his shoulders when the boy made a good play. The other children cheered, and Daphne thought her heart might melt.

That evening, Daphne strolled with Arthur along the Steine. The wide road was a fashionable promenade that passed in front of the prince regent's Royal Pavilion. But while the tourists were away, the locals enjoyed it as a pleasant thoroughfare. The pair had stayed at the picnic much later than Daphne had intended. Apparently Arthur was not one to leave when there were still people to assist with the after-party clean up. The longer she knew him, the more she discovered to admire about Arthur Grande. "How did you find the Annual Ladies' Auxiliary League Spring Picnic?" she asked. Aside from the tapping of his walking stick, her voice was the only other noise on the street.

"I loved every moment of it," Arthur said.

"Even the moments when Mrs. Libby recruited you for the bell-ringer's luncheon?"

"Especially those," he said with a wide grin. "She does have a way of convincing a person to do things."

"And you have a way of not refusing."

"I fear you're right," he said. "I shall have to work on that." He sighed. "And wasn't Little Ronald a wonder? So perfect and so tiny. He seemed to prefer me, I think."

"Yes." She smiled at his enthusiasm for the baby. "You were the one who tickled him the most." They turned to walk along a smaller road toward her house.

"Do you imagine you'll be at the assembly?" Arthur asked. "I would very much like to dance with you."

"Perhaps." She was glad for the evening shadows that hid her face. "You shall love Brighton in the summer, Arthur. The theaters open, and there are cricket games and . . ."

Her voice trailed off at the sound of raised voices. The noise made her uneasy. "We should take a different route," she said.

A man yelled, and though she could not make out the words, she knew by their tone that he was angry. Daphne pulled on Arthur's arm, wanting to get away.

A woman screamed, and instead of moving away, Arthur ran toward the sound.

Daphne followed.

The sound led them behind the lodgings in a neighborhood that Daphne knew to avoid. Jim Garrick stood in a narrow alley, his fist raised. Below him, his wife, Sally, was on the ground. The woman cowered away, holding her cheek. Their children were crying.

Arthur wasted no time. He charged at Garrick, grabbing him around the waist and knocking him off balance. He twisted the man's raised fist behind his back and held him tightly.

Daphne knelt beside Sally, pulling away her hand to see the damage to her face. The woman's cheek was swollen and red, her lip split open and bleeding. "Oh, mercy." She could not believe a husband being so cruel.

"What do you think you're doing?" Garrick bellowed, turning his head to see who held him. "You've no right to interfere in my business."

"Sir, I can hardly stand by and allow you to assail this woman." Arthur spoke calmly, but there was anger beneath his tone.

"Assail?" Garrick squirmed, trying to get his arm free. "She's my wife. I have every right to—"

Arthur pulled the man's arm tighter, and Garrick's words stopped as he gasped in pain.

Daphne used a handkerchief to wipe the blood. She brushed the strands of hair out of the woman's face. "Sally, do you have somewhere to go tonight?"

She nodded, glancing toward her husband with fearful eyes. "My sister's."

"We'll make sure you get there safely," Daphne said.

"Lad, fetch a constable," Arthur said. His voice was commanding, but he still managed to sound kind.

"Go on, Davy," Sally said.

Davy ran off, and the other boy rushed into his mother's arms.

"Get yer hands off me." Garrick grunted. "You have no right."

"That's enough, sir." Arthur said.

Mr. Garrick let loose a string of profanities that made the young boy cover his ears and his wife's sobbing increase.

Constable Humphries arrived with Davy.

He looked around the alleyway, taking stock of the situation. "Shoulda known it would be you, Garrick." He sighed. "Had a few too many again, I see." He took Garrick's other hand, slipped a cuff onto it, tightening the pin, then motioned for Arthur to release the other so he could cuff that wrist as well. "Come along, then. We've yer usual cell all ready."

"Not many would have interfered," Constable Humphries said to Arthur. "Glad you did, sir. Don't often see these situations end happily."

"I'm happy to help, Constable," Arthur said.

"You'll see to Mrs. Garrick and the lads, Miss Dayley?" the constable asked.

"We will." She helped the woman to stand.

The constable tipped his hat and gripped the back of Garrick's collar to lead him away.

"You have no right, Grande," the cuffed man yelled. "This is my family, and I won't forget what happened here—"

"Ah, stop yer yellin'." The constable gave a shove, making him stumble.

Daphne felt ill. Jim Garrick was certainly the type to hold a grudge, and with the man's propensity toward violence . . . She shuddered, fearing he would seek revenge on Arthur.

Once Sally and her children were safely delivered to her sister, Daphne and Arthur turned their steps back toward her house.

"I must say, this was a very eventful day. I am utterly exhausted, and I imagine you are as—"

Daphne slid her hand into his, and his words stopped.

He glanced down at her and gave her hand a squeeze, one corner of his mouth pulling in a smile.

"I'm frightened for you, Arthur," Daphne said.

He squeezed her hand again. "While I appreciate the sentiment, there is no need for it."

"But you heard Jim Garrick. He is likely to seek revenge."

Arthur shook his head. "Men like Garrick will hurt people weaker than themselves because they are cowards. I do not fear him at all."

She considered what he said, wishing the words would soothe away her worries, but they did not. "Most people would have run the other direction," she said. "You are a good man, Arthur."

They stopped in front of her door.

"Am I?" he asked. "Did you not call me the most infuriating man you have ever met?"

She smirked. "Well, you still are that."

"Oh, that is a relief," Arthur said. "I should not like to lose that distinction."

"I do apologize for the things I said and the judgments I made before I knew you. I was hasty and prejudiced." She held his hand in both of hers. "You really are all the things everyone believes about you."

"I assure you, I am not perfect, Daphne."

"Well, I intend to apologize all the same. I'm sorry for yelling at you and for calling you a cold-hearted tyrant."

"You did not call me a cold-hearted tyrant." His lips twitched.

"Well, perhaps not to your face."

Arthur chuckled. He leaned his walking stick against her doorframe and lifted her gloved fingers to his lips.

Daphne's breathing stopped, and her heart pounded. When Arthur's gaze held hers, the intensity in his eyes made her throat go dry.

"Good night," she said, opening her door and hurrying inside. She kept her gaze averted from his. "I've a big order tomorrow and need to begin early."

"Until tomorrow, then."

Daphne closed the door and stood still in the darkness as her breathing and heartbeat returned to normal. Something had changed in that moment when Arthur looked into her eyes. Something bigger than she could fathom. Could anything ever be normal again?

7

ARTHUR KEPT A WATCH on Our Dayley Bread as the day progressed. Even from the worksite, he could feel a heaviness in the air, and whether or not it was simply a projection of his own emotions, he wasn't certain. The little shop appeared to have more customers than usual today as people made their final purchases and said farewell.

In the late morning, Mary walked outside with a customer, giving the woman a warm embrace, then wiping her eyes before returning into the bakery.

Arthur felt a pang of sadness and wondered how Daphne was managing. He was certain she maintained a steady pace, smiling, working, and stoically pushing down her own emotions. He debated whether or not he should go to her but decided he would wait and allow her privacy this morning.

A warmth burst in his chest each time he thought of their parting the night before. Her blush and her worry for him. The feel of her hand in his as they walked. Though it was impossible to believe, after only a week, he was smitten with Daphne Dayley.

Finally, midday drew near, and Arthur walked with Mr. Fawcett to have a final meat pie. He felt a bittersweet pang at the sound of the bell over the door.

Mary waved from behind the counter. Her eyes were red,

but she still gave a bright smile. "Mr. Grande, Mr. Fawcett. Good day to you, gentlemen!"

"Good day." Arthur glanced at the hook by the door and saw Daphne's bonnet.

"Hello, Mary." Mr. Fawcett tipped his hat. "Oh, chicken pies today. My favorite."

"I prepared a special meal just for you." Mary pulled out a plate of pies and muffins from behind the counter for her favorite customer.

Mr. Fawcett took his plate to the table and immediately began eating, but Arthur remained at the counter to talk to Mary. "How is Miss Dayley managing today?" He kept his voice low, not wanting Daphne to overhear and think he was meddling in her affairs.

Mary's expression turned serious. "As you might imagine, sir. She puts on a strong face, but it is difficult." She ran her hand over the countertop. "Lot of memories in this place. For Daphne, it must feel like severing a link with her parents."

Arthur nodded, his throat feeling tight as he glanced up at the portrait of Daphne and her family behind the counter.

"She's preparing your order today," Mary continued. "Wants to do all of it herself. I think the poor dear needs something to keep her mind and hands busy." She glanced back toward the kitchen, shaking her head. "All that kneading . . . she'll be sore tomorrow."

Arthur took his seat but stood up after only a moment when Daphne came out of the back room. Flour dusted her hair and apron. "I thought I heard you," she said. "Do sit down, gentlemen. How do you do today, Mr. Grande?"

He scrutinized her face, trying to determine her state of mind, but her expression was closed. "Very well."

"I'm glad to hear it. And Mr. Fawcett?"

The older man dabbed a bit of gravy from his lip with a napkin. "Splendid, Miss Dayley. These chicken pies are delicious. I may just have another."

Daphne smiled, and even though it was a very small thing, it relieved Arthur greatly. "Please tell Mary if you need anything at all. If you'll excuse me, I still have a lot of work to do for your order, Mr. Grande."

"I appreciate it, miss."

"It will be ready at four. Shall I bring it to the worksite then?"

"I will come and fetch it." Arthur said.

"I would like to deliver it for you." She blushed, glancing at Mr. Fawcett. "For your workers."

Arthur thought he would never become used to the thrill her blush gave. "Thank you."

At four o'clock exactly, Daphne, Ruth, and Mary arrived, each carrying a crate of loaves. The women set the delivery beside the large door of the old furniture factory.

Arthur thanked them, and Mary and Ruth left.

Daphne remained. She set the last crate next to the others and brushed her hands on her apron. She hadn't bothered to put on her bonnet or gloves. Strands of hair had fallen from their pins and hung loosely around her face, glowing in the late-afternoon sun.

Arthur looked over the crates. Although each loaf was wrapped in paper, the smell still drew glances from workers who passed. He lifted one of the parcels and inhaled. "Cinnamon?" he asked.

"Some," she said. "I made ten of each: cinnamon, rye, currant, and yeast."

He set the loaf back into the crate. "Daphne, this must

have been an enormous undertaking. I didn't realize you intended to do all the work yourself."

She shrugged and gave a shy smile. "I was happy to do it."

He reached toward her but remembered they were in a very public place and thought better of it, clasping his hands behind his back instead. "Thank you."

"I wondered ..." Daphne looked up at the warehouse and gave him a sidelong glance. "If you are not too busy, perhaps I might have a tour?"

He blinked. "You wish to see the building project?"

"Only if you have the time."

Arthur had not expected Daphne to ever make such a request. Especially on the day before she must vacate her bakery. Seeing that she was serious, he grinned and bowed, spreading his arm in an extravagant gesture toward the warehouse doorway.

She stepped inside, and he came up beside her, making an arch with his walking stick. "Daphne Dayley, I present to you, the future Grande Hotel by the Sea." He lifted her hand onto his arm and led her forward, then turned them around, dramatically pointing toward the door where they'd entered. "Imagine dark oak doors with inlaid stained-glass windows and polished handles, opened for you by doormen in top hats and tails." He turned the two of them back around. "Once inside, you will gasp at the enormous gas chandeliers filling the opulent lobby with modern light and making the marble floors and brass fixtures glisten." He pointed with his walking stick along the top of the warehouse walls. "Above, a balcony surrounds the lobby, with two grand staircases, one at each corner."

"It sounds marvelous." She giggled at his performance.

"Just wait." Arthur grinned as he led her forward, trying very hard to contain his excitement, but it was difficult when he spoke about the hotel. "The reception desk will be here, directly in front of you, and on either side, doors that lead out into manicured gardens with flower beds, walking paths, and a pond."

The pair turned toward the east side of the warehouse. "Here we will have sitting areas." He waved around his walking stick. "Plush chair and sofas spread over thick carpets, interspersed with statuary and tables of hothouse flowers."

"And leafy palm plants in painted pots?" Daphne said.

Arthur looked down at her, uncertain of where the suggestion came from. "I hadn't thought of it..."

"I saw workers delivering tall palms in beautiful Oriental pots to the prince regent's pavilion," she said. "They were so elegant..." She shook her head. "But perhaps they won't suit for what you have in mind."

"Daphne, if tall palms in Oriental pots please you, then tall palms in Oriental pots we shall have."

She gave him a playful push, rolling her eyes and smiling. "Tell me, what is this here?" She pointed to the wall of the warehouse building, or more specifically, the enormous hole where the wall used to be. Beams held up the ceiling, and through the opening they could look into the former dressmaker's shop. Some workers were moving away the debris from the wall, and others were nailing support beams into place.

"These beams are only temporary. Eventually pillars will run down both sides of the lobby," he said. "Through here will be our dining room." He led her through the hole in the wall, helping her to step carefully over broken bricks, rubble, and scraps of wood. "The engineer tells me the building next door is not in good enough repair, and so it will be completely torn down, and this room expanded." He pointed to the rear of the shop. "The kitchens will be built further on that way, and the business offices."

"That is where you will work," she said.

Arthur shook his head. "The plan is for my office to be above, on the first story, so my windows face the sea."

Daphne nodded and glanced up at the shop's ceiling. "A benefit of ownership."

"Precisely," Arthur said.

He led her back through the demolished wall into the warehouse. "The ceilings of the different shops will need to be adjusted to a uniform height. Of course, the apartments and rooms on the upper stories will be torn down and completely rebuilt to allow for the new plumbing and a suite-style layout."

They walked through the building in the other direction.

"More seating areas here?" Daphne guessed.

"Yes, and in this corner, a grand piano."

"Oh, I like that very much," she said. "You really have thought of everything."

He studied her face, surprised at her enthusiasm for the project. But perhaps she was simply being polite.

"And here we have the gentlemen's smoking room." She motioned toward the broken wall on the west side of the building, through which they could see the empty shop that shared a wall with the bakery.

"Yes," he said carefully.

Daphne released his arm and stepped through the opening. Boards were piled against the far wall, ready to shore up the ceiling when the workers broke through into the bakery.

"Use caution, Daphne." He pointed to a coal stove the workers used to heat the wood varnish. "It may still be hot."

She stepped away from the stove and looked at the wall for a moment.

Arthur watched her closely, worried that she might break down into tears, but she seemed to be simply thinking.

She turned back toward him slowly. A sliver of light shone through a gap in the boards of the wall, making dust motes sparkle in the air around her. "You must do this," she said softly.

He studied her, his nerves on alert as he considered exactly how to reply. Was she preparing to yell? To weep?

She crossed the room, taking his hand. Her fingers were warm in his palm. "This is your dream."

"It is," he said.

"And you will make it the most magnificent hotel in the world."

"Well, hopefully in Brighton at least."

"I am happy for you," Daphne said.

He watched, waiting for her anger or her tears. "Are you happy?" he asked slowly.

"For you." She looked around the dusty warehouse. "Your passion for this project shows in every word and gesture. I can see how strongly you want this, how you've worked for it. I was wrong to be angry."

"You were hurt."

She nodded. "I don't want to see you break the bakery wall," she whispered.

He pulled her into an embrace. "I know."

She held onto him tightly, and he could feel her tension. Her shoulders were shaking. "I need to leave now," she said, pulling back. "But I wanted you to know I'm not angry. Not any longer."

Her face was tight, and he could see she held back tears. She started toward the door, her pace rushed.

"Shall I accompany you?" Arthur touched his fingers to her lower back as he walked beside her. He felt helpless, watching her battle with her emotions.

"You've bread to distribute." She tried for a smile, but her lips trembled. "And if you please, I just want to be alone for a bit." Her last words came out as a whisper.

She hurried through the warehouse door and toward the bakery.

Arthur watched her go, feeling a wave of emotion. If he'd been asked a week earlier to describe Daphne Dayley, he'd have said she was a beautiful woman with a fiery temper and a sharp tongue. But somehow, over the days he'd known her, he'd discovered there was much more. She was kindhearted and thoughtful, with a quick wit and a charming humor. She cared for those around her, even though she might not say it outright; he saw it in the way she worried for his safety, her tolerance of Mrs. Libby's nosiness, how she'd ensured her employees had jobs when the bakery closed, and that Arthur knew she did not bear him a grudge. Somehow, all of these things served to make her even more beautiful, and there was no doubt in Arthur's mind that he was in love with her. Which made what he planned to do all the more difficult.

8

DAPHNE SCRUBBED OUT THE inside of the ovens, then wiped her rag over the handles and cast-iron doors until not a speck of dust remained. She scrubbed the preparation table and the kitchen side table, then took down the baking pans and pots and scrubbed them as well.

As she worked, memories flooded her mind, and her tears fell freely. She remembered the stool she used to stand on as she helped her grandmother roll out piecrusts and the small loaf pan her father bought so she could make her very own bread. She arranged the spices in a neat row with their labels facing outward, just as her mother preferred, and made sure the lid on the flour was sealed. Once she was certain everything was in its proper place, she swept and mopped the kitchen, satisfied that the cleanliness was up to even her grandmother's high standards. She took her reticule to the dining area, hanging it on a hook by her bonnet and shawl, then moved to work on the service counter.

She took down the family painting and wiped the frame. Seeing the faces of her parents and grandmother, such a rush of emotion overcame her that she had to stop her work and just allow herself to weep. She sat on the floor, holding the painting as sobs heaved out of her chest, and when she finally stopped, she felt like she was wrung dry. "I'm sorry," she whispered. Knowing how disappointed her family would have been to see their beloved bakery close was physically painful. She winced when she stood, her legs stiff from sitting on the floor. More time had passed than she realized; the night was full dark. She hung the painting back on the wall by the kitchen door and lit lanterns.

Daphne got a clean cloth and wiped off the counter, making the glass of the display case gleam in the lantern light. She washed the trays and made certain to scrub away every crumb that rested in the shelves' corners. She wiped the tables and chairs in the dining area, dusted off the picture frames, and swept every inch of the floor, then filled a bucket.

When she returned into the dining area to mop, she saw Arthur waving at the front window.

She knew she must look a sight after her bout of weeping, but there was nothing to be done about it, and the thought of his presence was a comforting one. She set the mop head into the soapy water, balancing it in the bucket, then opened the door.

He winced when he saw her face. "Oh, Daphne, I'm sorry."

She nodded, too exhausted for a witty comeback. "Are you here for . . . ?" She tried to remember if she'd committed to something earlier.

"I just wanted to talk to you," Arthur said.

She held the door wide open. "Come in. I'm nearly finished."

"Can I help?" he asked.

She shook her head. "I'd like to do it myself. But I thank you for the offer."

Arthur hung his hat on the hook by the door and sat in a chair at one of the small round tables.

Although he waited, Daphne did not rush. She wanted every bit of the bakery to sparkle. Somehow, she felt she owed it to her family to leave it in perfect condition.

She was finally satisfied with the floor, and she put away the mop and emptied the bucket.

Arthur stood when she joined him. He pulled out a chair, and Daphne sank into it, mentally and physically exhausted.

He returned to his seat across from her.

"You wanted to talk to me?" she prompted.

"Yes." He hesitated, likely put off by her appearance.

She smoothed back her hair. "I am all right now," she said. "I just needed some time to feel sad."

He nodded, but his brows were still furrowed as if he was unsure whether she was telling the truth.

"It's strange how difficult it is to separate a place from the people who once inhabited it," she said.

He glanced at the picture on the wall, then leaned his forearms on the table. "Daphne, what will you do now?"

She frowned. "That is what you wished to speak to me about? My plans for the future? The bakery isn't even . . ." Her voice trailed off, and she sighed, unable to hold onto her anger when Arthur looked so concerned. "I don't know."

"But . . ." he grimaced.

She held up a hand. "I know what you are going to say. I've been aware for six months that I would quit the bakery tomorrow. Surely I have thought of something before now."

He nodded. "Have you?"

Daphne sighed again, not caring that she might be considered overly dramatic for doing so. "I've tried, Arthur. I've considered working for Mr. Cawston. I've considered reopening the bakery at a different location. I've even considered moving to Cornwall to live with my cousin. But I just . . ." She shrugged. "I just don't know."

"None of the ideas feel right," he said.

Daphne nodded. That was it exactly. "I don't know what I'll do. What do I do?" She looked out the darkened window in the direction of the sea and whispered the question, not really speaking to him but sending out a prayer to the universe.

"You should follow your dream," Arthur said quietly.

"This bakery is my dream." Daphne spoke sharply. She looked back at him, then down at her hands, feeling as if her words sounded like a reprimand. She hadn't meant them that way, but she was so tired of trying to answer this very question. And to be challenged on it today, of all days.

"Is it?" he asked, his tone gentle. He lifted one of her hands from the table and held it in his own.

"Of course it . . ." *Isn't it?* Now she didn't know. If not, would she be so upset? But there was another part of her—one she didn't acknowledge—that felt relieved at the bakery's closing. "It is all I know," Daphne admitted at last. Just saying the words made her feel like even more of a failure.

Arthur took her other hand, holding them both and capturing her gaze. He looked extremely serious and . . . nervous. His shoulders were stiff as if he was bracing himself. "Daphne." He took in a deep breath. "You should go to France."

"France?" She blinked, trying to comprehend what he'd said. "You want me to leave?" Surely she'd misunderstood.

He squeezed her hands. "To attend culinary school and train to be a pastry chef."

Daphne's heart started to beat fast, and she pulled her hands away. "How did . . . who told you? It was Mary, wasn't it?"

"It doesn't matter who," Arthur said. "Listen to me. You have always done what everyone else wanted you to do. Finishing school in London for your father. The bakery for your mother and grandmother. But now it is your turn to decide. You have the chance to choose your own path." He glanced around the bakery and then looked back at her. "That is why none of your choices feel right. You can't decide because the thing you really want—it's too big, and it frightens you."

He stopped talking and watched her closely, looking as if he was nervous for her response.

Daphne's hands shook. She folded her arms across her chest. Her thoughts were spinning, and her pulse beat loudly in her ears. "I can't just go to France," she said. "What will... I mean, I don't know anyone there." She rubbed her arms. "And you're right, I am afraid." She looked down at the table. "What if I fail?"

"I know." Arthur touched her wrist. He took her hands again, leaning toward her across the table. "I felt the same. Investing my father's money in... this"—he pointed with his chin in the direction of the warehouse—"I was terrified. What if it failed? What if the hotel couldn't be built and I lost not only my father's and my uncle's money, but that of the investors I'd convinced to believe in the project... in my dream?" He pulled her hands toward him. "But now... now that it's happening... Daphne, it's the best feeling in the world. And it's what I want for you. To see you follow your dream, learn what great things you're capable of."

Daphne suddenly couldn't sit still. She stood, moving behind her chair and pacing toward the counter and back. The idea sparked something inside her, as if it had unearthed a long-buried treasure that she'd forgotten she'd hidden in the first place. Her breathing came fast, both out of excitement and fear. She couldn't do this—could she?

"But I can't leave Brighton," she said, voicing just one of her arguments against the idea from her growing list. "It is my home."

"And it always will be," Arthur said. He'd risen from his

seat when she stood, and he rested a hand on the chair back, watching as she paced. "The town will be here when you return, Daphne. Nothing will change."

"Except me," she said. She stopped walking and faced him, nerves tingling.

"Well, yes." He smiled softly and stepped toward her, putting one hand onto her shoulder and lifting her chin with the other. "But I do hope you won't change too much. What if Mrs. Libby should decide that we are no longer suited?"

His lips twitched, but he didn't smile. Instead, he bent close and kissed her. The confused thoughts spinning around her head stilled and dropped away completely, until the only thing left was the sensation of his lips on hers.

Arthur slipped his hand into her hair, cupping her head as his other hand wrapped around her, holding her tightly against him.

She slid her arms around him, thinking she couldn't hold tightly enough. Arthur was solid and steadfast, and in his arms, her worries and fears vanished.

He pulled away, resting his forehead against hers. "Don't change too much," he whispered.

"I can't do it," she said, but her tone was far from convincing.

"Consider carefully," Arthur said. He stepped back, taking her hands. "I would miss you dreadfully, but I promise, there exists no feeling worse than regret."

"I will think about it," she said.

"Good." His smile was sad. "Shall I walk you home? It is beyond late—nearly early."

She shook her head. "I should like to stay a bit longer." Seeing that he was about to protest, she pulled at his hand. "Don't worry. The fishermen leave early. I shan't be on the streets alone." She smirked. "And if it makes you feel better, I will bring my rolling pin."

Arthur brushed another kiss over her lips and took his hat from the hook by the door. "I nearly forgot." He pulled a packet of bills from his pocket. "For the order today—the men were very grateful to you. And my special owner's price is the same? Double?"

"Of course not." She waved her hand.

"I insist." He pushed the money into the reticule that hung beside her bonnet. "Good night, Daphne." He gave a bow, put on his hat, and departed.

Daphne watched through the window as he walked away, down the street toward his hotel, a warm glow filling her up from the inside. Was it from the kiss? Or the spark of a new purpose?

She took a lantern into the kitchen and dug beneath the stack of papers and documents until she found the pamphlet for the culinary school. The paper was worn and yellowed, but she could read the words clearly, and though it terrified her, she felt peaceful. Could she really do this? Leave Brighton? She would be gone for months—perhaps longer. If only she were brave enough. She went into the dining room and looked at the family portrait, but as always, her parents and grandmother gave no advice. *What am I to do?* If she only had some sort of sign.

Returning to the table, she sat and looked over the pamphlet, her mind spinning with scenarios until her eyes grew heavy.

Something was wrong, but Daphne couldn't quite put her finger on exactly what. It itched at her, seeming familiar. There was something she must do. She tried to ignore the sensation, wanting to continue with her pleasant dream, but the feeling wouldn't leave. *Danger.* She blinked herself awake, pushing herself up from the table. She'd fallen asleep in the bakery's dining area.

As she grew more aware of her surroundings and considered what had awakened her, she realized smoke filled the room, and she jolted out of her chair. She glanced at each of the lanterns, then rushed back to check the ovens, but the kitchen wasn't the source of the fire. She coughed, hurrying back into the dining room and through the front door.

Instead of fresh air, the smell of smoke surrounded Daphne out in the road. She peered through the haze illuminated in the pre-dawn light and realized the thickest smoke was coming from the warehouse. Between the slats of the walls, she saw a menacing glow. "No, no, no." The entire structure was built of wood. All of Arthur's work and his plan—his dream. Fire would destroy every bit of it. She rushed to the warehouse door. The lock had been broken. Daphne's stomach felt ill, and panic made her breath short. Where was the night watchman? "Fire!" she yelled into the night. "Fire! Call up the fire brigade!" Someone else must smell the smoke. Perhaps fishermen on their way to the boats would hear her yell.

She cast around, deciding on the best course. Should she run for help herself? Or try to put out the fire before it grew? She hurried to the main entrance of the construction site. The door was ajar. *Is somebody inside?*

She pulled on the door, opening it enough to slip through. Smoke stung her eyes, but it wasn't thick here. Coughing, she searched for the source of the fire. "Hello?"

There was no answer. She prayed it meant the building was empty.

A glow came from the west side of the warehouse, and as she moved closer, she could see it was located beyond the broken wall, between the old furniture warehouse and the bakery. The light seemed to be contained to that area. Perhaps, if the fire hadn't fully grown, it could still be extinguished.

Pulling up her apron to cover her nose and mouth, Daphne stepped through the warehouse, careful to avoid tripping over debris in the partial light. Could she smother the fire? She saw a drop cloth in a corner and grabbed an edge, dragging it toward the glow. When she reached the broken wall, she stepped through. The stove was open. Glowing embers were clumped with smaller bits of wood beneath the pile of boards, and burning rags were pressed between the slats of the wall. Even as she watched, flames grew and spread throughout the room. The drop cloth would be useless, and she let it fall. A wave of heat pushed toward her. She stumbled back, coughing and blinking her tear-filled eyes. If the supports fell, she'd be crushed.

Daphne ran back through the main room, hearing something crash behind her. The fire was growing, and within moments, the entire building would burn. Sunlight from the high windows and the firelight behind illuminated the room through the smoky haze. She remembered seeing plans and documents on a table by the door and hurried that way. At least she could save those.

She coughed again, choking, and crouched down to where the smoke was thinner. Her eyes stung, but she could still see her way well enough. The table was just where she remembered.

Yells came from outside, and a bit of the heaviness in her chest eased. Help had arrived. *At last.*

She rolled up a stack of plans and snatched up the papers around it, not caring that she crumpled them in her haste.

The doors pulled open, and through the haze, she could make out figures coming in. "Is anyone inside?" A voice yelled. "Miss Dayley?"

"I'm here," she called, coughing at the breath she'd drawn to yell. She knew the voice. Rodney Thomas was the captain of the local fire brigade.

He found her almost immediately. "Daphne, what are you . . . ?"

"The papers . . ." She clutched the rolls and wadded sheets in her arms, reaching toward those remaining on the table.

"Leave them." Rodney seized her around the waist and pulled her to the door.

More men charged inside, some leading a wheeled fire pump.

Where was Arthur? Had he come as well? Daphne blinked but found it difficult to make out details through the smoke and her bleary eyes.

Outside, a crowd had gathered. Men ran back and forth in an organized chaos. A bucket line stretched from the sea to the warehouse.

Rodney handed Daphne off to Mrs. Forbush and turned back immediately to the fire, calling out orders as he went.

Daphne closed her eyes against the burning and let Mrs. Forbush lead her away from the smoke and heat. With the older woman's help, she sat on a crate away from the commotion. Still holding the papers, she rubbed her eyes onto her sleeve.

She muttered a thanks as someone put a blanket around her shoulders and pressed a cup into her hand.

The water felt cool on her throat. She watched the townspeople fight the warehouse fire, and her heart hurt, imagining Arthur's devastation at the sight of his project going up in flames.

9

A BANGING CAME FROM Arthur's hotel-room door, shaking him from his sleep. He pulled on trousers and crossed the room. Upon opening the door, he found a man he recognized as one of Mr. Simper's workers.

"Fire, sir!" the man said in a panicked voice. "At the warehouse."

A boulder dropped in Arthur's stomach. He crammed his feet into his boots, grabbing his coat and hat as he bolted out the door. "What damage is there? Was anyone hurt? How did it start?" He fired questions at the man as they ran from the hotel and down the street to the waterfront.

"I don't know, sir." The man panted as he spoke. "Mr. Simper sent me to fetch you as soon as I arrived. I only saw smoke before I raced away."

As if speaking about it made him aware, the smell of smoke reached Arthur, and dread turned his thoughts frantic. If they lost the warehouse, the hotel would need to be built completely from scratch, which would cost months of extra labor, not to mention the supplies. "What about the fire brigade?" Surely Brighton had a volunteer fire company at least.

"Sorry, I don't know, sir. But Rodney Thomas, the brigade captain, lives close to the waterfront. I imagine if they've not come already, they'll be there soon enough."

When they arrived at the construction site, smoke surrounded Arthur, impairing his vision and choking his throat. He squinted, scanning the scene, assessing the severity of the situation. Men operated the cranks on a fire pump, shooting water into the warehouse. A chain of people stretched over the beach, passing buckets along the line. It seemed the crowd's heaviest concentration was at the west side of the warehouse, near the bakery.

A new question occurred to Arthur, sending a jolt through his chest. Had Daphne been in the bakery when the fire started?

He pushed his way into the smoke and crowd and through the bakery door, choking as he swept his gaze through the shop. Water dripped from every surface, and broken glass crunched beneath his feet. Billows of smoke poured from the west wall, where the fire had been mostly extinguished. Embers glowed in the charred remains.

A fire brigade volunteer chopped at the wall with an axe, and another tossed a bucketful of water onto the hole, making a cloud of steam and smoke. The furniture had been thrown to one side and the glass display cases shattered either by the fire or those fighting it.

Daphne's bonnet, shawl, and reticule hung on the hooks just inside the door. At the sight, cold terror shot through his veins. "Daphne!" he yelled. She must be in the kitchen. Had she been hurt? Was she hiding? He started toward the back of the shop.

One of the firefighters, a stocky man with a ruddy complexion and ash in his hair, hurried toward him. "Not safe in here, sir."

Arthur pushed past him. "Daphne Dayley. I must find—"

The man caught Arthur's arm in a tight grip. "She's not

here. Found her in the warehouse earlier trying to salvage some papers." He gave Arthur a shove, turning him toward the doorway. "Dangerous business, that. A lady has no place near a fire."

Arthur pulled away his arm. "She's safe, then? Unharmed?"

The man handed out the empty bucket through the door and grabbed onto the handle of a full one. He motioned out the door with his chin, a bit more gently this time. "Inhaled a bit of smoke, but she's not hurt."

"Thank you." Arthur breathed out a sigh. He grabbed Daphne's things from the hooks, but instead of exiting, he turned back.

The man had taken the fresh bucket and tossed the contents onto the fire, then brought it back to the doorway.

"Sir, what is your name?" Arthur asked.

"Rodney Thomas."

"You are the captain of the fire brigade," Arthur said, remembering the man's name. He held out his hand. "Thank you, Mr. Thomas for your service to me."

Rodney Thomas shook his hand and gave a shrug. "'s my duty, sir." He reached through the doorway, exchanging the bucket.

"But I thank you all the same," Arthur said.

"You're welcome," Mr. Thomas grumbled, and he gave him another push. "Now, go find Miss Dayley and leave the brigade to our work."

Arthur left the bakery. He glanced at the warehouse, but his worry for the building project had shifted down his list of priorities. *Where is she?*

After a short search, he found Daphne seated on a crate at the other side of the road. A blanket lay over her shoulders. She clutched parchment rolls and loose sheets of paper to her chest, watching the fire with a dazed expression. Seeing her unharmed, Arthur's tension released, leaving his knees feeling soft. He crouched before her, placing a hand onto her arm. "Daphne."

She turned her gaze to him. Her face was dirty and her hair a mess. She shook her head as if coming out of a stupor. "Arthur, I'm so sorry. Your hotel." She blinked swollen eyes and gave him the stacks she held. "I couldn't get them all. I didn't know there was a fire until I smelled smoke in the bakery, and by then, it was too advanced for me to put it out."

Arthur took the piles of papers from her hands. "You smelled smoke and went *into* the warehouse?"

"I wanted to help. But I could do nothing but grab these." She motioned to the papers he held.

Arthur needed a moment to calm himself and gather his thoughts. Daphne could have easily been killed. What had she been thinking, running into a burning building? What if . . . He breathed deeply and put the papers into a stack on the ground, setting a rock on top to hold them in place. He found a crate further along the street and brought it alongside hers, sitting on it.

"Daphne, no document is worth . . ." He took her hand in both of his, turning his knees toward her. "My dear, you should have run *away* from the danger, not toward it." He kept his voice gentle, not wanting his fear to be interpreted as chastisement.

"I couldn't just sit by and allow it to burn." She squeezed his hand. "Not when it means so much to you."

The tension returned, and he pinched the bridge of his nose. "Daphne, it's just a building—bricks, boards, and nails. Compared to you, it matters not at all." He put an arm around her shoulder, pulling her against him. "What if I'd lost you?" he whispered. He was surprised she'd not mentioned the damage to the bakery once.

Daphne leaned her head on his shoulder, resting against him as they watched the brigade extinguish the last of the fire.

The morning sun rose higher, brightening the beach as the smoke dispersed. Men who'd moved quickly in panic stood around in groups or worked slower now, cleaning up their equipment and departing.

Mr. Fawcett approached at a quick pace. "Mr. Grande, there you are." He rubbed his forehead, and his eyes darted around, taking in the scene. "Bad business, this," he said. "That red-faced fire captain won't allow anyone inside—not even Mr. Simper—until he's certain the building's sound." He paced with short steps. "And where is the night watchman? Is all lost?"

"Not all." Arthur stood and picked up the stack of papers, handing it to the solicitor with the plans.

"Gracious. How did you ever . . . ?" Mr. Fawcett shuffled through the pages, muttering as he reordered them.

"Miss Dayley saved them," Arthur said. He helped Daphne to stand.

Mr. Fawcett looked up. "Oh, Miss Dayley, what quick thinking." He put the rolls of plans beneath his arm and lifted his hat, bowing. "We're in your debt, miss."

Daphne inclined her head and gave a small smile.

She looked exhausted, and Arthur realized she must not have slept at all. "If you please, Mr. Fawcett, would you send for a cab? I'm going to see Miss Dayley home." He pointed toward the warehouse with a lift of his chin. "There's nothing more to be done now. I'll send for you if you're needed."

Mr. Fawcett gave a brisk nod. "Very good, sir."

Daphne was silent during the carriage ride, and Arthur didn't disturb her. His mouth tasted sour as he thought of the blackened walls of the warehouse. How much damage had been done? And how had the fire started? Discouragement made his limbs heavy, and he imagined Daphne felt the same.

A quarter of an hour later, Arthur helped her from the hackney. He paid the driver and accompanied her to the door.

She turned a key in the lock.

"Will you be all right?" He cupped a hand beneath her elbow, thinking she looked so exhausted she might just fall over. "Can I assist you? Or shall I send for someone?"

"I just need to rest." Her smile was tired, and her brows were drawn together in a pensive manner. He wondered what she was considering so deeply.

"Might I call on you tomorrow?" he asked.

"Yes, thank you, Arthur." She focused her gaze on him, looking as though she was pushing away the other thoughts. "And again, I am so sorry."

He lifted her hand, brushing a kiss on it. "Sleep, Daphne. Things will seem better when you wake."

She nodded, drawing her brows close again. "Yes, I will. Thank you."

As he walked back to the site, Arthur wondered what she was pondering so intently. Or was it simply weariness that occupied her mind?

The next morning, Arthur, Mr. Simper, Rodney Thomas, Constable Humphries, and Mr. Jenkins, the head engineer, walked through the building site. The engineer pointed at the ceiling, talking about joists and beams, but Arthur found it difficult to concentrate on his words. His heart thudded dully as he stepped through the soup of water, ash, and charred wood and let his gaze travel through the space. Sunlight gleamed through holes in the walls, caused by both the fire and the fighting of it. Black stained the wood in uneven patterns that reminded Arthur of lashes, and one section of ceiling had nearly completely caved in, leaving a pile of soggy debris beneath. Aside from the engineer's voice, the warehouse was silent. Workers awaited approval of the building's safety before they could enter. He kicked aside a hunk of blackened wood.

"Well, that is good news, isn't it, Mr. Grande?" Mr. Fawcett jotted something in his notebook.

"I beg your pardon," Arthur said. "What is good news?"

Mr. Fawcett squinted, a concerned expression moving over his face. He glanced at the other men. "Mr. Jenkins says the framework is sound. We may resume construction immediately." He spoke slowly, looking closely at Arthur as if to assess his mental state.

Arthur cleared his throat and straightened his back, remembering that he was the leader of this project. Enough feeling despondent; he had a hotel to build.

"You are absolutely certain the building is sound?" He spoke directly to Mr. Jenkins, inflecting his voice with authority. "If the integrity of the structure is at all compromised, I'd rather tear it down than risk any lives."

"The building will not collapse," Mr. Jenkins said. "But the original plans will need some modification for reinforcement." He motioned toward the majority of the damage on the east side. "And the bakery will need to be completely rebuilt."

Arthur swallowed the pang his statement caused. "How will it affect the timeframe, Mr. Simper?"

"Shouldn't set us back too far, sir." Mr. Simper said. "I'll tell the men they can return to work."

Constable Humphries cleared his throat, stepping forward. "Once the investigation is completed, gentlemen." He tipped his head toward the fire captain. "Mr. Thomas, your findings?"

Mr. Thomas motioned toward the east side of the

building. "If you come with me, Constable, Mr. Grande, I'll show you."

"Very well," Arthur said. "Mr. Simper, coordinate the changes with Mr. Jenkins, please. And Mr. Fawcett, arrange with Mr. Miller to revise the plans."

The men parted, and Rodney Thomas led Arthur and Constable Humphries through the wall into the building between the warehouse and the bakery. This area was most certainly the most damaged. What remained of the space was blackened, and the majority of the roof was in a pile of broken and burned boards at one end. The same small cast-iron stove Arthur had warned Daphne about the day before lay on its side, its door open. Holes of various sizes riddled the wall that separated the shop from the bakery. The appearance of the room was haunting, reminding Arthur of a skeleton. The lingering smoke smell was so strong that even with the open air, it felt stifling.

Arthur coughed.

"This room is the point of origin." Mr. Thomas crossed to the remains of the far wall. "You see here." He indicated a bit of drooping ash poking out between the boards. "Rags or pieces of cloth stuck in here . . ." He pulled out the black substance, and rubbed it between his fingers, crumbling it into a powder. He sniffed his fingers. "Some sort of alcohol, I imagine for accelerant."

Arthur and Constable Humphries stepped closer to see what remained of the cloth.

Mr. Thomas kicked aside some boards and crouched down, motioning for the other men to join him. "Coal." He pointed to a black lump and then to another a short space away. "Probably from the furnace there." He poked a finger into the ashes beside the coal, flicking them over and peering closer. "And kindling set around it." He stood, brushing off his hands. "This was no accident."

Arthur stood as well, his head dizzy. He felt both overwhelmed and furious. Could someone have truly started this fire on purpose?

"That is in accordance with the witness's statement," Constable Humphries nodded. He poked at the coal as well.

"Witness?" Arthur asked.

The constable rose, wiping the ash off his fingers onto his trousers. "Miss Dayley. She came by this morning to deliver a statement."

"Oh." Arthur was glad to hear that she was awake and apparently feeling better, but a small part of him was jealous that the constable had heard from her when he'd not.

They walked back through the warehouse to the main entrance, stepping outside to where Mr. Simper was talking to Mr. Fawcett and the vicar, Mr. Libby.

The men greeted the vicar.

"See here," Mr. Thomas said from the doorway, returning them to the investigation. "The lock was broken."

Constable Humphries nodded. "Miss Dayley corroborated that as well." He bent forward, peering at the lock. "Based on her testimony and the evidence, we can be sure this fire was set deliberately."

Arthur inhaled sharply. Hearing it said aloud felt like a punch.

"Do you suspect someone?" Mr. Thomas asked, peering at the lock as well.

"Of course it's Jim Garrick," Mr. Simper said. He planted his fists on his hips, motioning over his shoulder toward the docks with a flip of his head. "You all know what sort of man he is."

"We can't be certain," Arthur said. He didn't want to believe anyone capable of this—especially not in a place he'd come to think of as home.

"Garrick was dismissed from the crew, I've heard," Mr. Thomas said. "But he has no grudge against Mr. Grande personally."

Constable Humphries and Arthur shared a glance. "Actually . . ." the constable said, "he might at that."

The others looked curious, but neither Arthur nor the constable elaborated.

Mr. Libby put a hand on Arthur's shoulder. "I know I speak for the parish when I say we are saddened that something like this happened here in Brighton. This is not who we are. We consider you very much a part of our community, Mr. Grande."

Arthur's throat constricted. "Thank you, sir." He did not doubt the vicar's words at all. He'd been nearly overwhelmed by the outpouring of condolences and well wishes from the other townspeople. Not to mention the multitude of meat pies, fresh bread, and puddings that had been delivered to his hotel room. He'd never be able to eat it all; however, Mr. Fawcett was making a valiant effort on his behalf.

"And I hope your building project will continue in spite of this . . . this horrible incident?" Mr. Libby asked.

"It will." Arthur gave a sharp nod. "Mr. Jenkins believes the bones of the structure are still sound."

"Found your night watchman sleeping off the effects of a belly full of whiskey in the alley," Constable Humphries said.

Arthur scowled. That the man would choose this night of all nights to drink himself into oblivion felt suspicious.

"We are very lucky the fire brigade arrived in such a timely manner," Mr. Fawcett said.

"Luck had nothin' to do with it." Mr. Thomas frowned. "If Miss Dayley hadn't screamed—raised the alarm—we might have lost the whole building."

Daphne had saved more than the pile of papers after all.

Arthur felt a rush of gratitude and something that was becoming more common as he thought of Miss Dayley. A warm kind of happiness that made his heart skip and his stomach feel light.

"She'll be glad to know that," Mr. Libby said. The vicar looked at Arthur and opened his mouth as if he would say more, but he must have changed his mind, and he closed it again.

"I'll take my leave now." Mr. Thomas tugged on the brim of his cap. "Good day to you, gentlemen."

The fire captain started away, but Arthur called for him to stop. He took a few quick steps, catching up to him. "Mr. Thomas, I thank you again for saving my property."

"No need for thanks." He shifted his gaze, looking uncomfortable.

Arthur continued anyway. "I should like to repay you and your men."

"Not necessary, sir. We're just doing what we trained for."

"I wonder," Arthur said, "if I might be permitted to join the fire brigade. I've no experience, but I am willing to learn."

Mr. Thomas gave a solemn nod and extended his hand. "We'd be pleased to have you, Mr. Grande."

The two shook hands, and Arthur felt a measure of relief that he'd be able, in a small way, to repay the debt to the town of Brighton.

When he returned to the other men, Arthur found that Mr. Simper and Mr. Jenkins had departed and Constable Humphries was taking his leave. He bid the man farewell and thanked him for his assistance.

Mr. Fawcett followed the officer up the street. "You must find this . . . this . . . despicable . . . criminal and punish him to the full extent of the law . . ."

"I am glad to have a moment alone with you," Mr. Libby said, motioning for Arthur to follow him a short ways away. He opened the satchel that hung on his narrow shoulder and pulled out a paper-wrapped parcel, from which there emanated a delicious smell. "First of all, Mrs. Libby sent this for you with her deepest condolences about the fire."

Arthur took the parcel. "Thank you."

Mr. Libby drew in a deep breath. "And this is for you." He handed Arthur a letter. It was addressed to him, but the pattern of the wax seal gave no clue as to the sender.

Arthur assumed the letter was from Mrs. Libby as well. He smiled his thanks to the vicar and slipped it into his breast pocket.

"Miss Dayley came to see me this morning," Mr. Libby said.

He spoke as if he were starting a conversation that he didn't want to have. The hair on the back of Arthur's neck prickled. "And she is well?"

"Yes, yes." The vicar pinched his lip. He glanced to the side, then to Arthur. "She spoke very highly about you. And I must say you've been a good friend to her."

The uneasy feeling grew, making Arthur's stomach tight. "Sir, what are you telling me?"

"Well, I'll let her speak for herself." He tapped Arthur's chest where the letter sat in his pocket. *It's from Daphne.* But why would she send a letter? And why ask the vicar to deliver it? It all felt wrong, and a new sort of fear moved into his thoughts, setting his nerves on edge.

Arthur bid the vicar farewell, not knowing the words he used. His thoughts felt slow as he stepped inside the ruined bakery and righted a chair. One of the legs sat unevenly on the shards of glass, but he didn't correct it. He took out the letter, running his finger beneath the edge to break the wax seal.

Dear Arthur,

Please excuse the impersonal nature of this letter. I feared that if I spoke to you in person, my courage would fail.

When you read this I will be gone. I plan to take the mail coach to Dover and from there, the ferry to Calais and onward to Paris.

Yesterday I did something that terrified me because I could not bear the idea of you losing the thing you'd worked so hard for. I couldn't bear to see your dream destroyed. And as I watched the bakery burn, I realized that you were right all along. The bakery isn't what I want, and my own dream no longer seemed so frightening.

I thank you for your friendship to me this past week and your encouragement to pursue my passion. While I shall miss my friends and home, I think the thing I shall miss the very most is you.

Arthur paused, blowing out a heavy breath and rubbing his eyes before he continued.

I believe with all my heart that The Grande Hotel by the Sea will be the most splendid structure in all of Brighton and will make the prince regent immensely jealous. I cannot wait to see it for myself when I return.

Mrs. Libby was very pleased when I informed her that you'd happily participate in a theatrical performance during the Ladies' Auxiliary League's harvest luncheon. And I do hope your hat stays where it belongs.

With warm regards,
Daphne

In spite of the lump in his throat, Arthur chucked at

Daphne's parting tease. He read the letter again, feeling very proud of Daphne and very sad for himself.

Encouraging her to leave had been one of the most difficult things he'd ever done, and yet it had been the right thing for her. If only that assurance eased the ache in his heart. He leaned forward, resting his elbows on his knees and his face in his hands, knowing without a doubt the pain wouldn't disperse until she returned.

10

Thirteen Months Later

DAPHNE WALKED UP THE familiar road, feeling at home and lost at the same time. So much had changed in a year, and yet Brighton was the same town—her home—and she was thrilled to be back.

The smell of the sea breeze and the sound of birds crying and waves crashing brought back a flood of memories. Brighton's tourist season was at its height. Bathing machines had taken up their positions on the beach, and visitors filled the shops, restaurants, and walkways. The town held an air of amusement and relaxation.

Daphne took the route she'd walked for years—along the beach road toward where the bakery used to stand. With each step, the nervous flutters in her stomach became more pronounced. What would she find when she arrived? Would he—? She shook her head as questions flooded into her thoughts. She'd not contacted Arthur in over a year, unsure of exactly what to say. And, save for a parcel containing a silk scarf at Christmastime, he'd not contacted her either.

She'd left suddenly, and she expected he may have been offended. Was he hurt? Angry? Had he moved on? Was he married? Would he even remember her? The questions returned, and try as she might, she couldn't silence them.

Daphne came around a bend, and suddenly there it was, The Grande Hotel by the Sea. She stopped, and her thoughts froze as she took in the sight.

The building was made of whitewashed brick and stone, with large windows and balconies. It stood three stories tall, somehow managing to look imposing without being ostentatious. Manicured hedges and ornamental trees adorned the front and lined the walkway to the main doors. The building that had once been the bakery blended flawlessly with the rest of the structure, and although she'd expected it, Daphne felt a hint of sadness not to see the *Our Dayley Bread* sign.

The nervous quivers returned when she noticed the guests walking in and out of the hotel. All wore the fine trappings of high society and moved with an air of sophistication. Daphne hesitated, but she reminded herself that her gown was of the latest Paris fashion. She held her head high and climbed the steps.

A doorman in a top hat and tails pulled on the polished brass handle, giving a bow as he opened the door. "Good morning, miss."

"Thank you." Daphne stepped inside, and for the second time that day, her breath was stolen away. It was exactly as he'd described, but the sight was even more splendid than her imagination had conjured. The gaslights of the chandeliers glowed through enormous globes, making the marble floors and brass fixtures shine. Straight in front of her stood the reception desk, made of carved mahogany and staffed by two formal-looking gentlemen. Thick carpets covered sections of the floor, and above, a balcony with a marble balustrade ran around the upper level of the lobby. Deep chairs and plush sofas were arranged throughout the space, and among them, Oriental pots with large palms.

Seeing them, she blushed. Arthur had used her suggestion.

Walking slowly around the room, she ran her finger over a glass-topped table that held a vase bursting with hothouse flowers. Paintings of the sea and other sites she recognized near Brighton hung on the walls. She glanced into the dining room, noting the crisp linens and delicious aromas. Arthur had done it—all of this—and she felt immensely proud.

She walked along the rear of the lobby, past the staircases. The windows looked out onto a stunning garden. She paused, admiring the flower beds and statuary. Families walked along the paths, and children played in the shade of the trees. The scene was idyllic.

She continued around the lobby. Ahead, a woman played the grand piano. Daphne walked past and then braced herself to see the smoking lounge. Just a quick glance.

But when she looked into the space, she gasped. Instead of a gentlemen's salon, the layout of the room was almost exactly like the bakery—only larger and much fancier. She stepped inside, finding a dining area with wrought-iron tables and chairs reminiscent of a French café. The walls were papered a subtle rose color, and along them hung paintings of French street scenes. And the window treatments were striped in black and white. Beyond the dining area were new display cases, and on the counters, domed cake stands. All empty, as if waiting . . . Daphne's pulse pounded in her ears.

She lifted her gaze, seeing the painting of her family hanging in its spot beside the kitchen entrance. High on the wall behind the counter was a sign painted in elegant scrolled letters: *Dayley's Delectables*. He hadn't forgotten her after all.

Something thumped on the floor at her feet, startling her.

A man's top hat.

Daphne picked it up but didn't look around, using the excuse of dusting off the hat to compose herself.

Taking a breath, she turned.

Arthur Grande stood before her, and though she'd expected to see him, she'd not expected the mess of emotions that rose in her throat. He wore an elegant, custom-tailored coat, and on his cravat glowed a gold pin. He smiled, leaning on his walking stick and looking supremely handsome. She swallowed. "Arthur, what is all of this?"

"Do you like it? Rather presumptuous of me, I know. I just couldn't help myself."

"But—"

His brows pinched together. "Do not feel obligated in any way; that was not my intent. I just hoped . . ." He scratched his cheek. "I wanted you to have a place to come home to."

"It is . . . wonderful," she said. "More than I can say. I—"

He grinned. "Come, let me show you." He led her into the kitchen.

Daphne was stunned. The kitchen was entirely modern, with wood-topped preparation tables, a pantry of ingredients, shelves of copper pots, crocks full of utensils, stacks of painted dishes, and—Daphne gasped.

"Gas ovens," Arthur said proudly. "I'm told they regulate heat—essential for creating delicate pastries."

"Yes," she said, running a hand over the table, her fingers itching to start baking. "They—" She turned toward him. "It is all—so much more than I ever . . . Arthur, you did this for me?"

"Well, I do think a pastry shop will be profitable, but I did have some ulterior motives." He stepped closer, taking his hat from her hands and tossing it onto the table with his walking stick, then slid an arm behind her waist, pulling her toward him. "Éclairs." He smacked his lips. "I really do love éclairs."

Daphne laughed.

Arthur's grin softened, and he lifted her chin. "And that

was my other motivation. You said the bakery was your heart—and I rather wanted to take care of that."

Her cheeks flared in an exceptional blush. "Perhaps it was, but now I think my heart belongs somewhere else."

Arthur leaned close until his lips nearly touched hers. His hand moved behind her neck, and he tilted his head to the side, closing his eyes. "Oh? Where is that? I hope it's nearby."

"Very near," Daphne whispered just as his lips covered hers. She wrapped her arms around him, returning the kiss fully. All the tension and worry and wondering fled, and she poured all her emotions into her touch, wanting him to know without a doubt that she was here, she'd returned to stay, and he had her whole heart.

Arthur pulled back, leaving her breathless. He brushed a finger over her lips, then pulled her into an embrace. "I missed you, Daphne. More than I can say. I am so very proud that you went to Paris, that you followed your heart—but please ... don't leave again."

"I won't." She nestled into his arms, thinking no promise had ever felt truer.

After a moment, he pulled away, his smile returning. "Would you care for a tour of The Grande Hotel by the Sea?"

"Very much." His grin was contagious. Daphne took his arm, and he put his hat on his head, leading her back through the dining room and into the hotel lobby.

He strolled with his head held high, greeting guests they encountered. "Not much has changed, Daphne, since you left, with a few notable exceptions ..."

"Oh?"

"Mr. Fawcett and Mary Coombs are wed."

Daphne smiled at the news. "How lovely." The couple was perfect. She a baker, and he ... well, an eater of baked things.

"And Little Ronald says my name now, quite regularly. His mother claims the sound is just babbling, but he and I both know differently."

Daphne put her other hand onto his arm, holding it tighter and resting her head on his shoulder.

Arthur paused and turned her to face him. "Are you happy, Daphne?"

She shrugged and looked to the side, trying to look dispassionate, but couldn't hold the expression, and she smiled. "I am. Fine, you win. I am supremely happy."

Arthur gave an exaggerated smug smile and a bow. "I told you, once I put my mind to something, I do not fail."

Daphne took his arm once again, turning him to continue their walk through the lobby. "Don't go getting a big head."

Arthur laughed. "And now I'm putting my mind to a new goal." He tipped his hat to a couple they passed.

"And what goal is that?"

"Marrying the hotel's pastry chef."

Daphne gave an indignant scoff, even as her heart tripped. "Do you think I would be so easily ... won ... by a fancy kitchen and some pretty glassware?" She felt the blush return but held her head high as if she'd not noticed.

Arthur's mouth pulled in a smirk, and he covered her hand with his. "Dearest Daphne, you will never be easily won, and as for myself, I relish the challenge."

Jennifer Moore is a passionate reader and writer of all things romance due to the need to balance the rest of her world that includes a perpetually traveling husband and four active sons, who create heaps of laundry that is anything but romantic. She suffers from an unhealthy addiction to 18th- and 19th-century military history and literature. Jennifer has a B.A. in linguistics from the University of Utah and is a Guitar Hero champion. She lives in northern Utah with her family, but most of the time wishes she was on board a frigate during the Age of Sail.

You can learn more about her at AuthorJMoore.com

Signs of Love

Annette Lyon

1

"I WANT TO SEE if I can find some fossils before the tide comes in."

From behind her, fifteen-year-old Caroline scoffed. "Really, Julia. Why do you care so much about things that have been dead for thousands of years?" Her tone shifted slightly as she added to either Mrs. Fields or their friend Andrew, "Thousands, correct?"

Judging by her flirtatious tone, Julia suspected that Andrew was the recipient of the question. "I believe so," Mrs. Fields said, hazarding an answer anyway, her bygone duties never far from mind.

"Yes, thousands." Andrew had a smile in his voice.

Julia turned about, still walking but backward, and grinned at her little sister and Andrew, her lifelong friend. Unsurprisingly, Caroline was gazing admiringly at Andrew, to whom Caroline had taken quite a fancy, as if she'd only recently discovered that he was a handsome man rather than someone she'd known literally all her life.

"Science is fascinating!" Julia declared.

"Ugh. I cannot and will not ever understand you," Caroline declared. "Here we are at the most exciting place in England, with an invitation to attend a ball at the Royal Pavilion, and instead of finding the amazing pavilion interesting, instead of anticipating seeing the Prince Regent in attendance, you'd rather look at ancient fossils."

Julia slowed her step until she was in line with the trailing group of three. "Don't forget the chalk and flint cliffs. I find those utterly fascinating too." She glanced at Andrew and caught his amused smile. She smiled back knowingly.

Yes, the India-inspired Royal Pavilion was an impressive structure, and she did have a modicum of curiosity about seeing it up close and going inside. Yet she'd passed the stage of young womanhood when one's universe was comprised of handsome beaus and the next social event.

Julia remembered talking nonstop to her mother at the same age, so she felt quite sure that Caroline, too, would mature beyond the thrall of such superficial excitements.

In the meantime, bless Andrew for indulging Caroline's demand for attention, and especially her demand for *male* attention.

Heaven knew that Julia was at her wit's end listening to Caroline's gushing monologues about handsome young men, the most sought-after styles in dresses and hats, and other frippery.

She just hoped that Caroline wouldn't be heartbroken when "her" beau, Andrew, picked someone a bit older to marry.

They walked along in silence, listening to the lapping of the waves, breathing the salty breeze, and admiring the shore, with its alabaster cliffs on the left and a stony beach and shining waters on the right of the path. To be truthful, Julia and Andrew walked in silence, but Caroline did not. She couldn't stop talking, especially about the ball at the Royal Pavilion later that week.

"I hear there are dragons in every room," she cooed.

"Dragons, you say?" Andrew said, sounding properly impressed.

"Not real ones, silly." Caroline swatted his shoulder with

her free hand, clearly taking care not to remove her other hand from the crook of his elbow. "In the décor. I hear there are chandeliers with swooping dragons in gold and bright walls of all colors, just like in India."

"Hmm," Julia said thoughtfully. "I was unaware of India being so full of dragons and color."

Caroline stopped walking, making the other two stop as well. She gave Julia a pointed look, one eyebrow raised. "Mock all you wish, dear sister. Enjoy your fossils and chalky cliff. All I know is that I am going to thoroughly enjoy myself at the ball tonight. You don't have to attend if you'd rather make rubbings of your fossils. I'm sure Mother wouldn't mind at all that you're ignoring what might be the biggest social event of your life."

The twinge of pain in her voice made Julia immediately contrite. "Forgive me, Caroline," she said. "I didn't mean to tease. That wasn't kind of me."

"Well—th-thank you," Caroline said, clearly not expecting that response. "And I suppose I should apologize for poking fun at your interests. I'm sure science is quite ... fascinating ... to persons of a specific mind."

It was a touching attempt at an apology, and Julia wanted to encourage that kind of behavior in the future—it boded well for her sister.

She stepped in front of Andrew and reached for her sister's hands. Caroline reluctantly removed one hand from Andrew's elbow and allowed Julia to take them between her own.

"I have an idea," Julia said. "You're surely fatigued after our long walk. You and Andrew rest here for a spell, and I'll investigate the shoreline a bit farther on. I won't be long, and then we can all return to the inn in time for tea and for Mother to take us with her to visit friends of hers who are also on holiday in Brighton. That is, if such a plan is amenable to Andrew."

"It is," Andrew said hastily. "I would like to hunt for fossils before we leave Brighton, but I'm happy to cut the trip short today for your dear sister's sake." He nodded toward Mrs. Fields, the family's longtime governess, and added, "And for Mrs. Fields's sake too."

The somewhat portly middle-aged woman smiled gratefully. "My feet are a bit tired. Thank you."

"My pleasure, Mrs. Fields," he said with a nod that approximated a bow. "And Caroline and I—we'll have a rousing good time while we wait, won't we?" he added cheerfully.

"I suppose," Caroline said dully.

Julia pointed to a log that had washed ashore. "There. That is the perfect place to rest your feet while you wait for me. I won't be long."

The governess made tracks through the sand as she scurried to the log and sat with a grunt of relief. For her part, Caroline sighed, then walked over to the washed-up log and plopped herself down in what was a rather dramatic show of resignation.

Good enough. Julia threw Andrew a grateful look and made the sign meaning *thank you* to him as she walked away. Many years ago, Andrew had suggested learning deaf signs as a way to communicate secretly, and what little she remembered still proved useful at times. In response, Andrew made a sign that meant *you're welcome*, and then he waved.

Julia returned to the path, carrying the bag in which she kept her rubbing and other adventure tools, as she thought of them. Alone, she could walk at the pace she preferred, which was much more quickly than before. She didn't intend to go far, only to the end of the visible stretch of beach, but when she came to the spot where the cliff curved, hiding what lay beyond, the sound of men's voices drifted to her around the bend.

If Julia Hughes was one thing, she was curious, and about far more than science. Anything unexpected or unknown piqued her interest, and the conversation around the bend definitely qualified. The tones of at least two different voices pulled her forward.

The first words she could make out clearly came from a scruffy, low voice. "Ye expect me to keep the shipment here, where it could be found at any moment? Are ye daft, man? Have me sent right back to the workhouse up the road, ye will. I doubt they've had time to sweep it out since I was released, so they'll toss me back in when they find me guarding a stash o'—"

"Hush, man," a second voice interjected, one far more cultured and educated. The first broke off, muddled, as if the second person had covered his mouth.

Julia's eyes widened, and her step came up short. Were these dangerous men? Would they hurt her if they knew she was there?

"You mustn't say such things aloud," the second man said. "Not if you know what's best for you and the crew. That kind of thoughtlessness *will* land you right back in your cell, no question, but it won't be me sending you there. It'll be your own stupidity."

Despite the logical arguments in her head telling her to go back to Andrew and the others posthaste, she stepped forward and peered around the corner. The scruffy voice belonged to an equally scruffy and unkempt man who appeared to be in his forties, unshaved and uncouth. The other man, however, wore a proper coat, trousers, boots, and a cravat. His hair was neatly styled, pulled back into a ribbon.

Even after a mere glance, she knew she'd never forget their faces.

The handsome man shifted, and, fearing he'd spot her, Julia pulled herself out of sight, then backed up a few more steps to be sure they wouldn't see her, but she moved oh so slowly to remain unheard as well as unseen.

Now that she couldn't see the men directly, Julia could not make her feet move. What should she do? Thank heavens that Caroline hadn't come this far. But what should Julia herself do?

Leave, certainly.

Yet she remained, wanting to remain and flee in equal amounts, the two desires battling each other. In the end, her deep-seated curiosity won, thanks to her hiding place in the crook of the cliff. She *had* to find out who the younger, stronger of the men was, had to learn what crimes the older man was guilty of. Most importantly, she simply had to discover what they were up to here on the shore of Brighton, days before a ball with the Prince Regent.

2

JULIA STOOD JUST OUT of sight, back pressed to the white cliffside, listening. The men weren't talking, which made her chest constrict with worry. Had they seen her? She held her breath, half expecting either—or both—of the men to march her way and threaten her.

Finally, the younger man spoke. "Did you hear something just now?"

He must have removed his hand from the older man's dirty face, because the latter replied. "A 'course I did, yeh simple git—yer voice, mine, the birds squawking about, and the water makin' its noises." The words were impudent, though he'd lowered his voice slightly, as if agreeing with the wealthy-looking man that they needed to be discreet.

Would the younger come to search out the noise? The noise she knew well was made by her own slippers, her own weight shifting pebbles under her feet. Julia scarcely dared breathe, as if that, too, would create sound and raise suspicion.

These men were criminals, the older one by his own admission a moment ago. The younger one, though ... he didn't look the part of a criminal, not at all. He looked like a landed gentleman, possibly even a titled one. Could he be a duke or earl, or even a relatively speaking lowly baron? Such men had morals and standards.

Had the noble-looking man said anything that

implicated him in a crime? She didn't think so; that was the older man. She tried to remember precisely what she'd heard.

I should hurry back to the safety of being with Andrew and Caroline, admiring the sun glinting off the water, she thought. This was no place for a gentlewoman to be walking alone and unchaperoned, vulnerable to who knew what all. *Apparently, to criminals.*

Would they hurt her if they knew she had seen them and was listening? Perhaps she could quietly slip away, one careful step at a time, until there would be no one for them to spy even if they did round the corner; she would have returned to the others with no one the wiser.

Her harried thoughts and indecision made her miss a portion of the conversation between the men, which had begun again. She deliberately abandoned thoughts of Andrew and Caroline and leaned in to hear every word she could from around the bend.

"I'm tellin' ya, Silas, I don't feel good about this; we're too close to the Prince Regent, we are."

"You will call me Mr. Hayward," the gentleman said. "And I'm telling you that the Prince Regent will support us in our endeavor."

Julia's interest was suddenly piqued even further. Could these men be involved with the war efforts in some fashion? Perhaps they were here to deliver an important communiqué.

But the older man dashed that idea with his next words. "The Prince Regent likes his wine as French as the next man, I've no doubt. But smuggling it across the Channel, so near the pavilion? Are ye daft? Ye've left me with half a dozen crates of French port right here in the open. How d'ya suppose I go about hiding them so they aren't seized before we can sell 'em?"

"Durham, stop worrying," Silas—rather, Mr. Hayward—

said. His tone was coaxing. "They're already sold. That's the beauty of this: we aren't bringing in large amounts of goods that could hamper the war efforts. No, no, we're providing a service to the noble classes, the lords in government, and even the Prince Regent himself—to those who need good port as they make critical decisions for the rest of us."

Durham snorted. "I mightn't have the book learning you got, but I'm no imbecile. Parliament and the Prince Regent don't need booze to run the country. Fer that matter, getting them all sloshed would only help France. So don't pretend that what we're doin' is somehow noble or patriotic. This is to line our pockets, it is—or rather, it's to line yours."

Mr. Hayward cleared his throat, and if the regular crunching of sand and gravel was any indication, he began pacing. "You will benefit too, my friend," he said. "You already have. Don't forget."

"Yeah, yeah. But a few days free don't mean nothin' if I end up right back in my cell."

"You won't," Mr. Hayward assured his partner. "And the ... more *sensitive* element of our campaign will bring us nothing but reward from the Prince Regent when he realizes that we've identified a supposed ally who has traitorous intent."

The older man humphed. "I have half a mind to walk back up the street and ask to go back in so I don't have to be arrested and sentenced again."

"Don't you trust me?"

Someone—likely Durham—spat. "Trust yeh? Hah. Not without some reason to. Give me a way to know I can trust yeh—or I might just trot myself right over to the pavilion now and tell Prinny himself what I know."

Sudden shuffling and grunts registered. Had Durham attacked Silas? The other way around? Julia's heart began pounding. She'd always prided herself on being an independent woman, unafraid of anyone or anything, but her bravado had evaporated, leaving her wishing she hadn't gone on ahead alone. Wishing that she could at least call out to Andrew and Caroline without being detected, so she could have the safety of their presence. The idea of being a lone woman near smugglers made her feel as vulnerable as a kitten.

They probably have weapons, too. The thought was utterly unhelpful, but it appeared of its own accord. *Knives? Guns?* The hair on the back of her neck stood on end, and a shiver zipped through her.

"You'll tell no one a thing," Mr. Hayward said, his voice threatening.

Gasps for air followed. Was Durham being choked? Julia's hands flew to her own neck as if her turn was next. She waited, listening and trying to determine the best course of action, all while pressing herself against the cliffside.

"I need—assurance," Durham squeaked out.

After a moment for Mr. Hayward to contemplate, Julia heard stumbling and a gasp of air. Slowly, she peeked ever so slightly around the cliff with just one eye. She couldn't *not* look, but at the same time, she prayed she wouldn't be spotted.

Mr. Hayward was walking her direction, but with his face downturned, so he didn't see her. His hand stroked his chin in deep thought. She froze, certain he was about to spot her. With a sudden movement, he spun around, spraying pebbles and sand—and allowing Julia to breathe again. He reached into his waistcoat pocket, then held out whatever he'd plucked from it. Durham sat on the ground, one hand rubbing his neck where Mr. Hayward had gripped it.

"What's that?" Durham asked, jutting his chin toward the object.

"My pocket watch. You keep it—hidden, mind you, until this is all over."

"Why would I want that?"

"For assurance," Mr. Hayward said. "If you take it, each of us has a way to betray the other. No one would listen to you if you were to accuse a gentleman with the so-called crimes some may think we're committing. But *with* it, you'd have some basis for your claims. You won't need to use it, because as I said, our business will be over before you know it. You will be paid handsomely—more than the watch is worth—so there's no use in running off and selling it."

Durham reached out tentatively, then snatched the watch and peered at it. "More than this is worth?" he said in awe. His chin trembled, and then he coughed as if trying to speak while holding back tears. "I'll be able to pay off my debts and return to my family."

"Yes," Hayward said. He knelt on one knee and placed a hand on Durham's shoulder. "This whole venture will be good for both of us. Good for England. Good for your family."

In reply, Durham nodded but at first said nothing. He cleared his throat again, then, with a wobbling voice, said, "Thank you, sir. I won't let you down."

"I know you won't." Mr. Hayward stood and wiped his palms together, as if removing sand. "Now go hire that wagon to transport the crates. I'll meet you here on Friday eve, one hour before the ball, with further instructions."

"Yes, sir." Durham scrambled to his feet—several seconds' worth of work, as the gravel and sand did not provide much purchase—and then bowed and scurried off down the shore trail away from Julia.

Hayward watched him go, and Julia watched Hayward. He stood tall—a hand taller than Andrew, if she guessed correctly. He had broad shoulders. Dark hair that would need to be cut soon and a jawline that hadn't seen a razor yet today; the shadow made him look mysterious and powerful, like a hero from a Gothic novel.

In a manner of speaking, she already thought of him as a hero of sorts. He was helping a man who had fallen on hard times. Even if the same deed lined his own pockets a bit, she couldn't help but admire him. Technically he was breaking a law, but he was right; the entire upper class drank French wine despite the blockade. He seemed to be doing something good, or at least, nothing particularly bad.

With each second, she felt drawn to him, and while she imagined what it would be like to talk to him, she would never have been so foolish as to attempt such a thing. Even if they'd had a proper introduction, she couldn't very well reveal herself after overhearing the scene with Durham.

Mr. Hayward gazed out toward the ocean, and the morning breeze sent his coat alight and ruffled his hair. Goodness, he was handsome.

Mr. Silas Hayward, she thought, cementing the name in her memory.

Who knew that she'd find something on the cliff path that would interest her more than fossils?

3

FORTUNATELY, JULIA CAME TO her senses the moment Silas Hayward began to turn. Just as his coattails shifted with his weight, she pulled back, out of sight, breathless at nearly being spotted.

Now what? Would he come her way, walk the path along the cliffside, and find that she'd been eavesdropping? With her mouth suddenly dry and her frame trembling with panic and excitement, she tiptoed carefully through the stones as quietly as she could manage, trying to get as much distance between herself and Mr. Hayward as possible before he rounded the corner and saw her.

Wait a moment, she thought, suddenly realizing her error. If he came around the bend and saw her withdrawing, he'd know for certain that she'd been witness to his encounter with Durham.

She looked about frantically, then realized a solution. She quickly left the path and ran toward the shore. Her steps would make some sound, but she walked purposefully and deliberately—and slowly—doing her utmost to appear as if she'd been admiring the ocean view and the sun as it reflected off the water, sending streaks of gold and orange and red across the surface. Julia set her face into what she prayed looked like an enamored, dreamy expression, and lifted her face to the sky as if relishing the breeze, even though the salty tang was mixed with fishy smells, which weren't so enjoyable.

Andrew, Caroline, and Mrs. Fields were far enough away that she'd have to call loudly for them to note her, but near enough for Mr. Hayward to assume—rightly—that she was part of their group and—wrongly—that she'd only just wandered ahead of them.

Julia arranged her wrap about her shoulders a bit more, noting the morning chill and hoping to catch a glimpse of Silas out of the corner of her eye. He wasn't there. She turned toward the stones on which Andrew still sat, waiting for her return as Caroline stood and chattered, gesticulating as she told him another story of who knew what about whom.

With the water on her left and the path on her right, Julia had a good view of Andrew. She could tell the moment he'd spotted her, as his posture straightened in expectation, and then he stood and smiled in the way that could always light up a room.

"Sit down, Andrew," Caroline said, tugging on his coat. "I wasn't finished."

"Of course. My apologies," he said, resuming his position. "What were you saying about the ball?"

Once more, Caroline continued her chatter, but Andrew continued to look at Julia. He unobtrusively held out his fist thumb up, put his other hand palm up beneath it, and made the sign *help*.

Julia had to hold in a laugh. Dear Andrew. Even now he lightened her mood and eased her anxiety, even when he didn't know about her worry: whether Silas would figure out that she'd seen him and knew things she should not. She began walking toward him, the water on one side of her and the cliffside path on the other.

Out of her peripheral vision, she noted movement by the cliffs and instinctively turned. There was Mr. Hayward walking along with a purposeful gait, as if on the way to an important meeting. She gulped, then quickly schooled her face, hoping to seem as casual and unaffected as a stranger would, but he noted her and slowed his step. For a heartbeat or two, they stared into each other's eyes—his cobalt-blue ones held her gaze fast. They seemed to bore into her mind, reading her very soul. He looked as if he had a deep and complicated past that demanded someone—some woman—learn of and love him for it. He nodded and touched the brim of his top hat in acknowledgment, an action that stunned her into clumsiness.

She didn't realize that she'd been staring at him for several seconds until her slipper caught on a large rock and she stumbled, nearly falling onto the stony ground. After she caught herself, she smoothed her skirts and wiped off any dirt, blushing furiously. By the time she looked back up at the path, Mr. Hayward was gone, still visible but much farther along the path.

Either he knew she'd witnessed his encounter with Durham and didn't care, or he had no idea about it, and her ruse had worked. At the moment, she wasn't sure which to hope for most; she was merely grateful that he hadn't confronted her with the angry tone he'd used with Durham. She felt quite certain that she wouldn't withstand two seconds' interrogation from him. Though he was quickly growing smaller in the distance, Julia kept looking his way, curious about him, though now sure to check her footsteps to ensure that she wouldn't trip again.

When she'd crossed about half of the distance to Andrew, he jogged along the stony ground to reach her. "You're back," he said, taking a spot beside Julia as she walked the rest of the way. He held out his arm, and she slipped her hand into the crook.

She eyed him mischievously. "Do I detect a hint of relief in that statement?"

Andrew laughed aloud, throwing his head back, which, with a gust of wind, sent his hat flying and mussed his reddish-brown hair. "Oh, you sensed far more than a *hint* of relief," he said, reaching for his hat on the ground. He smoothed his hair back and replaced his hat in its place. "She is a like a sister to me, truly, and yet . . ."

When his voice trailed off, Julia offered, "Yet younger sisters do have a tendency to wear on one's nerves . . . only on occasion, of course."

"Precisely. Only on occasion," Andrew said, still smiling, though he faced forward. Julia could see him in profile now and was glad to see the dimple in his cheek.

"I believe I can make a relatively accurate prediction about our dear younger sister—though she's your sister in name only, of course—"

"Of course," he said with a mock-solemn nod.

"I think it is quite safe to suppose that Caroline will be insufferable for the entire time we are at Brighton, and that she will not stop talking nonsense until we've returned to London and a full fortnight has passed."

"God save us all." Andrew sounded almost as if he meant it as a genuine prayer, something Julia could appreciate entirely, though his response was so unexpected that she laughed aloud and nearly lost her balance on an uneven portion of the beach.

She stumbled a few steps, making her grasp Andrew's arm with both of hers. He, too, stopped and bent over, holding on so she wouldn't fall. When the downward momentum had halted, Julia found herself staring at the ground and awfully near Andrew. His boots were right there, below her eyes, and his arm felt warm and secure around her—waist. The latter realization sent a thrill through her, though Mrs. Fields would be shocked and appalled by such a forward gesture, even though it was instinctual and entirely for Julia's safety. Andrew wouldn't be able to act untoward even if his future livelihood depended on it.

All the more reason that Julia, for the briefest of moments, didn't want to straighten and keep walking. She let herself enjoy the moment of feeling his hand about her waist, the warmth of his body near hers, the scent of sandalwood from his skin.

"Are you quite all right, Miss Hughes?" he asked, reverting to her proper name.

Mrs. Fields must have drawn near. Sure enough, when Julia looked up, there she was, standing at a distance with her hands upon her hips, looking for all the world as if Julia and Andrew were misbehaving children or outright scoundrels. The governess's disdain would have looked the same for either situation, Julia was quite certain.

"I'm fine," she said, straightening. "Thank you so much for your help, Mr. Gillingham," she added, reverting to his proper name.

Mrs. Fields and others did not approve of using Christian names with those one was not intimately familiar with. Yet that was precisely the thing that Mrs. Fields did not understand: Andrew had been part of Julia's and Caroline's lives for literally as long as they could remember. They'd grown up together, their mothers having been good friends and their families having settled in the same area. Their fathers were partners at a thriving bank, and since his father's passing a year ago, Andrew had moved in with the Hughes family as he studied under their father in preparation to take his own father's position at the bank. In many respects they were very much like siblings.

Though truth be told, Julia was grateful for the fact that they *weren't* related, for they could interact in other ways that such a relation would have made difficult. She dreaded the day that Andrew found a wife, for marriage would inevitably change their long-standing friendship. No longer would Andrew be able to be her confidante. No longer could they take walks together without society papers whispering about it. A wife—or husband, in her case—would be highly unlikely to view their friendship as something worthy of continuing.

Julia herself could scarcely bear the thought of marrying, because that would almost certainly mean moving away from London to some estate, possibly in the country, to be the mistress far from where she had always called home.

Until either of them married, all could continue as they had for years and years. But seeing as Andrew was four and twenty, he'd almost surely marry within the year. Society—and his family—would demand he settle down soon.

As for herself, Julia was already two and twenty, which meant she was nearing spinsterhood. If she was lucky, perhaps she'd escape the need to marry. Her father's estate could provide for her in her later years, and beautiful Caroline would almost surely make a good match.

Perhaps I can live with Caroline in my elderly years.

She smiled a bit at that thought right as they reached Mrs. Fields and Caroline, who now put a hand on her hip, much like the old woman. "Why are you grinning like an imp?"

Julia thought quickly. She had a plethora of reasons to be smiling right then—escaping Mr. Hayward, *seeing* the handsome Mr. Hayward at all, enjoying and appreciating Andrew's friendship, his saving of her when she tripped, and, yes, the thought of living with Caroline as she grew old and gray and got to spoil Caroline's children beyond measure.

In that moment, however, she smiled most at the memory of the dashing and exciting Mr. Hayward, who had an aura of mystery and danger about him.

"I'm thinking of this week's ball at the Royal Pavilion with much anticipation, that's all," she told Caroline—likely the first flagrant lie she'd ever told her sister, and hopefully, it was the last.

JULIA HAD FULLY EXPECTED to find her patience tried exceedingly by her younger sister as they got ready for the ball, but instead, she found Caroline's excitement contagious. As they walked down Old Steine on their way to the Royal Pavilion, it lay ahead of them, stunning in its white glory. Lit by candles and lamps so it glowed against the darkness of the night, the radiance reflected back from the water, making an even more awe-inspiring scene. Julia could not help but feel slightly giddy at the prospect of going inside.

Andrew walked between the sisters, each of them on one of his arms. Unsurprisingly, Caroline was abuzz with anticipation, to the point that Julia doubted the Prince Regent himself would be able to get in a word edgewise if he tried to.

Would they meet the Prince Regent? The thought was thrilling to Julia, though until yesterday, she hadn't any desire whatsoever to meet him or any other royalty. Something had changed, and she knew what it was: the scene she'd witnessed the other day between Mr. Silas Hayward and Durham.

Caroline did a little hop as they walked. "I cannot *wait* to see for myself how the inside is decorated. I wonder if there are many halls and rooms or one large open area. Oh, I hope there really are dozens of dragons. I've looked forward to finding as many as I can. That had better not be a rumor, or I'll be so disappointed."

"I've heard about the dragons from several sources," Andrew said encouragingly. "You shouldn't be disappointed on that count, at least."

"Oh, I'm so glad to hear it!" Caroline tossed some dangling hat ribbons over her shoulder. "I cannot wait to return to London and tell the James sisters all about the Royal Pavilion and the ball. They'll be sick with envy, I tell you!" With a start, she released Andrew's arm and spun around to face the sisters' parents, Mr. and Mrs. Hughes, who were following from the rear. "Mother," Caroline cried. "I forgot my brooch!"

Mrs. Hughes waved a hand in an attempt to console her daughter. "The Prince Regent will never know the difference, my dear. You look stunning."

Caroline ran to her mother's side, which made the entire party stop right there on the cobbled street. "Please, Mama. May we return to the flat to get it? My night will be absolutely *ruined* if I don't have my brooch. I've dreamt of this night for weeks, and always with my brooch. It simply won't be the same without."

Mr. Hughes and his wife exchanged knowing looks. "Very well. I'll continue on with Julia and Andrew, while you two ladies return for the brooch."

"Oh, thank you, Papa!" Caroline went on tiptoe and gave his cheek a peck before taking her mother's hand and trotting back up the street as fast as her mother could go.

Mr. Hughes waved Andrew and Julia along. "We might as well continue on our way."

They walked along, the pavilion growing larger and larger in the distance, and the sounds of music and the milling, growing throng reaching them like a murmuring wave from the sea. They stepped onto the long pier, at the end of which the pavilion awaited them. Neither Julia nor Andrew spoke for some time, each in their own thoughts.

Julia would never have admitted that her mind was fixated upon a single thought: *Will I see Mr. Hayward tonight?*

At last, Andrew broke the silence. "Did you find any fossils at the shore yesterday? You weren't gone for long, but I didn't know if that was because no fossils were to be had, there were so many that you found more than you needed, or something else."

She'd forgotten that she hadn't reported on her solo excursion—not a word about fossils or chalk or flint or anything else she'd been vocal about wanting to study. Until now, no one had asked about her silence, and she'd begun to think she'd be able to maintain it.

"I simply decided to turn back before I began looking for any."

She prayed the few street lamps dim and far apart enough that he wouldn't note how her face had paled out of guilt. She'd never lied to Andrew before, and now she'd lied to both Caroline *and* Andrew on successive days.

That wasn't a lie to Andrew, she argued with herself. She *did* decide to turn back before looking for fossils. That was true, if not the entire truth.

Still, guilt swept over her like sudden seasickness, a feeling she pushed away as hard as possible, and then she tried to lock a mental door so the thought could not return. For this magical evening to *not* be spoiled by such a mental intrusion, however, she needed to redirect Andrew's line of query.

A man her father knew from past business appeared from a side street and greeted them. She and Andrew were introduced to Mr. Lambert, and then they returned to their walk, her father and his associate lagging behind, involved in their own conversation. This left Julia and Andrew a modicum of privacy, which she wasn't sure whether to welcome or wish away.

Before Andrew could return to questioning what had happened at the shore the day before, she decided to approach the conversation from a different angle. "I've been meaning to thank you for not dismissing my interest in the sciences."

Andrew cocked his head and looked her way as their steps clicked and clacked against the cobbles. She felt herself blush under the weight of his stare. At last he looked away and replied, "I think every young lady should exercise her mind across any and all subjects she finds interesting. Such an endeavor can only expand her intellect and be a benefit to everyone in her sphere."

"Some people would argue that expanding a young lady's intellect, indulging in her curiosities, is reason enough to discourage studies beyond the traditional list of what it means to be an accomplished gentlewoman." Julia walked beside Andrew as she thought of how few people in her life viewed her love of learning with anything other than a negative eye. Her parents had always tolerated her thirst for knowledge but encouraged her to keep the expanse of it somewhat unknown publicly; they feared that a studious young woman would be less likely to attract offers of marriage. And perhaps they'd been right. The older Julia became and the more seasons that passed without an offer, the less they seemed concerned about her studies, almost as if they assumed she'd be a spinster now, and therefore, further book learning would do no harm.

After all, no one paid any mind to an eccentric spinster. Young ladies with marital prospects, however, were another matter.

"*Some people* are ignorant," Andrew declared. "Women, whether mothers or not, are a benefit to themselves, their families, and society as a whole. All benefit when a woman is educated. I say, educate all women, and more than the men."

"Careful, or someone will think you've gone mad," Julia

said. "Though I believe you are the most sane and intelligent of men to say so."

Part of her wished she could be secure in knowing what her future held: would she be a spinster with enough money to live on? If so, she'd be able to happily feed her mind without limit. She might be able to teach or explore or do any number of things to benefit society. Perhaps she might make a scientific discovery that would change the world.

"I'll take your opinion as a compliment," Andrew said. "I am like any man in the sense that I appreciate looking upon a beautiful woman. But beauty alone is not enough to tempt me."

"Oh?" Julia said. With a teasing grin, she said, "Do you then seek someone plain for a wife?"

"I did not say that," Andrew said, giving her a laughing side eye. "However, beauty, unlike marriage, doesn't last. And even if it could, I can think of no greater tedium than spending life with a woman who is beautiful but without anything of substance to recommend her."

"If beauty is not a requirement, perhaps being accomplished is." Some of the teasing had left Julia's voice. She found herself curious about the kind of woman Andrew would one day marry, hoping that whoever she was, his wife would be amenable to Julia's friendship with her husband.

"I don't put much stock into knowing every last bit of etiquette, being able to speak six languages, or knowing how to play any number of pieces on the pianoforte. Those things are lovely in certain instances, I suppose . . ."

When his voice trailed off and he hadn't spoken in three more steps, Julia repeated, "You suppose . . ."

"Those things are wonderful for public consumption, but when one is not attending a ball or other social engagement, what use are they? I'd much rather have someone who is my intellectual equal, with whom I can discuss Plato and Descartes. Someone I can read and talk about literature with. Most of all, a woman who doesn't pretend that her husband is somehow all knowing and always correct. I could not bear to experience counterfeit fawning."

Julia placed her free hand over the one already slipped through the crook of his elbow, so she was effectively holding his arm with both hands. "I have a suspicion that you are rather alone in your perspective. I no longer wonder at your bachelorhood."

"I suspect that other men feel the same, but I'll never know."

"I must confess, dearest Andrew, that you are a most curious, unusual man, which is precisely why we get along so well."

"I suppose I am odd," he said with a chuckle. "But I've never understood why women are supposed to be more alluring when they appear intellectually lacking. I find such women to be a trial of my patience."

"Even the prettiest ones?" Julia couldn't help but speak the thought; it popped out on its own. In her experience, the prettiest young women were also the most likely to have a filled dance card. They were the ones who behaved as Andrew declared he did not enjoy: they giggled around men, complimenting them on their physical and mental prowess, pretending they knew nothing and could do little without aid. She'd seen Andrew succumb to some such antics, although now that she thought on it, he hadn't been flattered into looking weak-kneed in the last year or two.

He didn't answer her question for several moments, but when she eyed him as they walked, waiting for a reply, he seemed to be contemplating her question deeply. At last he said, "I cannot deny that a woman beautiful of face has, at times, captured my attention, but 'tis a rare woman who *keeps* my attention. For while beauty may draw me near like a moth to a flame, if nothing substantive exists within the woman—no thoughts of her own, no intellect to challenge mine, no opinions that make me want to think and understand—then no matter how beautiful she may be, she will become dreadfully dull." They walked on a few more feet before he added, "Does that make the slightest bit of sense?"

Julia's usual instinct to tease didn't come to the surface, and she surprised herself by saying in a reflective tone, "Truthfully, your words make more sense than I ever would have supposed. I must say that your possession of such a mind must be why I like you so much: you don't find my curiosity and studying to be tedious or, worse, a threat to your manhood, as so many men seem to."

"I suspect your intelligence and determined nature are in good measure why I like you so much as well." Though his words contained a sliver of humor, his tone was reflective too, and they slipped into a comfortable silence for the rest of the walk to the Royal Pavilion.

Why couldn't life always be this easy and comfortable? 'Twas a pity she and Andrew couldn't spend their days as a bachelor and a spinster discussing all manner of topics for the rest of their lives.

Stringed music floated from the pavilion and seemed to fly up the onion-shaped domes, up into the night sky. The sight was magical. Caroline had been right in every respect. The Royal Pavilion was nothing short of amazing.

To her surprise, Andrew reached for her hands on his elbow and, turning for face her, held both of her hands in his and trained his warm brown eyes on hers. The heat and intensity of his gaze seemed to warm her from the inside out, and her knees threatened to unhinge altogether.

From behind them, the elder men caught up, and her father called to Andrew. "My boy, go inside with Mr. Lambert. He has much to tell you about his business with us."

"I'd be delighted to, Mr. Hughes," Andrew said, then nodded to the other gentleman. "Mr. Lambert. I'll be right in."

The two men went ahead, and Andrew faced Julia again. "May I have a dance tonight, Miss Hughes?"

The sound of her formal name sent an odd thrill through her, one she could not explain. Perhaps it was the romantic setting of the night sky, the glowing pavilion, the music and dancing within. Whatever the cause, Julia felt her heart pick up its pace in a delicious fashion, and she wished that her hands weren't gloved, that she could feel his skin next to hers.

"You may, Mr. Gillingham," Julia said, making sure to use his formal name as well. "I—I quite—look forward to it."

Had Andrew always been so handsome, or was it the flickering shadows that made him look so much like a Roman god? Why was she suddenly stammering?

Andrew bowed in her direction, kissing her glove. He looked up at her and, with a voice as smooth as warmed honey, said, "As will I, Miss Hughes. As will I."

"Come along, Mr. Gillingham," Mr. Lambert called from inside the doors.

Andrew winked at her, straightened, and entered the pavilion.

SHE HARDLY NOTICED HER father stepping to her side, taking Andrew's place. He held out his elbow to her. "Shall we?"

His voice pulled her back to the present moment, away from the spot where Andrew had slipped into the crowd with Mr. Lambert and disappeared.

Putting on a smile, she slipped her hand through her father's arm and said, "Let's."

Together they entered, and immediately Julia found several images of dragons—a few small statues and several others as part of the metalwork of a chandelier lining the long hall ahead of her. She and her father followed the queue along the luxurious red carpet, and she found similar dragons in other fixtures as well.

Her father leaned in and whispered into her ear. "How many townhouses do you think could fit along this hall, end to end?"

"I had no idea it would be this large," she whispered back. She felt as if she needed to speak softly, as if the pavilion itself might overhear anything she said and be dismissive if she was too impressed with its luxury. The rug alone must have cost more than her father would earn in his entire lifetime. She could not fathom what constructing the entire thing—pier, pavilion, decorations, landscaping—would have cost. Better not show that she was overwhelmed; that would only serve to prove to others that she wasn't part of the *ton*.

Her family lived comfortably compared to the majority of Londoners. But that did not make them wealthy, titled, or of especially good name. Her father had a respectable profession, but it *was* a profession—one he needed to be paid for. Their family had no inherited estate to manage or live off of.

How precisely had they gotten their invitation to the ball? Her father had explained at one point, but she couldn't recall the details now, possibly because they hadn't particularly mattered to her at the time. What did she care about the upper class and nobility?

Yet now, surrounded by colorful gowns of the latest styles and most expensive fabrics, she could not help but feel self-conscious in her simple, worn slippers. Compared with other ladies' footwear, visible as they stepped along the lush carpet, hers seemed ragged, and she was grateful that her dress hid all but the toes as she walked.

Julia had always scoffed at her peers' yearning for the latest in fashions, for a new hat each year, and at their constant worry about what others thought of them based on nothing but their appearances. Goodness, just moments ago, she and Andrew had shared a similar conversation—the outer shell of a woman mattered far less than what the inner part of her possessed in her mind and heart.

Had she turned into one of the foolish girls she'd always disdained? In some respects, she was afraid she had. No matter how it had occurred, she could not deny that standing there in the massive ballroom, with women and men from the highest places in society, she felt embarrassed over her simple dress of printed cotton. It had no stains and did not look worn, though she'd had it for five years already. She'd always loved this dress, which was a pale color somewhere between yellow and orange, one of the colors that splashed across the sky as the sun went down. Beside all of the other dresses—the satins, silks, brocades—hers looked simple, plain, and old-fashioned.

They entered the ballroom, which was even grander, with huge chandeliers, walls papered in red, gold, and green, and doors with intricate painted molding. She followed her father, who walked along the periphery of the room, greeting people as he went. Julia smiled at those they passed and curtsied with a proper "How do you do?" whenever her father introduced her to someone.

Where was Andrew? Between introductions and promises to dance with various eligible young men her father made sure she met, Julia surreptitiously looked about the room in hopes of finding him. He was the one person in all of Brighton who could make her feel comfortable and once more at ease.

"Miss Hughes, you say?" A deep, mysterious voice said her name, and Julia turned quickly to see who it was. *Silas*. She gathered her wits—or tried to—then amended silently, *Mr. Hayward.*

He had his hand out, as if expecting to take hers. Was her father making an introduction? How did her father know Mr. Hayward? He waited, hand outstretched, and one half of his mouth curved into an amused smile as he waited expectantly.

With his hand on her back, her father steered Julia closer to the man she'd first seen on the beach. "My dear, this is Mr. . . . uh . . . that is . . ."

"Mr. Silas Hayward, at your service." Hayward bowed to them.

Her father continued as if he'd merely forgotten the name of his associate. "Yes, Mr. Hayward, I am pleased to introduce you to my elder daughter, Miss Julia Hughes."

As she held out her hand, Julia felt certain that her father did not know Mr. Hayward at all and that the man had pretended an acquaintance to enable an introduction. She wasn't sure whether to be more shocked by the breach in etiquette or flattered at the efforts he'd taken to meet her.

"A pleasure," Hayward said, taking her hand and bowing. How would her father explain Mr. Hayward's connection? Julia's gaze slid quickly to her father's face and away again. His lips were pressed together, and his gray brows were bunched together as he thought—no doubt searching for any clue in memory about his supposed friend, Mr. Hayward.

Her father always assumed the best of everyone and would never have imagined that a man who looked as respectable and wealthy as Mr. Hayward would deceive. Father would simply believe that he'd forgotten. "We've done some business together," he managed, looking at Mr. Hayward hopefully. The latter nodded as if agreeing, and her father sighed in relief.

"Pleased to meet you, Mr. Hayward." Julia curtsied as she spoke and wondered if he could tell that her voice was tight with nerves. She was meeting a smuggler. No wonder her heart hammered in her chest.

"The pleasure, Miss Hughes, is all mine." He began to straighten, though he didn't release her hand. Instead, he stared at her with sultry eyes. "And it is *quite* a pleasure, I assure you." The strains of his voice seemed to vibrate something deep within her, as if a bass violin lived in her chest and something had plucked its strings.

"May I have a dance with you tonight?" Mr. Hayward asked.

"I'd be delighted," Julia said with a nod and small curtsy.

"Not your first dance, however." The speaker pulled up beside her with his rich, comforting voice—Andrew. "That one is promised to me."

She turned, pleased to see him. His presence popped the bubble of fantasy that had been building around Julia's mind and dropped her back to earth. She just looked at him and blinked a few times, trying to grasp what he'd said so she could make sense of the words.

Had she promised Andrew the *first* dance? That didn't sound like something he'd ask for, and it did not sound like something she'd promise unless it was in jest. Andrew must have sensed her confusion, because he stepped forward, held out his arm, and spoke again. "You'll recall that dancing with friends can be particularly enjoyable when compared with dancing with those who are only a step away from being strangers."

As he spoke, Andrew didn't look at Mr. Hayward. He didn't need to; his intent was quite clear. For her part, Julia's mind cleared enough to make sense of the moment. She and Andrew did indeed have a promise between them, and it did involve dancing together. However, it referenced his years-old promise to always rescue her from a potentially difficult partner. He'd done as much when she'd been practically trapped by a wealthy but very old man looking for a young wife, and on another occasion when an overbearing dolt droned on and on until he nearly made her fall asleep. In those cases, she'd been utterly grateful for Andrew's way of gently slipping into the situation and extricating her from it, with no offense taken on the gentleman's part, nor any trouble created in regards to her reputation.

The last time Andrew had used the ruse was months ago—nigh unto a year, if she wasn't mistaken. Why had he drawn out the old trick now? Couldn't he see that she'd been pleased to speak with Mr. Hayward—that she was indeed quite thrilled at the prospect of dancing with him? She wished to talk with him for longer than a dance would provide opportunity for. She hoped to take a turn about the room or the grounds now and perhaps later that evening.

Andrew couldn't have known any of that. The one truth he likely surmised was that Mr. Hayward had made a pretense of familiarity with Mr. Hughes as a way to meet Julia. She could hardly fault Andrew for growing suspicious on that count.

"I would be pleased to dance with you, Andrew." She slipped her hand into the crook of his arm and turned to Mr. Hayward. "May I save the second dance for you? Unless you're already promised for it, in which case, I can certainly wait until the third."

Dismay flashed oh so briefly across Andrew's face. Beside her, his frame tensed. She tilted her head to look at him better and was surprised to see such a strong expression on his face, one of distrust and something more—a warning to Mr. Hayward? Hoping to ease Andrew's protective, brotherly feelings, she patted his arm with her free hand. Hopefully he'd interpret the gesture as gratitude, even though this time a "rescue" hadn't been necessary.

Mr. Hayward bowed elegantly from the waist. "I shall look forward to the second dance, then," he said. "Miss Hughes." He nodded at her, then looked at Andrew, whose eyes flared with annoyance, and his jaw held tight. Hayward smiled as if he noted neither. "Mr. . . . I'm sorry, I don't believe we've been introduced."

"Gillingham. Andrew Gillingham." He spoke his name firmly, without inflection.

"A pleasure, Mr. Gillingham." Mr. Hayward gave a half bow, threw a smile and a wink to Julia, then walked away. The crowd seemed to instinctively part to make way for him as he drew further into the room, which was increasing in its giddy buzz.

Andrew grunted with irritation. "He is quite a cad."

He turned to leave, but Julia tightened her grip on his elbow. "You are not leaving me here," she declared.

"Why not?" Andrew said. "I stepped in so you needn't dance with a particularly loathsome man, but you clearly *want* to be stuck with that libertine. You have no need of me now."

Julia stepped closer to him and gazed intently into his dear blue eyes. "Andrew," she said quietly. "I will *always* need you."

He looked away and breathed through his nose, his jaw working.

She tried again. "You promised me the first dance. A gentleman wouldn't renege on a promise to a gentlewoman, would he?"

Andrew's stiff expression softened as he tried not to smile. "Are you insinuating that I'm a gentleman?"

Julia released a dramatic sigh. "I'm afraid so, Mr. Gillingham. Worse, you'll soon be a gentleman with a respectable profession and a thousand pounds a year." She ignored his laugh at the ridiculously large sum and continued. "Then *I* will be the one attending balls so that I may rescue *you* from the unwanted attentions of young ladies. Daughters of earls will be vying for your eye, and I'll have to beat them off with a parasol."

Andrew chuckled so hard he nearly snorted. "Let's dance then, you silly gentlewoman." He held out his elbow again.

She took it. "Yes, let's."

As they walked onto the dance floor, she breathed a mental sigh of relief; she never wanted to upset Andrew, but she also didn't need him behaving like an overprotective brother.

Especially when she *wanted* the attention of a certain Mr. Silas Hayward.

6

JULIA AND ANDREW TOOK the final spot in line just as the music began. She curtsied, he bowed, and they danced, weaving in and out of formations, coming back together, and turning in the patterns the quadrille required.

Midway through the set, Andrew struck up a conversation. "I've been meaning to ask you something."

"Oh? What is that?" Julia pressed her lips together in a small smile. She assumed he was still in the jocular mood of a few minutes before and expected a question along the lines of being gentlemanly or not.

A bright-blue cravat caught her eye, and she couldn't help but stare, nearly stumbling over her slippers as well as Andrew's boots while her attention was drawn to Mr. Hayward. He stood at the edge of the floor with a glass of port in one hand, his eyes on her. At first she questioned whether he was looking elsewhere, but when he noted her looking back, he raised his glass, his lips curved into an intriguing line that sent her heart pounding.

Another near trip over a different set of slippers—those of the woman beside her—tore Julia's attention from Mr. Hayward and back to the dance. She quickly murmured an apology to the unknown lady, then hurried to Andrew's side, still holding his hand but not entirely sure what part of the dance she'd missed or where to pick up. Watching the other couple for a measure solved the problem, and she slipped back into the correct step.

As she and Andrew promenaded down the center of their group, she remembered that he'd spoken before Mr. Hayward had drawn her attention. "You were saying?"

"It was nothing." His tone and expression weren't ones of anger, but distance. He seemed out of sorts, and Julia determined to figure out what, precisely, was bothering him. "Did you hurt yourself just now?"

"With my stumble? No, I'm quite well," she said. "Though I'm not entirely certainly the same can be said for the woman in the brown gown over there."

In answer, Andrew gave a weak smile, took her hand, and kept dancing, but his temperament seemed changed, and Julia guessed that the shift had something to do with her careless misstep a moment before.

"I'm truly sorry I got distracted," Julia said. "I'm quite sure that my incompetent dancing won't reflect poorly on your abilities."

"I'm not the least bit troubled by that, so long as you are unhurt." Andrew's shoulders went back as he straightened his stance, and he let out a breath that might have been a sigh.

Julia glanced over her shoulder, as if by seeing the spot on the floor they'd been standing on a moment before, she'd be able to witness the moment again and better surmise what had upset Andrew, for she knew he was upset. She'd known him long enough to recognize that weak smile for the mask it was, though the cause remained a mystery.

He'd been about to ask her something. She held that thought and dove back into the conversation, hoping to return the mood back to the pleasantness of a minute before. "What were you going to ask me?" She gave Andrew her best smile, and even with another flash of a bright-blue cravat from the side of the room, she did not trip or lose her focus at all.

"Merely what we brushed upon earlier on our way to the pavilion: what happened at the beach when you went on ahead yesterday morning."

Her stomach went sour, and she suddenly noticed that her grip on Andrew's hand was a bit too viselike. She forced out a chuckle. "Caroline had been complaining for some time about wanting to return to the inn, so I returned sooner than I otherwise would have."

"Ah," Andrew said with a nod.

They danced for several bars before either spoke again. This time, however, Julia was the one feeling out of sorts, desperately curious as to what Andrew saw in her to suspect that anything out of the ordinary might have occurred—and precisely *what* he suspected in that regard. Certainly not that she might have eavesdropped upon a handsome gentleman smuggler and a member of his crew.

She wove in and out of the couples, then returned to Andrew. "Why do you ask?" She hoped her voice was as airy as intended, but if she could sense from the slightest shift in Andrew's demeanor that something was awry with him, then he could most definitely sense the same in her. She'd wager that any other man, her father included, wouldn't have noticed anything different about her countenance when she returned from her solo walk. None would notice her pretense now, either. Only Andrew, unless she could feign lighthearted denial well enough to fool someone who knew her almost as well as she knew herself.

"You were rather flushed," Andrew said. "Cheeks bright pink."

"I'm amazed that you'd wonder at that, what with the morning chill and the fact that I was walking about—two things that naturally bring about color in a lady's face."

"But your complexion was a deeper pink when you

returned compared to when you left us. It went from cherry-blossom pink to the deep pink of your father's peonies."

She lifted an eyebrow in feigned disbelief and chuckled again. "Andrew, please."

"There's more."

Oh, heavens.

"Pray tell, what else?" Her smiles were beginning to feel like drying plaster and her laughter like a high note on an off-pitch violin.

Andrew's eyebrow went up, a twin to hers, only in curiosity. Drat. He'd noticed the tension in her voice and face. Of course he noticed. And if he hadn't already, he was about to note that her fingers had gone cold; he'd be able to feel their iciness through her thin gloves.

"You were breathing heavily, as if you'd been running—as if you'd been running *from* something. Or someone."

Hand in hand, they skipped and hopped along the dance floor, belying his serious tone. His hand tightened around her fingers protectively, though he couldn't have had any idea what had startled her or why she'd been afraid. The gesture crumbled her walls of pretense. Remembering the moment at the shore, and practically feeling the weight of Mr. Hayward's stare yet on her a moment ago, Julia felt heat creeping up her neck.

"Let's go outside," she said suddenly. "I need a breath of air." Whether she'd confess all to Andrew out of doors, she could not say, but she certainly needed to remove herself from the pressing heat and airlessness of the vast ballroom.

"Of course." Without another word, Andrew slipped her arm into the crook of his and led her off the dance floor, then wove through guests milling along the edges of the room until they reached the tall glass doors leading outside. A footman nodded as they passed through the exquisitely carved doorway and entered the elaborate gardens filled with shrubs and flowers that were unfamiliar to her. They walked several feet along a path, and then she turned to look at the pavilion and sighed in awe at the bulbous spires reminiscent of India.

"I've never seen the like," she said.

"Most impressive." Andrew placed a hand over hers at his elbow, and they walked forward in silence. She admired the view, amazed at how luxurious and fantastical the gardens and pavilion exterior were. The gentle sound of lapping water seemed to come from all around, a reminder that the pavilion was built upon a pier.

After a time, they reached a stone bench, and Andrew suggested they sit on it to chat. What should she tell Andrew? *Could* she safely tell him anything about what she'd seen and heard on her walk that morning?

"If you'd rather not relate what happened," Andrew began, "I understand. But I hope you know that you may confide in me about anything, at any time."

Dear, dear Andrew. She smiled again, only this time, it was as natural and genuine as an apple blossom. "I know I can."

Yet . . . his words seemed to imply something far more than the assurance that she could confide her troubles in a friend. Was it possible that Andrew had deeper feelings for her? The thought sent a swarm of wings alight in her middle—a sensation both delicious and unsettling. If he did see her as more than a friend, more than practically a cousin or a sister, what did that mean for her? For their friendship?

She'd never contemplated Andrew in such terms, yet now that the concept had been presented, she found herself drawn to it—drawn to him. For the first time in memory, she admired his jawline and the slight wave in his hair, near glowing under the silvery moonlight. The bright blue of his eyes—kinder and warmer than Mr. Hayward's icy blue—and the fact that Andrew was the perfect height for her to walk with, talk with, dance with, and even fall asleep beside. She'd done the latter in the family drawing room accidentally when the family was there after supper, reading and talking. One night in the winter, the crackling warmth of the fireplace had lulled her to sleep, and she'd wakened suddenly only to realize she'd slept with her head resting on his shoulder. They matched in so many ways, as if they were created to fit like puzzle pieces.

"Julia, I have something I must tell you."

A sudden fear of the unknown, of possible change, gripped her, and she broke in, unable to bear the loss of her friend. "Andrew, you'll never know just how grateful I am for you." Even as she tried to head off his attempt at changing their status quo, she felt betrayal in her own heart. Perhaps she should want such a change, should welcome it.

Before she could go on, before she could analyze her feelings at all, her words cut off, as did all thought, because Andrew was altogether so close, entirely filling her senses as he gazed into her eyes in a way he never had. For the space of several heartbeats, they sat in silence, side by side on the cool bench under the night sky, warmth—and something else, far more intense than she'd experienced with anyone else—passing between them. The sensation washed from him to her, engulfing her heart and senses, then returned to him in a wave, only to return to her a moment later.

What was this feeling? She could not think or speak, and while she wanted the moment to last and last, she feared its continuing as much as she craved it. Was it connection? Attraction? Love?

Could it be? Love Andrew? But he's my friend. A chum . . .

He's also a dreadfully handsome man.

She swallowed nervously, which broke the tension enough for her to inhale, then remember her name and his. Looking away, she stared at the grass bordering the path. For his part, Andrew kept his gaze on her, but she needed a moment without seeing his warm blue eyes to formulate her thoughts.

"Julia," Andrew said again, now taking both of her hands in his. Once more, the push and pull of wanting to be near him and wanting to pull away warred within her, forces of equal power. "We have known each other for some time, since we were but children, yet since my father's passing, since living with your family and learning the banking trade from your father, I have found our friendship to be one of both happiness and misery."

"A misery?" Julia scooted closer to him, terribly worried. "Andrew, how have I wronged you? Oh, please tell me; I cannot bear to think that I've offended or wounded my dearest friend."

"Dearest *friend*," Andrew repeated, a wan half smile settling onto his face. "Therein lies the misery."

"How so?" Julia asked, then immediately wished she had not. The fear of losing her friend, of settling for the commonplace when there were exciting, adventurous men in the world, began to be victorious over the new pull of attraction toward Andrew. In regards to excitement, Mr. Hayward outshone anyone.

"Every day I pray that you might look upon me with favor, that perhaps you might come to . . . to love me as I have found myself most ardently loving you."

She felt as unable to move as stone and wished she had not drawn quite so close to Andrew a moment before; she was all too aware of his presence, of his leg beside hers, his arm against hers, the warmth of his body . . .

"Julia?" he said after a moment. "Please say something. I can't bear the silence."

What could she say? She could scarcely form a thought, much less a coherent statement about her emotional state, when she did not yet know what it was for herself.

In the distance, she heard the door to the pavilion open, and she used the interruption to her advantage, turning from Andrew to see who was entering the gardens. Surely he wouldn't want witnesses to this private moment—though he'd apparently had no issue with the dozens of people meandering about the gardens already, each couple in a world of their own.

Instead of another pair emerging from the doors, a single man appeared—tall, with a dark coat and boots. He paused, seemingly looking about, then headed toward their bench. Light from a nearby lamp spilled onto his chest, revealing a bright-blue cravat. Such timing. Julia's mind raced for how to handle the forthcoming situation, but Mr. Hayward reached them before she'd formed so much as a kernel of a plan.

He stopped in front of them, his boots sending a few pebbles skittering away. "The second dance is about to begin, Miss Hughes," he said with a bow. "I believe the honor of being your partner is reserved for me?" He held out a hand expectantly.

"Alas, Miss Hughes is unwell," Andrew said. "She will have to enjoy your company another time. We retired from the quadrille because she needed air."

"Indeed?" Mr. Hayward said, his tone one of challenge rather than question.

"Indeed," Andrew replied with a stone face.

The two men seemed to stare daggers at each other, though neither wore a matching expression. Who knew so much could be communicated with nothing but one's eyes?

"I-I'm quite well now," Julia said, standing. Andrew

reluctantly released her arm. She turned to him, and their eyes locked, sending the same wave of heat and emotion over her. Mr. Hayward extended his hand further, and she took it. "Thank you for your concern, Mr. Gillingham," she told Andrew, but the look on his face sent a dagger to her heart. She'd wounded him, more deeply than anything she might have guessed at when he first began talking of misery.

What could she do now? She'd already promised the second dance to Mr. Hayward, and she'd already taken his hand and stood. She couldn't very well rebuff the man now.

The best she could do was a silent apology, which she did in the form of a hand sign, a fist over her heart, rotating it in a circle. She hoped he would accept her apology and understand. What she would say next time they spoke, she hadn't the slightest idea.

Andrew bent his fisted right hand at the wrist, an affirmative reply. She tried to smile, and he gave an even weaker one than before in return. The next thing she knew, she'd left Andrew behind and was taking her place for the reel with Mr. Hayward. He smiled, and his penetrating gaze sent a different kind of heat through her—one not entirely comfortable, though very exciting.

As she curtsied to begin the dance, she had the uneasy premonition of having left her childhood friend in the gardens. From that night, her friendship with Andrew would never be the same.

JULIA HADN'T BEEN DANCING with Mr. Hayward more than a few seconds before her thoughts and worries about Andrew vanished like butterflies in the wind. Something about the mysterious Mr. Hayward, from his dashing looks to his adventures and risk-taking drew her to him like a moth to flame.

I trust he will not doom me to the fate of a moth, she thought wryly, and, when Mr. Hayward led her into the next step, she returned his broad smile with her own.

"You will inform me if such a moment arrives in which you need a bit of air again," Mr. Hayward said, "won't you?"

"I do not think that will be necessary. I feel quite well." Julia felt somewhat better than *well*, a fact that made her feel not a little guilty over leaving Andrew behind as she had.

Knowing he was yet in the gardens was enough to convince her to *not* request fresh air; if she took a turn outside with Mr. Hayward, it would serve only to make Andrew feel worse than he did. She did not want the two men to have any additional harsh words between them, even if the general idea of two men fighting over her sounded romantic. Books with such stories were certainly enjoyable, but the reality wasn't at all pleasant.

What did happen between Mr. Hayward and Andrew? She couldn't be entirely sure—and thinking on it only muddled her mind further.

The reel ended, and after Mr. Hayward's bow and her curtsy, he led her off the floor. To her surprise, however, he did not release her at the edge of the throng, nor did he return her to her father's side or to Andrew's. She now spotted Andrew standing beside a table on which stood an elaborate floral arrangement. Mr. Hayward didn't slow at all as they reached the end of the dance floor. Instead, he firmly placed a hand over hers, ensuring that she could not easily withdraw it from his arm—not that she had any desire to—and together they took a turn about the room.

How fortunate to not have a third dance called for with another partner; she could stroll the room without interruption, and she hoped others might look upon her and note that she was on the arm of a wealthy gentleman. Julia could scarcely believe her situation. Women from relatively humble situations rarely found themselves both invited to a ball at the Royal Pavilion, where she would see the Prince Regent himself, and walking the room on the arm of a man who had prestige and influence.

Mr. Hayward nodded to all manner of guests: those with money, those with titles, and those who had influence in parliament and business. Her prior self-consciousness over her inexpensive, simple gown and her worn, stained slippers had all but vanished. She found herself able to walk with her head held high.

After nearly a full circuit of the expansive room, Mr. Hayward led her to one of the many refreshment tables. He fetched two tall glasses of punch, served in beautiful crystal goblets.

"Thank you," she said, taking the proffered drink.

He nodded. "Come." He led her to the rear side of a column, where they were partially blocked from view. He lifted his glass. She did the same, and then they sipped the golden champagne—perhaps from a bottle he had smuggled across the Channel. He subtly pointed out various individuals in the room.

"See that man over there with the long, pointed nose?" he asked with a slight tilt of his head, indicating the direction for her to look.

Julia nonchalantly took a sip of her drink as she scanned the room and turned back to him. "Thin face, long nose, wearing another country's military dress?"

"That is Charles Bernadotte, Crown Prince of Sweden."

She felt her eyes widen. "Truly?" She tried not to be too obvious as she looked at him and then away again, though she wanted to stare. The Prince Regent was known for hosting other royalty, but something seemed strange about this circumstance, though determining why took her a moment. A memory of her father reading a newspaper aloud and commenting on the latest battles with Napoleon returned to mind, and she understood her confusion. "Isn't Sweden an ally of France?" Why would the Prince Regent invite an enemy to his Royal Pavilion?

"Ah, that is the intriguing part. He's an enemy no longer." Mr. Hayward wore a rather pleased look, as if he knew he'd revealed information that she would be impressed by. "The latest reports say that he has removed his support from France and is now combining forces with England." He took a sip of his champagne.

"Fascinating." Julia turned to sneak another look at Crown Prince Charles. Or would that be Crown Prince Bernadotte? She didn't know the Swedish protocol for such things but was glad to know that he was an ally, not an enemy.

"People say that his choice may be the factor that utterly defeats Napoleon." He made a humphing noise.

"Wouldn't that be a relief," Julia said.

The wars had been going on for so long, and at a high price for the country in many respects: money, supplies, and most importantly, casualties. Countless men of several nationalities had been killed or seriously injured due to Napoleon's greed. 'Twould be good to end the bloodshed and vanquish the madman responsible for it. Would the Swedish Crown Prince's change in loyalties be key to changing the tide of the war?

Hardly daring to hope, she sighed. "We've thought that Napoleon was a hair's breadth away from surrender many times already. I hardly dare think such a thing is possible."

Mr. Hayward brought his glass to his nose and sniffed, then took a sip. "This time, I fear the rumors may be true."

"How so?"

Before answering, Mr. Hayward leaned close, so he could whisper in her ear. "I have communications with men from all fronts of the war. They say that the Crown Prince commands a battery with a new weapon: rockets that can fire long distances with accuracy that exceeds any cannon or rifle."

"Why, such a tool could definitely turn the tide." Julia could not remember how long she'd lived with the fear that her father might be compelled to fight or that Andrew would feel the need to enter the military. She'd lost several cousins to the war and more than a few neighbors. Few British families had gone through the years of Napoleon's reign and conquests unscathed. They all bore marks of war on their souls.

"Fascinating idea, isn't it?" Mr. Hayward said. He gave her a half smile, clearly pleased with her reaction. Is that why he'd told her the secret—so she'd be impressed? He already had her admiration, and yes, this new information only increased it.

A footman came to them and stopped, holding out a tray to collect their glasses. Mr. Hayward tipped his head back and downed the last of his drink, then reached out for her glass, only to realize she'd hardly partaken from it at all.

"I'm finished," she said, surrendering her glass.

Mr. Hayward set both on the tray. Instead of moving on as Julia expected, the footman spoke to Mr. Hayward under his breath. "Haven't been able to get close enough."

She knew that gravelly voice. The sound brought Julia's head around, and she peered at the man after having hardly noticed him before. He stood short of stature, with a crooked nose and dark hair. He was shaved clean, his hair was pulled back in a black ribbon, and he wore servant's clothing that was clean and pressed. Even with those changes, however, there was absolutely no mistaking: this was Durham.

"No excuses, man," Mr. Hayward said through his teeth, so quietly in a room humming with music and activity that she didn't quite trust her hearing.

Yet the corner they stood in, and the stone of the column, amplified his voice. She could hear them both, though their whispers indicated that neither suspected she listened or understood. She made a quarter turn and pretended to be fascinated with the dancing couples on the dance floor, though she kept her ear attuned to the whispered conversation only inches away, behind the column.

"I ain't makin' no excuses," Durham said. "Jus' reportin' back to yeh. I'll keep tryin', but he keeps waving away any drink I try to offer. I ain't sure I'll be havin' any success here. We may need another way."

Another way to what? Julia controlled her face, certain to smile and nod at guests as appropriate, though her mind was entirely consumed with Mr. Hayward and Durham behind her. She glanced over and noted that Mr. Hayward's jaw worked in annoyance. She quickly looked back to the dance floor.

Mr. Hayward gave Julia a look, as if seeing whether she'd heard anything. She deliberately focused across the room and watched blue, yellow, and green skirts brushing the exquisite marble floor, then turned her face to meet his, giving him what she hoped appeared to be an expression as innocent as a doe's. She couldn't let Mr. Hayward know she'd heard a word of the interaction—not for the world.

She wanted to learn as much as she could about their plans for defeating Napoleon, which she'd convinced herself was their aim. From experience with her father, she'd learned that not letting on as much as she actually knew tended to work in her favor. Chances were good that the same would apply to Mr. Hayward, so she pretended to be that cotton-headed girl she disdained—she knew nothing, and she'd heard nothing.

Mr. Hayward cleared his throat with a cough, and with his fist before his mouth, as if covering a cough, he murmured to Durham, "The position you're in gave you ample access."

"I can get the arsenic into 'im," Durham said. "Truly, I will. I just need more time."

Alarm shot through Julia, and she turned fully forward, hoping that Mr. Hayward wouldn't realize that she'd seen or heard a thing. *Arsenic? In the Crown Prince's drink?*

"Hush!" Mr. Hayward hissed, grabbing Durham hard on the arm. The old man sucked air between his teeth at the viselike grip. Mr. Hayward leaned in, nearly spitting in his face. "You keep your mouth shut, or I'll make sure you're silenced—permanently. Do I make myself clear?"

Durham nodded, face white as a sheet. Julia suspected her face looked about the same. She swallowed nervously. At last, Mr. Hayward released Durham's arm with a shove, and through his teeth said, "Give me the envelope."

Durham reluctantly reached into his coat and drew out a

small envelope of waxed paper, which Mr. Hayward palmed and slipped into his own pocket. Hayward released him, and the man scuttled away like a scared beetle.

As she watched him weave through the onlookers, chandelier light caught something gold, which she realized was the chain of the pocket watch that Mr. Hayward had given to Durham as "assurance." If she'd had any doubt of this being the same man as at the shore, the sight of the pocket watch removed all doubt. Now that she noted Durham, he was obviously out of place here. The Royal Pavilion possessed opulence and elegance in such quantities that even the servants looked highborn and cultured. Not Durham. His boots were too new; they had no sign of wear whatsoever, not even a hint of having been shaped by the left or right foot. They'd been purchased solely for this performance; she was certain of it. His suit was as fine as any, but his bearing and stride spoke louder of a poor, uneducated upbringing than any woolen suit could overcome.

What better way to hide a convict than as a servant? Julia suddenly realized the genius of Mr. Hayward's actions. Provided Durham performed his duties, he'd be largely unnoticed, invisible, no matter how many elite members of the ton and aristocracy were in attendance. He would have remained unnoticed by her, too, had he not spoken directly to Mr. Hayward.

Servants are much like women—we must both keep our peace and remain silent.

Silence was not a quality Julia naturally possessed, a fact that provided her father with no end of frustration and worry and one that provided Andrew with no end of entertainment. However, now that she knew, even vaguely, about Mr. Hayward's plans to do away with Bernadotte, she determined that so long as she remained in his presence, she would have to cultivate the art of remaining silent.

Doing so now, while keeping her arm through that of a man who appeared to be not a patriotic hero but in reality a villainous traitor, would be both an education and a motivation to learn the skill of silence well, posthaste.

Her life, and that of Crown Prince Charles Bernadotte, might well depend upon it.

8

MR. HAYWARD COUGHED, THEN tugged on his coat, straightening it out. Clearly distracted, he turned to Julia. "Thank you for the dance, my dear," he said, but though he'd glanced at her, his eyes scanned the large room. He stiffened almost imperceptibly, a reaction only a person very near, with deep-seated curiosity, would note. Someone like Julia. He blinked and looked back at her, then bowed slightly. "Perhaps we can dance again later this evening. For now, if you'll excuse me—"

"Oh, please don't go," Julia said, giving her best impression of her younger sister's energy and enthusiasm—things few people could say no to. She took Mr. Hayward's arm and began walking along the edge of the dance floor, bringing Mr. Hayward along with her. She'd heard some alarming things, which gave her three things to accomplish: first, ensure that Mr. Hayward did not suspect that she'd noted anything untoward between him and Durham; second, do her utmost to learn more about his traitorous plans regarding the Swedish Crown Prince; and third, stop any attempt on his life.

Mr. Hayward slowed their progress, stopped altogether, then attempted to unwrap her hand from his arm—an effort Julia found herself remarkably good at thwarting, simply by pretending to be ignorant of his intentions.

"You must excuse me, milady," he said, looking about the

room again instead of at her. His eyes flashed briefly—so briefly that she wouldn't have seen it if she hadn't been studying every tiny muscle on his face. Based on their proximity to the doors leading to the gardens, Julia suspected that someone Mr. Hayward wanted to follow or speak to had gone outside. The longer she held his arm, the more restless he became.

She stepped closer to him, then, again pretending to be Caroline, gazed into his eyes with what she hoped looked like dreamy attraction and said, "Care to take a turn about the gardens? It's so lovely tonight."

He broke his stare at the doors long enough to glance at Julia, who kept the sweet dreaminess on her face for his benefit. She found doing so far easier than maintaining a neutral expression, which she feared she'd fail at after hearing his traitorous intent. She simply could not allow even a hint of her real feelings to be revealed. The guise seemed to be working even though her heart had sped up, beating fast and faint, making her lightheaded.

"Very well," he said. "A turn about the gardens would be a pleasure." He looked at her in a way that an hour before, she would have found flattering but now found unnerving and duplicitous.

I could let him go into the gardens alone, then try to tell someone about Durham, she thought as they headed for the doors. Fortunately, the gardens were filled with guests; so long as she kept Mr. Hayward in areas lighted by lamps and near other guests, he couldn't hurt her.

For the second time that night, the chilly sea air raised the hairs on the back of her neck. This time, however, Julia couldn't help remembering her father's oft-repeated declaration that her curiosity would one day land her in trouble. He'd been referring to how easily she got distracted on explorations and his fears that she might twist an ankle while admiring the clouds, or that she'd fall off a cliff and break a leg while studying fossils.

Father had never imagined—nor had she—that she might one day risk her life by following a traitorous man into the Prince Regent's gardens. They walked a few paces from the door, and both looked about, Mr. Hayward seeking whomever he'd spotted before and Julia attempting to discern who that might be while appearing awed by the grandeur of the pavilion.

Some steps on gravel made Mr. Hayward's head come around, and Julia noted two men turning a corner around some shrubs, one of whom was in formal military dress. Bernadotte?

"Care for a drink?" Mr. Hayward said suddenly. Without waiting for a reply from Julia, he whirled around and approached a footman with a tray of drinks standing just outside the doors. After selecting two glasses of champagne, Mr. Hayward returned to her side and held out one for her. "Here you are."

"Thank you," Julia said, taking the delicate fluted glass. She pressed it to her lips but then remembered Durham's mention of arsenic and pulled the rim away again without a sip. She smiled, however, pretending that she'd had some and that it was delicious.

Mr. Hayward, she noted, did not partake of his drink. He gestured with it toward the very section of the gardens where the two men had withdrawn. "Let's take a stroll."

"Sounds lovely," Julia said.

With each step she took into the darkness of the night, farther from the lanterns, the more her insides knotted up. Perhaps she'd been hasty in thinking that accompanying Mr. Hayward outside would yield information she could use to thwart his plans. Her fingers tightened, the glass of the champagne flute feeling cold against her skin.

Instead of a slow, casual stroll, Mr. Hayward walked at a brisk pace, which only made the evening air feel that much chillier. A salty ocean breeze made her shiver. She almost asked him to slow down but knew he wouldn't comply. He wanted to catch up to Bernadotte, of course, and wouldn't risk losing him along the path.

She had to be ready to intervene to save Bernadotte's life. But how? She could hardly overwhelm Mr. Hayward. Her best and likely only option was to continue her pretension about being like her younger sister: acting foolish in intellect and childish in maturity, while being the opposite of both.

She began chattering on about the pavilion, using all of the many details and rumors that Caroline had shared and seemed impressed with. Mr. Hayward made appropriate noises and comments like "Mm, I see," and "Is that so?" but she doubted he heard a word. Goodness, *she* hardly noted a word that came out of her mouth. She simply had to keep talking, to stay with Mr. Hayward as long as possible and to learn all she could.

At a fork in the path, they paused, and Mr. Hayward listened, trying to determine which direction to go. As they stood there, she looked about and prattled on about the beautiful gardens and how much it all must have cost. As she went on like a dim-witted child, she prayed he did not note her watching him carefully, especially the moment she pointed out a shrub she'd never seen elsewhere, when at the same moment, he pulled the envelope out of his pocket and emptied the powdery contents into his champagne flute. Her stomach twisted.

"Let's go to the left," he said, slipping the now-empty paper into his pocket. The pavilion was large compared to most buildings, but not compared to an estate with sprawling landscapes. The gardens here were strictly limited to the pier on which the pavilion had been built upon. That meant a smaller area in which to take a walk, which should have been a comfort—Julia would never be too far from the ballroom and the murmuring crowd inside. Regardless, the gardens felt more like a cage, and Julia a bird unable to escape the gilded bars.

"Yes, let's," Julia answered, and they went to the left. She glanced over her shoulder toward the ballroom doors, knowing that the golden light spilling outside marked the door to her cage—that she could conceivably excuse herself and return to the ball—but she decided instead to stay with Mr. Hayward. She could not bear to think of him succeeding in poisoning the Swedish Crown Prince, or the guilt she would bear if his death meant losing the war to Emperor Napoleon.

Fortunately, Mr. Hayward didn't detect the slight hesitation in her reply, so they continued along the path until they reached a quiet corner created by some trees. The men at the end of the path, both of whom wore another nation's military dress, were almost certainly Crown Prince Bernadotte and one of his men.

Would she be witness to a murder right then? What would Bernadotte's companion do when his prince collapsed?

Was dying of arsenic quick or prolonged? What it terribly painful?

Perhaps she'd been hasty in choosing to stay in the cage, which seemed far less gilded with every step. She wanted to fly back to the ballroom, but the burden of potentially saving a life—and her country—would not let her retreat.

Help me get out of this moment alive, Julia prayed to the skies.

Moments later, the two men turned to face her and

Hayward, likely hearing their approach. They walked right up to the men, and Mr. Hayward greeted them. "Your Highness, what a pleasure it is see you again," he said to Bernadotte, bowing.

What should have been a moment of excitement for Julia—meeting royalty from another nation—was instead one in which she had to do her utmost to not faint right there on the path.

What have I done?

She offered the Crown Prince a curtsy and hoped she'd have the strength to rise from it.

9

SOMEHOW AN UNEXPECTED STRENGTH came into Julia's limbs, helping her to not only rise from her curtsy toward Bernadotte, but to stand tall and smile as if nothing whatsoever was untoward.

Mr. Hayward conversed with Bernadotte and his companion, and as he did so, gradually shifted position, taking a step forward, then waiting for Bernadotte to respond by stepping to the side or backward, and so on until Mr. Hayward stood in the corner looking out instead of the others. The move was deliberate, she was quite sure; from their vantage point, she could see most of the gardens and the ballroom beyond. It was Bernadotte who now could not see who might approach him from behind.

Julia herself stayed somewhat out of the corner, able to see toward the ballroom, but would Bernadotte realize his precarious position? Perhaps not; why would he suspect his life would be in danger in England, when he'd recently allied his nation with theirs?

Keeping one ear on the conversation, which so far consisted of banal talk, Julia gazed about the gardens with the eyes of an immature, starry maid. She held her champagne flute close, however, ensuring that it would not be tampered with.

"Ah, you there," Mr. Hayward said, raising his voice.

"Yes?" A footman replied.

"Come bring us a round of drinks. Crown Prince Bernadotte and his companion are parched. Besides, we need to toast the new alliance between our countries."

"Sounds delightful," Bernadotte said with a nod.

The footman bowed. "Right away, sir." He left on his errand, taking Julia's peace of mind with her. In a few moments, Mr. Hayward would take a new champagne flute from the footman's tray, then offer his own poisoned champagne flute to Bernadotte. What could she do to stop him from drinking it?

Still wearing a faux smile, she kept the footman in the corner of her vision, tracking his movements to know how much time she had to invent a way to keep Bernadotte from drinking from his glass, but she could not think clearly enough to conjure any ideas at all.

Behind the footman, a silhouetted figure crossed the path, glanced their way, and then stopped. Julia moved her focus from the footman in the background to the other man. Andrew. Her heart soared with relief. He was near. If he drew closer, she'd be able to tell him of the poison. A gentleman would find speaking to royalty much easier than a gentle lady. Andrew, however, could prevent Bernadotte from drinking, whether by saying something to the Crown Prince, or by physically preventing him from drinking the poison, neither of which she could do.

She surreptitiously slipped her hand free of Mr. Hayward's elbow so she could attempt to make a word sign with it, her left hand being occupied by her own champagne flute. Shaping her hand into a fist with the thumb facing up, she waited until she felt sure that Andrew was looking at her, then moved her hand toward herself. *Help.*

Could he see her signal by the light of the lanterns? Would he understand?

A weight struck her, bringing with it a new question. After the way she'd left him without an answer after he'd exposed his heart to her, would he come to her at all? He wouldn't imagine that her plea was of its dire serious nature.

Over Andrew's shoulder, she noted the footman returning with a tray containing two champagne flutes. He would be here any moment. Julia turned her attention to Andrew again, intently, and signed once more. *Help.* Then again. *Help.*

His figure straightened slightly. He'd seen and understood it. He turned his head and sipped from his own drink. When he looked over again, she put her opened palm to her chest and moved it in a circle in the air, as if marking a sore spot on her skin. At least, that's what she hoped Mr. Hayward would assume, but she was really signing, *Please.*

From that distance, she could not tell enough from Andrew's face to hazard a guess at what he was thinking or feeling, but her *please* elicited a much stronger reaction than plain *help* had. With one hand, Andrew casually made a sign of his own, not looking at her for more than a moment as he signed, *Now?*

Relief washed through her, and she found herself nodding several times in succession instead of answering with a hand sign. But she'd apparently given too much attention to Andrew, for she missed the footman's arrival. She turned back to the circle to see that Mr. Hayward had already handed Bernadotte his own drink, and he was taking a new one for himself.

Don't drink it! She wanted to yell the words but couldn't without looking mad.

Andrew was casually walking her way—coming, yes, but not rushing as she'd hoped, likely because she did not appear to be in danger. For the moment, *she* was not.

"A toast," Mr. Hayward said, holding up his new drink. Bernadotte and his companion, who was not in military dress, did the same, and Julia found her own glass rising to meet the others.

What to do? Think. Think!

"To allies and to peace," Mr. Hayward said, and he held out his glass.

Bernadotte echoed Mr. Hayward's words. "To allies and to peace." His companion did the same, and the two of them clinked glasses before drawing them to their lips.

"Oh!" Julia exclaimed loudly and stumbled forward, purposely knocking the champagne flute from Bernadotte's hand. She landed in a heap on the ground. She heard someone curse—Hayward, no doubt—then scuffling steps, and at last, a kind voice.

"Are you hurt?" Andrew asked.

She wanted to throw her arms about his neck and never let go. To kiss his cheek—his lips. Again and again. The thought was as pleasant as it was surprising. She remembered what had nearly happened and did her utmost to play her part to the hilt.

"I—I—" She weakly pushed herself to a sitting position, then pressed the back of her wrist to her forehead. "I feel rather faint."

"Let's get you inside." Andrew helped her to her feet, Julia putting far more weight on him than was strictly needed and gasping in imaginary pain when she tried to walk.

"Could you carry me, Mr. Gillingham? I fear I may faint away again."

"Of course."

Goodness, how I love him.

Had she truly just thought that word? And had she meant it in the same fashion as he'd used the term earlier that evening? Not the love one feels toward a sibling or a friend but something much deeper and richer? This was something that warmed her toes and made her want to be held by Andrew every day for the rest of her life.

"Thank you," she said, feeling herself blush. "I think that would be wise."

Andrew slipped a hand under her knees, and with a swoop of her skirts, she was in his arms. She reached out her hand, her glass outstretched toward Mr. Hayward, who looked so frustrated that the veins in his neck seemed to bulge above his cravat. "Would you take my glass, Mr. Hayward? I must apologize for this display. I am most embarrassed."

Bernadotte was the one who answered. "Do not worry for a moment. It's wise to go back inside and rest."

She nodded weakly. "I will, thank you."

Andrew nodded to Bernadotte, his companion, and Hayward, then turned and headed toward the ballroom with Julia in his arms. She didn't dare relax at all until they were some distance away, and then she rested her head on Andrew's shoulder. She savored the closeness, though she could tell that for his part, Andrew was tense. Why, she did not know; he didn't know what she'd just thwarted, so he couldn't be worried over her safety or that of Bernadotte.

The scent of Andrew so near again brought back the moment between them here in the gardens. And then she knew. Of course he was acting strangely; this was their first interaction since she hadn't expressed a reciprocation of his affections. He didn't know how to behave with her anymore.

Please don't forevermore call me Miss Hughes, she thought, even as she remembered, with a disturbing start, what she'd just foiled—and the terrifying reality that Mr. Hayward would likely try to assassinate Crown Prince Bernadotte again.

10

"Pray tell, what was that all about?" Andrew whispered—a delicious sound.

Her reaction sent a combined thrill and sense of wonder through her. How had she not realized sooner that she loved Andrew—how handsome and attentive and, well, how *everything* he was? She'd never before viewed him in such a light, but after he'd confessed seeing her in romantic terms, the same feelings had rushed upon her—feelings that she now realized had always been there but that she'd never acknowledged or given voice to.

This was not, however, a moment for relishing the warmth of his breath on her cheek.

"Are they watching us?" she whispered back. She wouldn't raise herself up enough to look over his shoulder but instead kept herself looking frail and injured, though she was neither.

"I believe they are," Andrew said, though he now spoke with his chin up; no one observing from behind would know that he was speaking to her. "I cannot know for certain without turning to look. Would you like me to?"

"Definitely not."

As they approached the doors to the ballroom, she wondered what people would say or think when Andrew carried her inside. The best possible scenario still involved dozens, if not hundreds, of people whose attention was drawn by the sight—the absolute last thing she wanted when a spy and assassin was wandering about. She preferred to find a hiding place in the shadows, where Mr. Hayward would be unable to find her. Granted, that assumed he would surmise that she'd learned of his plans. While she felt a modicum of assurance that he would not, she had no intention of testing the hypothesis.

Right before they reached the doors, she swallowed against a tight knot in her throat, which was filled with about twenty conflicting emotions, from fear to excitement to fatigue, and said, "I can walk in on my own, but I would prefer to leave the ballroom right away, in favor of a place to rest elsewhere in the pavilion." There had to be someplace they could go that would be available to the public yet not in such display of the attendees of the ball.

"Of course. I'm sure we can find a suitable location." He sounded dreadfully stiff.

She would have to find a time and a place to discuss the matter with Andrew, but not now, when Bernadotte's life—and with it the life of the country—remained in danger. Someone else, someone trustworthy, needed to know of Mr. Hayward's intent. That someone needed to be male if the message were to be received with any seriousness.

"There's something I must tell you in private," she said as they reached the door.

Andrew stared straight ahead, not looking at her, and they stepped through the doors. "Oh?" The single syllable cut her to the center. He likely expected to be rejected more overtly than he already had been.

"It's about Mr. Hayward," she said, hoping to ease his mind on that account.

In response, however, he straightened his back even more. "Of course it is." His tone said volumes more.

"Not in the manner you likely think," Julia said quickly. She slipped a hand about his elbow and gently tugged him to the side of the ballroom, toward a set of open doors that led back to the grand hallway. "Come." Would he hear the lightness in her voice that she tried to place there? Unlikely, seeing as she didn't feel light herself in any fashion except for relief at being near Andrew and away from Hayward. She had far too many other things to worry about.

He followed her lead to the right, then made a point of acting as if heading out to the corridor had been his idea. "Where would you like to go?"

Honestly? Home. Far, far away. However much she wished she could flee, doing so was not an option at the moment, even if she had a phaeton at the ready. Not when she had information critical to the nation's welfare. As an alternative, she would have liked to wander the streets of Brighton, but even that wasn't an option right now.

"It's also about the Swedish Crown Prince, Charles Bernadotte."

"Now *that* I did not anticipate." Andrew's voice had become inscrutable. "Does this also involve the third man you spilled champagne on? Four, if you count the footman, though I'm unsure if he was struck."

"Did I spill on them all?" She'd thought that the drink had simply splashed on the path, and she hoped that the glass had shattered so it couldn't be used again. Even after a washing, it might contain traces of the poison. She shook her head. "That's inconsequential."

They walked along the luxuriously decorated hallway. Now that it wasn't crowded with guests queued to enter the ballroom, the area looked very different—the chandeliers brighter, the carpets softer, the wallpaper more elaborate. She felt her mouth open slightly in awe, but then jerked herself back to reality. Gawking at the Prince Regent's Royal Pavilion could wait.

She drew Andrew into an alcove set apart with thick drapes that were held back with golden hooks that had carved dragon heads. Anyone standing behind the drawn curtain wouldn't be entirely hidden, but they would be largely out of sight and in enough shadow that with any luck, they would go unnoticed by guests walking by.

Inside the alcove, she pulled Andrew to the side, to be more concealed by the curtain. The closeness made her insides flutter and her heart race. She wanted to kiss him right then and there.

Perhaps that should take place after I've confessed my love for him, she thought. *And after we know the Crown Prince is safe.*

She had to push the feeling and the desire aside and focus on the matter greater than herself. "There is an assassination plot to kill Crown Prince Bernadotte tonight."

"I—" Andrew's voice cut off, and he pulled back slightly. "Beg pardon?"

"At the beach. You were right. Something *did* happen that I didn't tell you about."

The confusion in Andrew's face shifted to concern. He gripped her shoulders protectively and looked straight into her eyes—a gesture that sent warmth to her toes. "What happened? Please tell me."

For the first time since seeing Durham that night, she didn't feel unsafe or alone in her quest. The tension inside her bubbled over, and Julia found her eyes welling up with tears despite her attempts to hold them at bay.

Andrew pulled her into an embrace. "Whatever it was that scared you, it's over now. I'll be sure you're safe."

Holding him tight in return, she asked, "You knew I was afraid?"

"Of course I did." He pulled away slightly and looked into her eyes, which required him to bend his knees slightly. "Did whatever happened at the shore have anything to do with your pretended fall tonight?"

Her nose wrinkled. "Was it so obviously false?"

Half of Andrew's mouth curved upward. "Probably only to those who know and love you as I do."

For a brief moment that contained a lifetime, Julia let herself soak in his words as if she were in a hot bath. *He thinks I do not love him in return, but I think I do. Oh yes, I do. I do! Yet he still is protective and wants to care for me, no matter that I all but rejected him this very eve.*

"Are the two connected?" Andrew asked again.

"The . . ." Her emotions were so heightened that her thoughts were muddled, and she couldn't remember what two things he referred to.

"The shore and your fall tonight."

"They are very much connected, I'm afraid." Julia ordered herself to focus on the immediate concerns, which were far larger than a young man and a young woman who happened to be falling in love.

She recited the essentials of what she'd heard and seen at the shore, though she left out her initial inclination to think of Mr. Hayward as an exciting, handsome hero. Those feelings had long since been extinguished anyway.

"And that's the same Mr. Hayward who claimed the second dance with you?"

"One and the same."

"So he's a smuggler, and likely dangerous."

"Yes, but there's far more than that, I'm afraid." Now for the especially difficult part. "I heard him talking with his servant—Durham is here, dressed as one of the pavilion's footmen. Not thinking that I overheard or understood, they spoke about plans to poison Crown Prince Bernadotte."

"Whatever for? He's our ally now."

"Not Hayward's, apparently."

Andrew's brows drew together as he thought. "Wait a moment. The other day, Caroline was reading the Brighton society paper aloud, and there was a mention of the holiday of a wealthy Englishman, and I believe he was named Hayward. He had a French mother and spent much of his childhood on the continent and spoke the language impeccably."

"That would explain his French sympathies," Julia said.

"That is upsetting," Andrew said, now stroking his chin in thought.

"I learned that Bernadotte's alliance is hurting France. He has military strength *and* a new weapon that Napoleon needs. Now he's lost the Swedish army *and* the new weapon. The tide of the war will turn in favor of France. But without Bernadotte, the alliance won't stand, and Napoleon could conquer after all."

"We can't let that happen." Andrew raked a hand through his hair, mussing it up so it settled in the slightly haphazard way she loved.

Back to the urgent matter. She had to keep reminding herself to not get distracted. *I'm more like Caroline than I ever thought.*

"Durham had already failed once tonight," Julia explained. "Mr. Hayward decided to take matters into his own hands."

Andrew's eyes had widened. "Wait. Everything you heard between them was *before* your turn about the gardens, wasn't it? Please don't tell me that you put yourself in danger by staying at his side..."

"I had to. I had to learn whatever else I could. He'd already thought me a silly girl who paid no attention to serious matters and had cotton in her head. What else might he let slip, especially when I knew his intentions? I couldn't very well sit back and let the Crown Prince die."

"Of course you couldn't. I just don't want you hurt."

"I know," Julia said. "It was good I went along; I saw Hayward slip a powder into a glass of champagne, so I had to prevent Bernadotte from drinking it."

Understanding dawned on Andrew's face. "That's when you asked me for help. And when I didn't get there before the toast . . ." His voice trailed off, and she finished the story for him.

"I had to prevent him from drinking the poison, even if that meant looking a fool." She gestured toward her dress, which now had dirt stains from her fall onto the path. "He's going to try again, Andrew. We must stop him."

11

"You're absolutely right," Andrew said. "How do we stop him?"

Julia took his lapels in her hands forcefully. "You go find a way to get the message to the Prince Regent or his men. I'll go back to ensure that Hayward doesn't try again."

She released his coat and lifted her skirts to help her run, but Andrew caught her arm before she could leave the alcove. "Absolutely not," Andrew said.

"But Bernadotte! He is in danger, and even these few minutes away from him might have been too long."

Andrew shook his head firmly. "I am not letting you out of my sight. It's too dangerous."

Trying to bottle her impatience, Julia stepped back. "I comported myself well before, didn't I? And saved life to boot. All without Hayward having any suspicions that I might know a thing. I can do it again."

He couldn't argue with those points, and she watched his jaw work as he tried to come up with more reasons. "But—"

"No." She placed two gloved fingers over his lips. The gesture seemed strangely intimate and made her breath catch. Once more, she ordered herself to focus. "You'll hurry to get the message to the Prince Regent, of course, so I won't have to pretend to be a ninny for long, and I'm entirely ready to make a fool of myself a hundred more times if it means stopping Hayward."

"I don't like the arrangement at all," Andrew said below her fingers, which felt like a kiss.

She lowered her hand self-consciously. "I don't like it either, but it must be done, and the task falls on our shoulders. Yours and mine."

As he had before, Andrew took her hands in his, this time holding her fingers firmly and squeezing them as if doing so could bestow protection upon her from Hayward. "Very well, but I swear I will return to you as quickly as I possibly can."

"I know you will." She squeezed his hands in return and smiled encouragingly, hoping he'd believe her courageous. At least he couldn't see her trembling knees, which felt on the verge of knocking against each other. Maintaining her efforts toward outward confidence, she slipped a hand through the crook of his elbow, then nodded toward the corridor. "Shall we?"

"I'd be delighted," Andrew said, then added as they left the alcove, "or at least, I'll try to pretend to be delighted instead of escorting a piece of my heart to what could be argued to be her doom."

Julia chuckled quietly, though she knew he spoke the truth. His referral to her as a piece of his heart only served to warm hers. "You're worrying entirely too much," she said as they walked along the rug-lined hallway toward the ballroom. "Before we know it, our little mission will be complete, and we'll look fondly upon this night as one of adventure, where good triumphed over evil. It'll be a delightful tale to pass along to our children, one made grander with each telling."

She suddenly choked on her voice and blushed, realizing that her words could be taken to mean two distinct families of children, as well as the children borne to the two of them.

Which did I mean? She didn't know for sure, but the idea of having children with any other man suddenly held absolutely no interest to her. *A child of Andrew's might inherit his crooked smile and bright-blue eyes,* she thought. *Imagine a daughter with wavy hair like his. She would be a cherub.*

At the door of the ballroom, they paused. They both seemed to take a breath before crossing the threshold. Andrew patted her hand, released it, and whispered in an intimate tone that belied the formality of his bow, "Please be careful."

"You have my word," she whispered as she curtsied.

Julia watched him head for the other side of the room to find a representative of the Prince Regent. She sent a silent a prayer to the heavens, wishing Andrew success and safety. When he disappeared among the pressing throng, she turned her attention to the door to the gardens, screwed up her courage, and headed outside. With any luck, Bernadotte would still be outside, so she wouldn't have to search for him in the crowded ballroom.

The nighttime air nipped her cheeks. Either she'd gotten entirely accustomed to the warmth inside—and perhaps the extra warmth from being so near Andrew and feeling what she had in his presence—or the night had cooled very quickly. She walked beyond the golden orb of light from the lanterns at the door. She hoped that doing so would aid her sight in adjusting to the darkness, and that she'd be able to spot Bernadotte and Hayward more quickly.

A breeze kicked up from the sea, making her skin break out in gooseflesh. She looked back, hoping for a quick glimpse of Andrew, but he'd long since been swallowed up by the ballroom. The bravado she'd put on as an act for Andrew fell entirely, leaving her feeling utterly alone and afraid. There she stood, surrounded by opulence and some of the richest and most prominent members of the ton, but none of them knew her, and she didn't know them, either.

If things went poorly with Hayward, would anyone step in to help her, or would making an inevitable scene be below them? No matter. She had a duty to perform, and Andrew would be back at her side momentarily. She hoped.

Julia walked through the gardens, seeking out Hayward and Bernadotte, flushing with awareness at others who raised eyebrows at the sight of a young lady walking alone. Perhaps they were noting her threadbare slippers and gown, the style of which hadn't appeared on a fashion plate in three years at least. No matter. She kept her head high, imbuing herself with pride she did not possess.

Her first hint of the men she sought was nothing she saw but rather heard: Hayward's voice.

"Come now, Prince," he said, "let us go for a stroll. It's far too hot and suffocating indoors, and the sea air is so refreshing."

"I do enjoy the sea air," another, slightly accented voice said, whom she divined to be Bernadotte. "And when I return to the front, I will certainly miss it."

"I can imagine," Hayward said. Their voices began to grow fainter, so Julia hurried onward in hopes of catching up to them, careful to walk on her tiptoes to remain quiet. Hayward's voice continued from the other side of a hedge. "I imagine that battle brings very different odors, and many unpleasant ones."

"Indeed," Bernadotte said with a thoughtful tone. "War is a terrible thing."

The men continued walking, and Julia kept up, grateful for the hedge between them, yet it ended a few yards ahead. What would she do then?

Go to Bernadotte's side, of course, she thought. *That will block Hayward from trying anything overt.* The men didn't know that she'd overheard them, and if she played her part well, they would think she'd escaped an unwanted suitor in favor of another nation's royalty.

On her right, the hedge came to a well-manicured end, squared off like a wall. Beyond it lay the end of the pier and the ocean, which spread out before them like a silver blanket under the stars. She stopped and waited for the men on the other side to do something, to appear, to speak, to . . . she didn't know. Once again, she looked over her shoulder toward the pavilion, willing Andrew to hurry and find her, but she couldn't see anything along the hedge she'd walked by; all of that was dark. All she could make out was the glowing yellow light spilling from the pavilion doors in the distance.

It's up to me.

"I find it most interesting," Hayward continued, "that after years of supporting France, you've turned your back on the emperor and have allied with England."

"Do you doubt my loyalty to England?" Bernadotte asked. He stepped beyond the hedge, showing his profile in silhouette from the moonlight. He had a long face and a nose with a strong line to it. This was a man who did not appreciate being questioned.

"I said nothing of the sort." Hayward chuckled, a sound coming from his chest, as if the laugh masked a secondary emotion. He, too, stepped farther out onto the pier, and Julia held her breath, praying that neither man would turn around and see her, or that if they did, the shadows would conceal her presence. Even so, she leaned closer to the hedge to decrease the odds that they would spot her.

"I would have thought my decision would be one that a man like yourself would have supported," Bernadotte said. "But truly, I am not here to discuss politics or even the war. I should return to the ballroom so as not to be rude to the Prince Regent, my most gracious host."

"Alas," Hayward said, looking out toward the sea, "I have other plans for you."

His hand slipped into his coat pocket, and he withdrew a gun. He pointed the barrel at Bernadotte, who raised both hands in the air. Somehow, Julia kept herself from gasping aloud, but her eyes widened to the point that they felt as if they might burst.

"Now see here . . ."

Hayward didn't lower the weapon. "I was amazed to hear that you'd come tonight without any guards." He tsked and shook his head. "Foolish to think that you'd be safe even in the heart of your ally."

"What do you want?" Bernadotte said. His nostrils flared slightly, but his voice remained steady. "I can offer you money. Anything you wish for."

Hayward raised his other hand so that he gripped the gun with both. His chin jutted forward as he said, "I want my mother back."

"Where is she?" The Crown Prince's voice wavered, but so slightly that unless one was listening carefully, it would have been missed.

"She is dead, thanks to English doctors who would not listen to me, a fatherless boy trying to translate my mother's complaints. She spoke only French, and I learned the tongue at her knee. But no one would listen to a mere boy, so she died. All thanks to the arrogant English." He shoved the gun forward slightly; Bernadotte took half a step backward.

"What is that to me?"

"You were France's last hope for winning, for defeating the wretched refuse that is England. Now you have allied yourself with them. You've betrayed me and every other man with French blood in his veins." Hayward seemed to realize that he'd lost control and lowered his voice. "So long as England does not get your military strength—or your rockets—France can still win this war. And I can guarantee England gets neither by getting rid of you."

Julia watched in horror as Hayward slowly cocked the gun with a click. She could not allow this to happen, but what could she do? She'd assumed that spilling more champagne would be the greatest act she'd have to perform, not facing a loaded gun. Andrew was nowhere to be found. She couldn't merely appear from the hedge to flirt with Hayward; he would know she'd seen and heard too much and would simply kill her too. Her body, followed by Bernadotte's, would be washed out to sea with the tide, never to be found.

With the strength of urgency, Julia ran as hard as she could, driving her shoulder into Hayward's stomach. The shock was her greatest strength; he bent over with an *oof* and landed on his behind, tumbling backward with Julia landing atop him. The gun fired, but the shot went wild, and the bullet landed harmlessly in the water with a barely audible plop.

Hayward swore, first at the stray shot, then again at Julia. "Stupid girl!" He tried to pry her off of him, but she held on. "Look what you've done! Release me, you fool!"

Julia would do nothing of the sort. Under any other conditions, she would have scrambled off a man she'd found herself atop of, but this was no ordinary night. Her blood pumped through her veins, giving her strength beyond what should have been within her. Using his distraction with the gun to her advantage, she pressed her forearms against his neck, putting her entire weight and might into cutting off his air. Hayward looked stunned, staring into her eyes for a second as he tried to push her arms away and gasp for air.

Bernadotte leapt into action, wrenching the weapon from Hayward, whose arm was outstretched and flailing as he tried to aim again and get free at once. After seizing the gun, Bernadotte threw it off the pier, sending it spinning into the distance until it slipped below the surface and vanished forever. Then the Crown Prince dropped to his knees, seemingly unaware of potential damage to his expensive trousers, and helped Julia subdue Hayward. Already the scoundrel was losing strength, but neither Julia nor Bernadotte let up for a moment. Only when he fainted altogether did Julia climb off his still form.

"I'll go fetch help," she said, and she held up her skirts as she raced back up the path she'd come down from the pavilion.

She ran headlong into a figure hidden by the darkness and, in her panic, fought to be released, certain that Durham or another accomplice had caught her.

"Julia, are you well? The royal guards are coming."

Relief drained all her strength from before. "Oh, Andrew," Julia said, suddenly shaky and leaning against him so she wouldn't topple. "It's Hayward. He—he had a gun, and, and—" She couldn't say more; she gulped for breath and felt lightheaded from the exertion.

Andrew helped her to a bench, where she gratefully dropped. "Is the Crown Prince safe?"

"For now," Julia said. "He and I subdued Hayward, but he'll wake up soon."

"And the gun?"

"In the sea."

"The guards are on their way. I'll go meet them and show them where to find Hayward and Bernadotte." Andrew seemed to be bursting with energy, ready to gallop away to finish their mission for the night, but first he leaned in and kissed her forehead. "You are remarkable, Julia. Remember that."

Then he ran off into the darkness, calling for help.

12

AN ENORMOUS RUCKUS ENSUED, during which Hayward was dragged into the pavilion. A pair of guards escorted Crown Prince Bernadotte back to the pavilion, ensuring his safety in a manner that Julia felt should have been in place all evening. Hayward, now awake but looking unkempt and worse for wear, was soon restrained with metal cuffs, and he was dragged off to the jail on Market Street.

Julia stood beside Andrew and listened to a member of Parliament on a dais at one end of the room, addressing the crowd, with Bernadotte at his side. They stood near a large, slightly warped mirror, in which she checked her reflection, hoping her appearance didn't show evidence of her unladylike scuffle. Not that she regretted a second of it, but she didn't precisely wish others to think she'd arrived at the ball with her hair sticking out every which way either. She patted her hair, hoping to smooth out a few strays, and realized that she'd been perspiring; her fingertips came away wet.

"The Prince Regent has been informed of the events of this evening, most especially of the assassination attempt upon Crown Prince Bernadotte of Sweden, who is a valued friend and ally of England," the MP said. "His Royal Highness will recommend to the court that the would-be assassin receive a sentence of at least twenty years' transportation."

The crowd clapped in approval.

"His Highness also wishes to acknowledge the role of Mr. Andrew Gillingham in apprehending the accused." Applause followed, and the MP gestured for Andrew to join him on the dais.

Andrew took Julia's hand and tugged it. "Credit for this evening's success belongs far more to you than it does to me."

Together they went up the steps and stood beside the MP, where Andrew acknowledged the applause. "I aided in capture of the accused, but this gentle lady at my side, Miss Julia Hughes, deserves our gratitude far more than I do. It is thanks to her wit and willingness to risk danger to herself that the assassin was identified and captured." He released her hand and clapped, and the room followed suit, quickly showering Julia with praise.

She blushed, not particularly liking the attention, yet pleased beyond measure that Andrew had acknowledged her part. One more reason to adore the man. They left the dais, and the MP addressed the crowd once more. "As much needs to be done into investigating the crimes of those involved, His Highness deems the festivities to be over for this eve. Thank you for your cooperation, and good night."

With the ball thoroughly disrupted, the men and women murmured with a hum that almost sounded like the waves of the sea, a collective volume so loud that it would have drowned out the band, had it still been playing. But the musicians were putting their instruments back into their cases, and palace servants were trying to usher the throng out of doors. The guests seemed understanding, if disappointed, and they obeyed by gradually filing out. Julia wondered what her parents and Caroline would think when they realized she hadn't left with them.

She scanned the ballroom, hardly able to believe how utterly different this night had turned out from what she could have predicted. Now that the dangers of Mr. Hayward had passed—Julia herself was safe, as were England and Sweden, for the time being—her heart rate began to return to normal. She still felt hot, though; the events of the evening had definitely put a strain on her.

The ballroom had emptied considerably when she took a deep breath and turned to Andrew, smiling, ready to talk with him about how completely remarkable the events of the evening had been. But Andrew had suddenly grown stiff, as if he were a soldier in training. He clasped his hands behind his back and—at least it seemed—avoided her eye.

"Are you quite well?" Had Andrew been injured during the arrest? She wasn't sure what role he'd played, and the idea that Hayward might have injured him made her heart flare with anger.

Andrew's eyes seemed to wander, unsure of where to focus, though they landed on hers and glanced off again a couple of times as he seemed to struggle with words. "I am most grateful that things turned out as they did." His used his formal tone, something she did not like hearing at all.

She moved to step closer, to touch his arm, to feel his warmth and reassure him, but he moved backward an equal amount and held up a hand. Her step came up short. Brow furrowed with alarm, she looked up at him but held her ground. "What is it?"

"The last hour has been a diversion from the words spoken betwixt us earlier this evening. I am quite aware that my sentiments were sprung upon you and that they were not received as a prospective suitor might have hoped."

"I was surprised, yes, but—"

"No, please do not pity me or try to let me down easily. My pride needs a moment to mend before being the object of pity."

Object of pity, Andrew? Goodness, no. She hadn't known what to think or say, or even, in all truth, what she felt. But now, after he'd foisted the idea of love upon her and she'd had time to reckon with it . . .

"I regret that I did not respond as I should have," Julia began.

"I'll bid you good evening and goodbye. On the morrow, I will return to London."

Panic zipped through Julia's heart. "Why?" she asked, fearing the answer.

His neck was turning pink. He bowed his head, still avoiding her eye. "I will search out a flat to let. I believe that will simplify matters, making my tutelage under your father easier to give my attentions to, and . . . it will make daily life more . . . *comfortable* for you." He bowed deeply and quickly, then spun and walked out, leaving Julia behind and feeling quite sure that she'd broken his heart. If only she could go back in time and respond differently when Andrew had first spoken of his feelings.

Although if she could relive this evening and tell Andrew in that moment that she loved him in return, she wouldn't have heard Hayward and Durham talking, and Crown Prince Bernadotte would likely be dead.

Andrew slipped through the door on the far side of the room and disappeared. Her throat was so tight she could barely breathe, and tears burned in her eyes.

"Miss Hughes?"

She turned to look for the man who had spoken her name, a royal footman who stood ten feet off—but why would a servant of the Prince Regent know her name? Surely someone else had called her. However, the footman took another step forward and spoke again. "Miss Hughes?"

"Y-yes?"

"The Prince Regent witnessed your conversation with Mr. Gillingham just now, and—"

Stunned, she frantically looked at the door Andrew had disappeared through, then quickly scanned the room, but she saw no sign of the Prince Regent. "Pardon?" Surely she hadn't heard correctly.

The servant moved a step closer, and she realized that he was older than she'd assumed. This was not one of dozens of footmen. He was likely a long-time, trusted servant and adviser. He gave her a paternal smile, then tilted his head, indicating the mirror beside her. "The Prince Regent can watch the room from the other side of this mirror. It's made with a special paint that allows him to see out, but no one to see in."

Utterly tongue-tied, Julia gaped at the man, looking from him to the mirror and back again.

"He would like to know if you love the young man, Mr. Gillingham."

A most unusual question, but then again, she'd never expected *any* question, usual or otherwise, from royalty. Her feelings for Andrew swelled within her. "Oh, I do. I love him more than anything." Saying the words released her body of a horrible tension and allowed some warmth to move through her veins again. If only she'd been able to say them to Andrew. "But . . ."

"Yes?"

She looked toward the door he'd left from. "But he doesn't know that I return his love. You see, he confessed his feelings for me tonight, before all of this—" Julia waved her hand in a circle to indicate the events just passed. "And I was too surprised to respond. I fear he is returning to London in the morning, and I won't have the opportunity to correct the situation." She didn't realize she'd begun crying until a hot tear dripped off the side of her jaw. She swiped at it and sniffed.

"That is as His Highness suspected." The servant looked at the mirror and nodded twice.

Julia's eyes widened. "Is he still watching?" she whispered. Of course he was. She should have assumed as much.

"He is," the servant said. "And now you and I wait."

Julia's knees felt about as sturdy as tapioca. "May I ask what we are waiting for?"

"Patience, Miss Hughes. It won't be long."

From the hall, she heard footsteps and men's voices. The few remaining guests were ushered out by footmen just as the men from the corridor entered—two guards holding none other than Andrew between them.

"Oh, good gracious," Julia said. Visions of Andrew in a cell flashed through her mind. "He's done nothing wrong."

"You have nothing to worry yourself about, Miss Hughes," the servant said as he stepped to her side to face the guards with her. "You may call me Mr. Mayfair, if you'd like."

"Thank you," Julia managed, but his reassurance did little to ease her anxiousness. Once again she was unable to take in much air, to the point that if her life depended upon her ability to extinguish a candle, she mightn't have been able to.

Andrew looked panicked, his face and neck both drained of blood and white as wool. He was brought to stand before Julia, who shrugged helplessly and shook her head, palms upraised to let him know that she had no more of idea what was happening than he did.

No one spoke for a minute, an unendurable era. The ballroom was now entirely cleared of guests, and servants had closed the doors. Finally, the door by the mirror opened, and the Prince Regent appeared. Looking for comfort, Julia sought out Mr. Mayfair. He smiled knowingly, then looked ahead once more.

"I wanted to thank you both for your most patriotic actions this night," the Prince Regent said. One side of his mouth quirked up. "Even though it cut my event short."

Did one apologize in situations such as this? Julia curtsied and then stayed down, hoping that was correct. She'd never been taught the protocol for meeting with and speaking to royalty. At her side, Andrew bowed, then straightened again.

"If I'm not mistaken, such bravery deserves a reward," the Prince Regent went on. "I would quite enjoy bestowing a certain type of reward, one that my valet, Mr. Mayfair here, has investigated and learned would be welcome."

As if the matter were a puzzle in her head, the pieces clicked together, and she understood—he meant a reward for her and Andrew as a couple. But Andrew didn't yet know she shared his sentiments, and he likely felt spurned and hurt.

"I have already dispatched servants to find Miss Hughes's father, who, I am quite certain, will be quite pleased over discussing the terms of a marriage contract."

Andrew swallowed so hard that Julia couldn't help but notice the bob in his throat. "Your Majesty, we are not engaged."

"I am aware of that, Mr. Gillingham," the Prince Regent said. "And that is one reason I am speaking to you now—to set that little fact right."

"But—" Andrew clamped his mouth shut, surely after realizing how wrong he was to interrupt or contradict the crown.

The Prince Regent addressed Julia. "I must ask you to do something for me, Miss Hughes."

"Of course, Your Majesty," she said with another curtsy,

this one bobbing down and immediately up again. "Anything you wish." What types of favors could he possibly ask for when he already had the bidding of hundreds of servants and a nation at his beck and call? If he asked her to climb a mountain to deliver a missive to a sage living at the peak, she'd do it, and happily, if it meant Andrew not going to prison for some made-up offense.

"Tell Mr. Gillingham here what you told Mr. Mayfair a moment ago."

"Tell—oh." He'd asked the one thing that would be hardest of all: to bare her soul to Andrew right then and there. Her face went hot, and she was quite sure that it had turned a darker hue than Andrew's neck ever had. "Yes, Your Majesty."

She turned to face Andrew, feeling every inch as vulnerable as a soldier at a mark, with an entire army aiming their arrows at her. Was this how Andrew had felt when he first shared his love for her? Undoubtedly it was, and it had likely been even harder, for he hadn't known that his love would be requited, and she did.

"Andrew," she said, then she glanced at the Prince Regent and corrected herself. "Mr. Gillingham." She cleared her throat. Oh, what she would give to be on the other side of this moment, to have it in the past, and to be in Andrew's embrace again, with the promise to be able to be within his arms for the rest of her life.

"Miss Hughes, you needn't do this," Andrew said earnestly.

He did not want her to shackle herself to someone she did not truly love—one more reason to love him even deeper.

"Mr. Gillingham," she said, heart hammering against her ribs. "I am afraid I must confess something I failed to express adequately earlier: my utter love and devotion for you."

For the first time since before he'd left the ballroom, he

looked right into her eyes and did not look away. "Truly?" The single word contained threads of doubt and hope in equal parts.

"Truly. I can imagine loving no other for the rest of my life." Another hot tear tumbled down her cheek, this time from joy.

Joy replaced any stiffness, as if Andrew were shedding a cloak. He simply glowed as he stepped toward her and took her hands in his. "Then perhaps we should listen to our ruler and become engaged?" His lighthearted voice was back, but she heard his earnestness threaded through it.

"I think that would be wisest," Julia said, maintaining their mock-serious interchange.

Whereas not long ago, she'd been ready to collapse under her own weight, she now felt as if she could run all the night long, singing of her happiness, and never tire.

"Then it's settled," the Prince Regent said with a clap of his hands. "I'll provide handsome rewards for the actions you both took tonight, including a three-month tour of the continent as a wedding trip, a townhouse equipped with three servants for you to live in, and a nice sum of pin money for the future Mrs. Gillingham."

Neither could believe their fortune. Both clung to each other's hands and grinned like fools.

"However!" The Prince Regent's voice boomed. He held up a finger, and the couple quelled their excitement to hear him. Julia and Andrew stood meekly, heads bowed. "None of that will come to pass unless one last oversight is corrected."

They soberly waited for his command. Unexpectedly, the Prince Regent walked up to Andrew, placed a firm hand on his shoulder and said, "Come now, Mr. Gillingham. It is past time that you kiss your betrothed."

Their worry melted into the happiest of grins. "I'd be

happy to, Your Majesty." Andrew stepped closer, took Julia by the shoulders, and pressed a chaste kiss to her cheek.

When he pulled away, she shook her head. "That will not do, Mr. Gillingham. We must obey the Prince Regent." She reached up, held his face between her hands, and kissed him back, thoroughly.

Annette Lyon is a *USA Today* bestselling author, a 6-time Best of State medalist for fiction in Utah, and a Whitney Award winner. She's had success as a professional editor and in newspaper, magazine, and technical writing, but her first love has always been fiction.

She's a cum laude graduate from BYU with a degree in English and is the author of over a dozen books, including the Whitney Award-winning *Band of Sisters*, a chocolate cookbook, and a grammar guide. She co-founded and was served as the original editor of the *Timeless Romance Anthology* series and continues to be a regular contributor to the collections.

She has received five publication awards from the League of Utah Writers, including the Silver Quill, and she's one of the four coauthors of the *Newport Ladies Book Club* series. Annette is represented by Heather Karpas at ICM Partners.

Find Annette online:
Blog: http://blog.AnnetteLyon.com
Twitter: @AnnetteLyon
Facebook: http://Facebook.com/AnnetteLyon
Instagram: https://www.instagram.com/annette.lyon/
Pinterest: http://Pinterest.com/AnnetteLyon

The Reluctant Heir

Donna Hatch

1

Rowan Law, the newest Viscount Hadley, had been abandoned. He stood like a statue in the middle of the field, watching the family carriage drive away.

His father wouldn't leave him here alone with no money and no idea where to go... would he?

Overhead, a gull wailed. Rowan trudged back toward the road. Very well. He'd been out of line. He'd apologize to Father, eat his humble pie, and try to be more civil. Nothing Rowan said or did would change the Earl of Leiderton anyway.

He practiced, "Father." Hmm. Perhaps he ought to resort to more formality. "My lord, I apologize for my conduct. I vow to show due respect and to obediently learn how to manage the estate, even at this breakneck pace and ill-planned timing..."

The wind carried away his words.

They were meaningless anyway.

Rowan had never been strong or wise or dependable. His brother had been the heir—and the favorite—for a reason. Instead, Rowan prided himself on being fun and witty and charming. One race had changed all that. Now, he could only drag himself through each day in a mindless blur.

After an hour, Rowan continued to walk alone. Father certainly was taking his bluff further than Rowan expected. He crested a hill sprinkled with shrubs and stopped. Ahead, the wide expanse of the ocean shimmered like a long-distant friend. Endless and impassive, the water sparkled in the sun and spread out in a panorama of white cliffs and long, sandy shores. Timeless. Majestic.

Rowan closed his eyes and lifted his face to the sun. A flirtatious breeze carried the briny scent of the sea. For a moment a sensation akin to peace came over Rowan.

How dare he experience anything like peace?

The thought shattered the undeserved emotion, leaving a hole wide enough for raw, sharp pain to tear its way back inside.

Clawing at his composure, Rowan fisted his hands and swallowed hard. If only he could cover himself in the safe blanket of numbness that had protected him that first horrific week after Hadley's death.

Rowan continued toward the town of Brighton. Brighton. His brother, Hadley, had met Ann here, the only girl he'd ever loved—a girl so far beneath him in social status that Father forbade Hadley to marry her.

Did she know of Hadley's death? If only Rowan could send her a personal message—or tell her himself—before she learned the news another, less personal way.

A muffled mew caught his attention. Was that a cat? A rustling noise lead him to a sapling. At the trunk, a calico kitten struggled against a string snare, twisting and jerking. The kitten let out another mew.

How well Rowan identified with the small creature, caught in a snare not of its making, destined to strangle while fighting against the noose.

Rowan knelt. "Here, little one. I'll free you."

Grasping the kitten's body, he loosened the string and removed it from the furry neck. Then he lifted the kitten into his arms and held the squirming body close. He hadn't held a kitten in years. The little creature snuggled against him. Judging from the cleanliness of its fur, it either had an attentive mother or belonged to a home.

"I guess we're both lost souls," he said to the little ball of fluff.

The kitten studied him with blue eyes. As Rowan stroked the soft fur, a purr rumbled the small body.

"Here, kitty, kitty!" a feminine voice called. "Mimi? Where are you?"

Rowan turned. From behind a spreading elm tree across the field, a woman stepped out. At this distance, Rowan had no guesses as to her identity, but her trim figure clad in a light-colored gown moved at a steady clip along what was probably the road on the other side of a hedgerow.

"Mimi? Here, kitty, kitty!"

Rowan looked down at his handful of fur and said to the kitten, "I assume the lady belongs to you?"

"Mew." The little creature watched him, unblinking.

"I thought so." Rowan headed toward the womanly figure looking for her cat.

"Mimi!" The woman paused and turned a full circle.

Rowan trotted towards her. When she paused, her bonnet pointed in his direction, he waved. "Ho, there! Are you looking for a kitten?"

She paused, her stance alert. If he were to wager as to her age, he'd put her somewhere between seventeen and twenty. As he neared, her posture relaxed. "Oh, there you are, Mimi."

The young lady glanced at Rowan and returned her gaze to the kitten in his hand, but not before he caught her glance of appreciation. She pushed at one of the dark curls peeking out from underneath her straw bonnet and blushed prettily. He might have changed in many ways over the past few days, but at least he had not lost his appeal to ladies.

"Thank you, sir." Her voice rang out in a clear contralto with the cultured tones of a lady. "Wherever did you find my kitten?"

He waved a hand over his shoulder in the direction of the tree. "Caught in a snare."

She reached for the furball. "Oh, you poor little thing! Naughty kitten, running off like that," she gently scolded.

Rowan handed over the kitten without taking his gaze off the young lady. *Pretty* didn't seem to quite fit. She was lovely in a way that a clear brook with sunlight glittering on the playful surface is lovely. Of course, brooks don't generally bear a pair of kissable, full lips. A stirring inside him pressed against his barrier of sorrow.

Her gray eyes fixed on Rowan, and the girl smiled, a blast of white and joy and cheer. "Oh, good sir, how can I ever thank you?"

"A kiss would be a very nice thank you." He turned on his most alluring expression.

Instead of blushing in shocked delight, she laughed—not the giggle of a coquette but a sound of true mirth. "It might be nice for one of us, but I daresay that wouldn't be me."

In a low, sensual voice, he said, "There's only one way to find out." He took a step forward.

Her expression shifted to amused patience. "You, sir, do a fair job portraying the rogue. I'm duly impressed. However, I think perhaps a cup of tea and a slice of lemon cake might be what you really need, Mr. . . . ?" She raised her brows.

"Law," he supplied. "Rowan Law."

He kept quiet about his new courtesy title. It sounded ridiculously self-important to use it when introducing himself. Moreover, Viscount Hadley didn't fit. It might never fit. Hadley was his brother's title and name for as long as Rowan could remember. To apply it to himself was . . . wrong.

A girl like this one, with disturbing resistance to his charm, would surely be even less impressed with a title, anyway.

She bobbed a crisp curtsy. "Pleased to meet you, Mr. Law. I am Isabella Montgomery. Follow me, please."

She tucked her kitten into one arm, turned with the grace of a ballerina, and practically skipped to a dirt road skirting the edge of the field.

Shaking his head over her neat sidestep of his scandalous suggestion, Rowan scrambled to keep up with her. He must be losing his touch. Usually women found him irresistible.

He'd best find his father so they could resume this inane trip and face up to the inevitable courtesy title and the staggering load of responsibilities that came with it. The quicker he completed touring their properties, the sooner he could return to the family seat, where Father and he had left Mother and other family members grieving.

"Is the nearest coaching inn up this road?"

"Not this road, no. You'd need to go to the main highway."

Where would his father have gone to await him? Really, Father was taking this lesson rather too far.

Miss Montgomery glanced over her shoulder at him. "Are you in need of transportation, Mr. Law?"

"I have transportation. I simply need to find my father. We were traveling together and . . ." He paused. How much to tell her? "I got out to stretch my legs and lost my way. I thought he might wait for me at the next inn." The tale bore a vague resemblance to the truth, anyway.

"Where was your final destination?"

"Crestwood Manor, a day hence, but we were to stay the night somewhere a few hours away."

She stopped walking and turned to him. A disturbingly searching gaze came from her. "Perhaps he stopped along the road and is waiting for you to catch up."

"Perhaps."

The girl's curiosity seeped out of her continual glances, but she had the good breeding not to ask prying questions. "Our vicarage is up ahead. If you come for the tea and lemon cake I offered, we can watch for your coach from our parlor window."

Vicarage? He'd attempted to steal a kiss from a vicar's daughter? He almost smacked his own face. Instead, he donned his most polite manners. "I would not wish to impose, Miss . . . Montgomery, was it?"

She nodded. "I invited, if you'll recall, and it's the least I can do to thank you for finding my kitten." She pursed those deliciously full lips while her eyes laughed at him. "Really, the very *least.*"

He pretended not to catch her meaning. "Very well. Thank you. A spot of tea and lemon cake may be just the thing."

The girl beamed at him. Was she still silently laughing at him? The kitten tucked its furry head into the crook of her arm.

As they climbed yet another low hill, Rowan pointed with his chin at the kitten. "What did you call the wee beastie?"

"Mimi, today. Yesterday, I called her Butterfly. The day before, she was Music. I cannot seem to find just the right name for her."

The girl was either mad or charmingly eccentric. "How about Patches?" he suggested.

She made a scoffing noise. "That was my brother's unimaginative name for her—no offense. He also suggested Callie since she's a calico, but that's too obvious. To spare his feelings, I did try both of those, but to no effect. I'll find the right name. I'm fond of Mimi, but we'll see how I feel tomorrow."

"She may never learn her name if you change it every day."

She grinned. "Most cats don't respond to their names anyway, but I suspect it's because the owner doesn't choose the *right* name. Don't you think so, Mimi?" She peered down at the sleeping kitten, who made no response. "Hmm. Perhaps not Mimi, then. I did like that, though." Her curious gaze flitted to Rowan. "Have you any pets, Mr. Law?"

"My father has hunting dogs—he's excessively fond of them." More than he'd ever been of Rowan. It rankled to acknowledge that. "Mother has a canary. There are cats in the stables, but they aren't pets; they're mousers."

"Not a pet of your own? A pity. Pets give us great joy." The spring in her step suggested she found joy in many ordinary things.

"What gives you joy, Miss Montgomery?"

"Oh, most things. We were put on this earth to find joy, even in spite of hardships."

She seemed absolutely pure and untouched by hardship.

Without missing a beat, she said, "At the moment, my greatest hardship is my brother. He sorely tries my patience. I'm also quite distressed at not having found the right name for my kitten. Quite a difficult hardship." She grinned at him to show she spoke the absurd words in jest.

He smiled politely, but it probably looked tight.

"Most of all, I'm also desperately trying to paint a masterpiece—one that will gain me the notice of a local art master who accepts one new student this year."

"I have no talent for art, but I admire those who do. I wish you luck."

They reached a gray stone cottage about the size of the vicarage in his family's county seat, yet this one appeared to be at least a century older. Flowers bloomed from every patch of dirt, and the yard appeared neat and tidy, from the cleared path to the weed-free flower beds. Humble but loved.

She trotted ahead to the front door. "Aunt Missy," she called. "I hope you don't mind, but I've found another stray."

"Very well, bring in the poor creature, and let's have a look," came a woman's laughing voice.

Grinning, Miss Montgomery wiggled her brows at Rowan as if they shared a private joke and led the way inside. Removing his hat, Rowan blinked in the dim interior. The girl's light-colored gown guided him through the entryway into a dark-paneled room with an assortment of furniture and odd curios. It created a chaotic warmth.

A plump woman stood. She might have reached Rowan's shoulder if she rose up on tiptoe. The diminutive woman tucked a strand of gray hair into a white cap. "An unusual stray, indeed." She laughed. "Do introduce me to your companion."

"This is Mr. Law. He was kind enough to help me find this little scamp." Miss Montgomery indicated the sleeping bundle in her arms.

"I'm relieved you found her." The older woman beamed at the kitten.

Miss Montgomery made the introductions. "Mr. Law, this is Mrs. Williams, my . . . well, I call her Aunt Missy, but she and the vicar took us in out of the kindness of their hearts."

Mrs. Williams waved her hand. "You make it sound nobler than it is. Come in, Mr. Law, and welcome. I've just rung for tea."

Mrs. Williams gestured at an overstuffed armchair next to a window. Once the ladies seated themselves, Rowan accepted the offered chair.

Mrs. Williams wasted no time. "Mr. Law, I've never met a 'stray' quite like you. And I've not seen you hereabouts."

"Er, no, ma'am. My father and I were passing through. We got separated."

"Ah, well, some boys just don't seem to learn not to wander off from their parents." Mrs. Williams chuckled at her own wit.

Miss Montgomery interjected, "I told Mr. Law he might watch the road from this window in the hopes his father's carriage comes this way."

"Of course." Mrs. Williams nodded. "In the meantime, do accept our hospitality, Mr. Law. Anyone who will take the time to return a lost kitten is a friend of ours."

Rowan offered a debonair smile. "It was my pleasure. If I had known the kitten would lead me to such a pair of lovely and charming ladies, I would have done so with greater haste."

They both smiled, but while Mrs. Williams's was merely a polite acknowledgment of his compliment, Miss Montgomery's smile, coupled with a shrewd gleam in her eye, told him she saw through his flattery and was not impressed.

If they knew his father had abandoned him because he'd been disrespectful, these kind ladies might not be so hospitable. And what would he do if he failed to find his father?

An idea sprouted. He could use the time to search for his brother's lost love and inform her of Hadley's fate. Any girl who could capture his brother's heart must be remarkable. She deserved to know the truth—before she heard it in passing or read of it in the newspaper.

2

Over the brim of her teacup, Isabella watched her guest, a gentleman with all the town polish of a charming rogue, the kind that often came to Brighton in search of diversions once the London Season had ended. Many such gentlemen had plied their tricks on her, but with Aunt Missy's guidance, Isabella had outmaneuvered them with her heart intact. She would resist this one, too.

Though this stranger seemed different, he carried too much air of mystery to be entirely trustworthy. Of course, his black attire and stark-white shirt, in addition to his dark hair and eyes, only added to the starkness of him. Perhaps that was the source of his image of danger. He spoke eloquently but never with any true animation, as if haunted by great sadness.

Aunt Missy seemed equally intrigued but had not yet put up any of her defensive guards that she usually did when confronted with a rake.

"Where is your home, then, Mr. Law?" Aunt Missy asked.

"My family hails from Sussex, ma'am."

Not a complete answer. While petting Mimi, who slept in her lap, Isabella took a bite of lemon cake and glanced at Mr. Law again. The darkness of his eyes suggested secrets she longed to discover. Though windswept, the style of his dark hair, neatly trimmed on the sides while longer and wavy on top, gave him a polished appearance. His clean-shaven face had stronger lines than those truly patrician features she so often saw among the gentlemen who visited Brighton. But his mouth, oh how it captured her attention. Each motion, each pucker, beckoned to her.

She had resisted all manner of rogues, rakes, and roués. She would resist this one as well. Shame on him for suggesting she ought to kiss him! Still, his playful expression as he'd uttered the scandalous words had aroused her amusement instead of her ire. Perhaps he was a flirt rather than a true libertine.

Aunt Missy tapped her finger against her chin. "Law family from Sussex. Hmmm. I don't believe I know your people."

"A grievous oversight on our part, to be sure, ma'am," he said.

Oh, what a charmer! Isabella barely managed not to roll her eyes. And again, he'd sidestepped Aunt Missy's implied question. What was he not telling them?

"And where were you bound?"

"Crestwood Manor, a day's ride from here."

"I've heard of it." Aunt Missy nodded.

The front door slammed, and heavy footsteps neared. Her brother George strode into the room. "I have decided to challenge Sir Reginald to a duel!"

Mimi lifted her head and offered a startled mew. Mr. Law choked and coughed into a napkin.

Isabella stroked Mimi's fur. "George, really! That will be your third duel this week."

They grinned at each other. Isabella petted Mimi until she went back to sleep.

Mr. Law said, "Sir Reginald? That popinjay? Whatever for?"

"He has stolen the love of my life!" George put a hand over his heart theatrically.

Isabella asked their visitor, "You know Sir Reginald, Mr. Law?"

"Yes, I've met him on occasion in London," the mysterious Mr. Law said. "I'm surprised that silly fop could rouse himself enough to court a lady."

"I think he's sweet," Isabella said. Although she too found his fascination with fashion and his flowery compliments to everyone a tad overdone.

"By all means, duel the silly peacock. I hope you're a good shot."

George grinned at Mr. Law as if he'd found a long-lost friend. "Perhaps it will be swords, my good fellow. So much more satisfying."

Quickly, Isabella made the introductions. "Mr. Law, may I present my brother, George. You'd never know it, but he's nearly three years my senior." The siblings exchanged a grin. "George, this is Mr. Law, visiting from Sussex."

The enigmatic Mr. Law stood and offered a bow worthy of a greeting to a Peer of the Realm.

"You've been to London?" George asked the visitor exuberantly.

"I assure you, it isn't as glorious as it's made to sound. You clearly lead a much more exciting life, what with all the duels and such." Mr. Law raised his brows as if impressed, but a twitch of his mouth revealed he was playing along.

George sighed. "I haven't actually fought any duels."

"No? A pity."

George nodded mournfully. Aunt Missy looked on with an indulgent smile.

Isabella gave her brother a sympathetic pat on his arm. "Perhaps you'll meet another love of your life at the public ball."

George perked up. "Indeed."

Another love of his life. How wonderful it must be to love so easily. Isabella could only imagine how that must feel.

"Are you in school, George?" Mr. Law asked.

George swallowed a bite of his sandwich. "Just graduated from Oxford."

"Ah. Which college?"

"Exeter."

"I did as well," Mr. Law said. "Did you have Professor Keynes?"

George let out a scoffing noise. "His class was a good place for a nap. I think he is the son of the sandman."

Without missing a beat, Mr. Law said, "He's old enough to *be* the sandman."

They shared a comradely grin—or rather, George grinned, and Mr. Law's mouth curved slightly. But more importantly, faint light brightened Mr. Law's eyes. He quickly snuffed out that light, as if he felt it somehow inappropriate to enjoy a moment of true merriment.

Could he be in mourning?

As she took another look at him, the small black band around his arm that blended in with his black tailcoat became apparent. Poor Mr. Law! Whom did he mourn?

While they chatted like old friends, Mr. Law surreptitiously kept watch on the road, but no carriage passed. As only a young man not yet twenty-one could do, George devoured enough tea, sandwiches, and lemon cake for four people.

George stood. "Well, I'd best be off. I promised Molly I'd write to her every day."

"Another love of your life?" Mr. Law asked.

"To be sure. I really ought to be a sailor with a girl in every port."

Panic rose up in Isabella's chest. "Don't you dare become a sailor!"

George froze. Slowly, he said, "No, of course not. I wouldn't really go to sea, you know."

Isabella took a shaky breath. "No. I know. Forgive me." George was safe. She folded her hands together and did a slow release of air, letting go of her panic.

Mr. Law watched her with assessing eyes. He probably thought her a ninny destined for bedlam, who had fits of madness on a regular basis.

"Er, anyway." George glanced at each of them in turn. "Good afternoon, Mr. Law. I'm happy I met you."

Mr. Law stood and offered another formal bow. "I am as well. Good afternoon."

George sauntered out of the room.

Resuming his seat, Mr. Law's expression shifted into the kind indulgence one often wears when watching a child at play. "Likeable lad."

"I suppose he's tolerable when he isn't severely trying my patience," Isabella said in an exaggeratedly mournful tone.

"I'm sure an angel such as you has an abundance of patience." Again came that flirty curve of his mouth.

Angel. Bah! Who did he think he was fooling? She'd heard all those flowery phrases from other so-called fine gentlemen who thought they were irresistible.

Mr. Law was too flirtatious. How many ladies had fallen for his charm? He had too many secrets. And he clearly thought himself such a catch that any girl would fall all over herself to kiss him.

The object of her thoughts glanced first at the road outside the window, then at the clock on the mantle. His posture deflated ever so slightly. Unconsciously, he started bouncing one knee, a clear indication of anxiety.

He must have been truthful about becoming separated. But why all the secrecy? Did it have anything to do with his being in mourning? Perhaps rather than secretive, he was merely private. She would do well not to pry.

Gently, she said, "Mr. Law."

He gave a start as if he'd forgotten her presence. A tiny, rueful smile twitched his lips but didn't erase the sorrow in his eyes. "How may I be of service, Miss Montgomery?" Always that air of refinement and charm.

Should she trust his sincerity? "Perhaps you'd enjoy seeing the gardens and sitting under the willow tree? We can face the road so you may continue to keep watch. Or," she added impishly, "we could enjoy a more exhilarating diversion and go for a swim in the pond."

He lifted a brow as a smolder entered his dark eyes. "We?"

"*We* as in, you and my brother." She waited for his reaction.

Amusement lifted the corners of his mouth, but nothing lit the dullness in his eyes. "Of course. Your brother." He glanced at Aunt Missy but said nothing further.

Primly, she said, "I stopped swimming with boys at least a year ago."

A brow lifted. "I stopped being called a boy much longer ago than a year."

Aunt Missy interjected. "As far as I'm concerned, any male younger than thirty is still a boy."

Mr. Law bowed in polite defeat. "I suppose I'm a boy for another four years, then." He turned his dark eyes to Isabella. "I'd be delighted to see your garden." He nodded again to Aunt Missy. "Ma'am, it was a pleasure to meet you. Thank you for your hospitality. I hope our paths cross again."

With true warmth, Aunt Missy reached out and took his hands before giving them a squeeze. "I do as well, Mr. Law."

He blinked at the contact and then gave her a lopsided smile that almost banished the sorrow in his eyes.

Isabella carefully picked up the sleeping kitten from her lap and replaced her on the divan. "There, Mimi, you may rest here." Without looking at Isabella, Mimi stretched, jumped off the divan, and trotted off. "Hmm. Perhaps not Mimi, then. I must think up a new name for her."

Mr. Law stood and held out a hand to invite her to lead the way. In the garden filled mostly with wildflowers, Isabella and Mr. Law strolled along the paths that followed the fence by the road. At one point, he looked up and down the road.

"Are you worried about what has become of your father?" Isabella asked.

"No, I don't believe something has befallen him." He cast a quick, cautious glance at her before returning his gaze to the ground. One of his booted toes swiveled in the gravel path below their feet. "We were not on the best of terms. He might have left without me. Deliberately."

Isabella's mouth dropped open. "He abandoned you?"

"I thought it was an idle threat and that he'd wait for me at the next crossroads, prepared with a lecture." He let out a huff of cynical laughter. "I have never understood him. I understand him less now. It's clear I won't find him here, so I will bid you good day. Thank you for your hospitality."

"Where will you go?" As she stood next to him, their difference in height became apparent, as did the breadth of his chest. The breeze carried his scent, strong and clean and oh, so provocative.

"I'll follow the road." He bowed. "Good day, Miss Montgomery. It was a pleasure."

"I wish you luck."

He bowed again and strode to the gate leading to the road. She watched him walk, tall, confident, and proud. After the briefest pause, he chose a direction and headed down the road. How could she let him leave without knowing how to find his father? Yet what could she do?

Uncle Joseph rode up from the opposite direction. Wearing his vicar's cassock, her guardian glanced at Isabella and then at Mr. Law's retreating back. "Did we have a visitor?"

She nodded as an oddly unsettling sensation of loss edged into her usual cheer.

"You seem preoccupied, child."

Isabella indicated the shrinking figure on the road. "I found him walking the road. Apparently, his father . . . well, they became separated." Revealing that his father had left him would reflect poorly on both father and son.

"You found another lost soul to rescue?" Uncle Joseph's eyes crinkled in a kind smile.

She shrugged. "It seems so."

"And you're concerned about what may become of him."

"Well, yes. He's all alone."

Uncle Joseph swung down off the horse and said in a conversational tone, "Do you think he is of good character?"

She considered. "I think so. He is mysterious and reluctant to talk about himself. But I think it's because he's grieving, not because he is up to mischief. He was wearing a mourning band. I worry what will become of him."

Almost to himself, Uncle Joseph quoted, "'For I was an hungred, and ye gave me meat: I was thirsty, and ye gave me drink: I was a stranger, and ye took me in.'"

Isabella watched him. "Are you thinking of taking in this stranger?"

"I should discuss it with Missy first, of course." He handed her the reins to his horse. "Be a good girl and walk Noah, would you?"

Taking the reins, Isabella clicked her tongue and walked the horse around the house. Through open windows, Uncle Joseph's voice mingled with Aunt Missy's. A few minutes later, Uncle Joseph returned, took the reins, and swung into the saddle.

"Set another place for dinner, m'dear." He urged Noah to a canter toward Mr. Law's distant figure.

Isabella hugged herself in an attempt to quell her excitement at spending time with Mr. Law again, possibly for days. Really, she ought to be merely concerned for his welfare, not thinking about the shape of his lips or his manly scent or how tempting it had been to give him his requested kiss.

3

Rowan stared blankly at the vicar who'd ridden to him. Surely he'd heard him wrong. "You want to *what*?"

Of a similar height now that he had dismounted, the older man who had introduced himself as Mr. Williams held his gaze steadily. "You heard me. Is it so hard to believe that I'd offer a bed to someone who's a bit down on his luck?" The older man smiled, his eyes kind.

Rowan chuckled darkly. "It wasn't exactly luck that brought me here."

Mr. Williams raised a pair of gray eyebrows. "Have you a place to sleep?"

"I will when I find my father."

Mr. Williams considered him as if he toyed with whether or not to divulge a secret. "Was your family coach black with red wheels?"

Rowan went still. "Yes." It came out more like a question.

"I saw it at the coaching inn up ahead." He pointed with his chin. "A gentleman wearing a yellow coat came out of a private dining room and entered that coach. They left perhaps two hours ago."

Two hours ago? His father had left. He'd had a meal and then simply driven off, knowing Rowan was alone in an unfamiliar place, without friend or money.

Rowan ran a thumb across his chin. "I see."

After all that talk about how Rowan, as the new heir, was so important and how they had much to do—a declaration that began mere hours after Hadley's funeral—his father had simply left.

Had Rowan pushed him too much?

If Father had indeed ceased his attempt to educate Rowan on the aspects of how to properly care for their estate—the properties, tenants, crops, and holdings—then who was Rowan to argue?

Perhaps, freed from Father's unwelcome attention, Rowan would enjoy a much-needed respite here in Brighton. A holiday at the seashore might do him good. He might even find the mysterious love of his brother's.

Rowan pressed a hand over an inner pocket of his jacket, where he kept the tiny oval frame containing a miniature painting of an eye, complete with lashes and brow. The Lover's Eye, along with a lock of golden hair and the name Ann, provided the only clues to the identity of his brother's love. Would they be enough?

In order to do that, he needed a place to sleep. Still . . .

Rowan drew a breath. "That's very kind of you, sir, but I couldn't impose."

"Not at all. Our vicarage once housed nine children. Now it only houses two young people. It's surely more humble than you're accustomed to, but you are welcome to stay until you are reunited with your father—or until you can make other arrangements. Let's give it a week, shall we?"

A week under the same roof as the delectable Miss Montgomery, and the chance to locate his brother's Ann. This vicar's hospitality seemed a perfect answer. "Very well, sir. I thank you for your generosity."

"Excellent." Leading his horse, Mr. Williams walked next to Rowan as they headed back to the vicarage. "I should tell you that I'm particularly protective of my ward, Isabella. Though she's not my blood relative, I feel great responsibility toward her and her brother. I expect you not to trifle with her heart or her virtue."

"Sir, I would never—"

Mr. Williams held up a hand to silence Rowan. "It's easy to say that now, and I'm sure you mean well, but I was your age once and I know how young men's thoughts run when a pretty maiden is close at hand. If I even *suspect* ungentlemanly conduct on your behalf, all my goodwill toward you will vanish in the blink of an eye. Are we understood?"

"Yes, sir." No stolen kisses. Understood. Not that he really would, tempting as it had been. Besides, she'd already made it clear she would not succumb to his advances. Clearly, she was no ordinary girl.

They reached the vicarage, and Rowan took a better look at the abode that would be his haven for the foreseeable future. A two-story building made entirely of brick with white trim sat in the sunshine. It seemed to smile at him.

Inside, Mrs. Williams welcomed him warmly and showed him to his bedchamber. A tiny yet comfortable room greeted him. Sunlight streamed through a window overlooking the front of the house. A cool breeze blew in, stirring crisp, white curtains at the window. A cheerful quilt covered a bed that looked barely large enough to fit his frame. He'd have to be careful when turning over. The soft green carpet, though faded, appeared free of dirt and stains. This family may not be wealthy, but cleanliness and care reigned in this little home. The small, quaint space seemed to breathe with light and cheer.

He turned to Mrs. Williams. "I'm sure I'll be quite comfortable here. I cannot tell you how much I appreciate your—"

"Tut tut, Mr. Law." She waved away his words. "No need for all that. We've all needed a friend now and again. You rest now, and we'll call you for dinner shortly."

He glanced down at his dusty traveling clothes and boots. "I fear I have nothing appropriate for dinner."

"We'll have an informal dinner *al fresco*." She beamed at him and left him alone, closing the door behind her.

Rowan took out the Lover's Eye and lock of hair, his clues to finding his brother's beloved Ann. Where would he start? He knew nothing about her—not even a last name. The vague reference to Father deeming her unsuitable was no help. She could be a member of the impoverished gentry, with no dowry. Or an innkeeper's daughter.

An hour later, Rowan met the family in their small parlor. The moment he caught sight of Miss Montgomery, Rowan checked his steps. A fresh loveliness about her called to him.

Mr. Williams's previous warning rang loudly in his head.

Rowan took a seat on the opposite side of the room, where he'd have to turn his head to look at her. Moments later, a housekeeper old enough to have been alive during the Roman Empire toddled in to announce dinner.

Mr. Williams escorted his wife out of the room, followed by the Montgomery siblings, who flanked Rowan.

"I hope you're hungry," Miss Montgomery said. "Our cook was so excited to have a dinner guest that I think she prepared enough for twice as many people."

Rowan glanced at the lovely girl. "I'll do my best to eat enough to let her know her work is appreciated."

"No doubt George will finish whatever you don't."

"Eat quickly," George advised Rowan with a grin.

Outside, under a deepening blue sky, they dined at a table set up under a tent. Linens, china, and silver graced the table.

The western horizon blazed with a setting sun, and the birds serenaded them as sweetly as any string quartet. Rowan sat at the vicar's left, with the lovely Miss Montgomery on his other side. So as not to give his host reason to doubt his word, Rowan kept his focus on the menfolk and his food. Miss Montgomery's calico kitten wandered about, sniffing at flowers and chasing bugs.

As if separated from them by a filmy curtain, Rowan observed the family conversing with familiarity and affection punctuated by laughter and good-natured ribbing. An ache opened up inside him.

He'd never known it until now, but he'd longed for this all his life. Even while visiting home during school holidays, he'd never enjoyed this comfortable warmth around a dinner table with his family. They'd been too busy wearing impeccable clothing and using impeccable manners.

Rowan glanced at the lovely Miss Montgomery. Well, he'd meant to glance, but he couldn't look away. The curve of her cheek, the elegant tilt of her head, and each motion of her mouth captivated him.

She caught him looking at her. "Have you been to Brighton before, Mr. Law?"

"Only briefly. I should like to see more."

"I believe an outing to the seashore is in order," the vicar said.

George perked up. "Jolly good."

The matron of the family clasped her hands together. "Shall we plan to go on the morrow?"

Four pairs of eyes focused on Rowan as if awaiting his agreement.

Rowan spread his hands. "As it happens, my social calendar is open tomorrow, and I cannot imagine a more pleasant diversion with a more charming group of people."

"It's settled." Mr. Williams nodded.

Excited voices filled the air as each member of this makeshift family chimed in about things to do and places to see in a happy cacophony. How unlike all the various places he'd referred to as home, depending on which estate they were residing at the time. A sense of familiarity about this humble vicarage stole over him. A tight knot in his chest loosened—one he had never noticed before now. He took a deeper breath than he had in years.

As the light faded, the ancient housekeeper and a girl-of-all-work came out and lit the lamps. They returned moments later with a cake before quietly retreating.

Apparently, the vicar had few servants, but he and his family seemed to live simply without the army of staff that his father's estates required.

"Oh, and we'll have to take you by the prince's Royal Pavilion," Miss Montgomery said as she served a slice of cake to Rowan. "We aren't allowed inside, of course, but we can peer at it through the fence. Perhaps we'll catch a glimpse of the prince himself."

"No, we won't, silly," her brother protested. "He never shows himself. They say he has underground tunnels from his house to a fenced-off area where he rides." He directed his next words to Rowan. "He doesn't want anyone to see him—probably because he's so fat that he knows people will mock him."

Before Rowan could reply, Miss Montgomery interjected. "Or he's a private person. Can you imagine what it would be like to have everyone watching you and judging you?"

"That's right," Mr. Williams said. "We may not approve of his lavish and indolent lifestyle, but we must not judge him. Only God can see into a person's heart." He tapped the air with a finger to punctuate his point. Perhaps he was one of those vicars who pounded the pulpit during his sermons.

The vicar's wife spoke up. "I think Prince George acts that way because he has a broken heart."

They all turned to her.

The matron looked at each of them in turn. "Well, can you imagine what it must have been like to have his beloved wife torn from him, to have his marriage declared invalid, and then to be forced to marry another woman whom he obviously doesn't love? He is probably trying to forget his sorrows with all the pleasures of the world, when really his heart cries out for true love."

Mr. Williams picked up his wife's hands and kissed the backs of them both. "You, my dear, are a romantic."

She certainly was. Of course, the prince made no secret of keeping his former wife as a mistress, nor did he apologize for all of his other lovers, not to mention his exorbitant spending, but Rowan kept that to himself.

Mrs. Williams smiled. "Can you blame me for being a romantic?"

"Not at all, my dear."

Though darkness enveloped the land outside the cheery rings of lamplight, the family made no move to leave.

"Aunt Missy," Miss Montgomery said. "Do you think it would be appropriate to bring Mr. Law to the public ball?"

"Of course. No one would object to having another gentleman in attendance"—she looked at Rowan—"if you are in agreement?"

Wryly, he said, "Since I have no idea how long I will be here, I am afraid I cannot make any promises. However, I would be delighted to accompany your family anywhere you wish to take me while I'm here. Consider me at your disposal."

"Let us hope you will spend at least a week in Brighton, then," Mr. Williams said.

Miss Montgomery asked her uncle, "Might we pick up some more paints while we're out tomorrow?"

Mr. Williams nodded. "Of course. Are you working on a new piece?"

Miss Montgomery's expression lit up. "I already have it sketched. I need more blue paint, though, before I can paint it."

"How many are you entering?" her brother asked.

"This will be my fourth," the young lady said. "Surely one will take Mr. Corby's notice."

After attempting to piece together their conversation, Rowan asked, "Is there an art contest?"

Miss Montgomery's eyes sparkled with an inner vivaciousness. "Mr. Corby is a master artist who lives here. He only accepts one student a year based on the entries in his contest next week."

"Ah, yes—the art master you mentioned earlier," Rowan said.

"I would love more than anything to study under him." She clasped her hands together.

"I hope you'll show me your art sometime."

"Of course. You can tell me if you think any of them are good enough to enter."

Was she teasing him or in earnest? Rowan held up his hands. "I do not consider myself an expert and would never presume to advise you."

"Well, if my work is truly awful, then I wouldn't wish to embarrass myself by entering it so you must tell me if you dislike it."

Honestly, he said, "I cannot imagine you doing anything truly awful."

"You should hear me sing." A wry smile curved her delicious lips.

Rowan almost returned her smile, but his mirth slipped away. Surely he ought not be so jovial so soon after losing his brother. Or ever.

4

ISABELLA SWUNG HER HAT by the ribbons and sang "English Country Garden" as she strolled along the garden path. Overhead, a pink sunrise faded to purple and then blue skies. Scampering along behind her, stopping to sniff a rock or chase a frog or butterfly, her kitten kept her company. When the calico trailed too far behind, Isabella called, "Come, Gypsy."

The kitten ignored her. Perhaps she needed time to adjust to the name Isabella was trying on her today. Or it wasn't the right name.

As she rounded a bend in the garden near the willow, a figure lounging on her favorite wooden bench came into view. Mr. Law stared upward as if fascinated by the changing colors. His dark hair and black clothing stood out in sharp contrast against the pastel colors of the garden and sky.

She sauntered towards him. "Good morning. I don't normally find others out so early."

He stood and effected a half bow. "Good morning."

Isabella bent her knees in a curtsy and continued toward him. "Do you always rise so early?"

"Not normally, but I find it difficult to sleep in an unfamiliar place."

She took a seat on the bench so he would not, as a gentleman, feel he must stand. Patting the bench next to him in invitation, she studied him. All manners and grace, he sat next to her but lost the relaxed posture he'd had before her arrival. Nearby, Gypsy stalked a lizard.

"In all our excitement, we may have talked you into going on an outing you'd rather not attend," she said.

"Not at all. I look forward to a diversion." He trailed off as if he wanted to say more but changed his mind.

"Was there something else you'd like to do while you are here?"

He glanced at her as if to gauge her reaction. Oh dear. He wasn't about to ask for something scandalous again, was he? She might have to turn him down this time with a right hook like her brother taught her.

His expression remained serious. "I'm hoping to find someone."

She leaned forward. "Who?"

"A girl."

She might have known. "I see."

In halting tones, he explained, "Her name is Ann, and she lives here in Brighton—at least she did two years ago." He reached into his coat pocket and withdrew something, then opened his hand. In his palm lay a curl of hair the deep, rich gold of old coins, and a miniature.

Isabella peered at the miniature. A tiny, delicately painted eye set in a narrow gold frame looked up at her. The golden-brown brow arched over a honey-brown eye rimmed with surprisingly thick eyelashes. She'd never seen a Lover's Eye so beautifully painted.

She mused, "Brown eyes and blonde hair? An unusual combination."

"It's all I know of her. I must find her. She doesn't know . . ." He paused and swallowed, then turned his head and coughed softly.

Barely above a whisper, Isabella asked gently, "What doesn't she know?"

"What happened to my brother."

His brother. That explained the mourning band and his sadness.

Very gently she asked, "What happened to him?"

He swallowed again. "Accident. Steeplechase." A long pause. "Ten days ago."

He must be positively grief-stricken. She wanted to hold him and offer solace.

In a soft voice, she prompted, "Ann was special to him?"

He nodded. "He told me once that she is the only girl he ever loved. But my parents wouldn't sanction a union between them."

"How tragic."

He said nothing.

"Was she impoverished gentry? Working class?"

He exhaled. "I only know she was deemed unsuitable. She has probably not yet learned of his . . . death." He stumbled a bit over the word.

"That is very thoughtful of you to tell her personally." Perhaps she had misjudged him. Though obviously a charmer with enough town polish to impress even the fussiest *grandes dames* of society, here sat a grieving gentleman whose top priority was not finding a way back to his mansion but finding a stranger to inform her of his brother's fate, despite her obviously inferior social standing.

He'd lost a brother. So had she. This common loss opened up a new connection for the gentleman.

She picked up the Lover's Eye and studied it. "I cannot recall seeing eyes like this, but it is difficult to say without the whole face. I'm not certain I'd recognize my own brother if I only had a painting of an eye to identify him."

Perhaps she was foolish to want to help Mr. Law. But help him she would, if possible.

Of course, that meant she would have less time to devote to her paintings, and she had at least one more to finish before the art show. Surely Mr. Corby would see her talent and accept her as a student this year.

"I'd be happy to help you search for this blonde, brown-eyed girl named Ann," she promised.

He tucked away the lock of hair and jewelry. "Thank you."

She stood. "I do believe I'm in need of breakfast. Have you already eaten this morn?"

He rose to his feet in a fluid motion. "Not yet."

As they ate, Isabella questioned Mr. Law on anything else he could remember about the girl he sought, but he knew nothing more. Sipping her tea, she turned over in her mind every blonde who might be the right age to have caught the eye of a wealthy young gentleman but not high enough in status to be deemed eligible. There weren't that many blondes in the area. Surely finding Ann would not be so difficult.

An idea came to Isabella. "There's a wealthy merchant with a blonde daughter about my age. I cannot recall if she has brown eyes or not, nor do I recall her name. I will ask Aunt Missy if she remembers."

He nodded. "A cit would certainly not please my parents."

"Do you mind if we enlist Aunt Missy's help—or Uncle Joseph's?"

"As I don't know how much time I have here, including your family would be wise."

Aunt Missy arrived in the breakfast room. "Good morning, my dears. Are we ready for an outing?" She picked up a plate and began serving herself from the buffet.

"Yes, indeed," Isabella said. "Aunt, can you think of any girl—of any class—here in Brighton who is blonde, has brown eyes, and is named Ann?"

Aunt paused and lifted her brows questioningly, then furrowed them in thought. "Ann, with blonde hair . . . hmmm. The Joneses have a pretty blond girl. I cannot recall her name . . ."

Isabella tapped her chin. "I believe you are right."

"It's been some time since I last looked in on them, and I heard Mrs. Jones has been poorly. I shall prepare a basket and take it to them."

"Might you go before we leave for our visit to the seashore? It's important."

Aunt Missy paused, then shrugged. "As you wish."

In the kitchen, Isabella helped Aunt Missy prepare the basket with bread, cheese, apples, a jar of soup, and a small tin of tea. "Aunt, when you are there, please take notice if their daughter has brown eyes as well." She quickly explained Mr. Law's goal to find his brother's forbidden love.

"I'm always happy to help."

After Aunt Missy left with basket in hand, Isabella helped the cook assemble the baskets for their picnic at the seashore and store them in the buttery to keep them cold. Then she gathered up her sketch pad, pencil, and other art supplies she'd need if a view at the shore inspired her.

When Aunt Missy returned, Isabella pounced on her. "Well? What is their daughter's name?"

"Her name is Margaret. And her hair is more red than blonde."

"Oh." Isabella drew a breath. "Very well. Now we have one less place to look."

Aunt Missy patted her arm. "We'll do all we can to help him, but it may not be possible to find her."

Isabella ensured her kitten—Gypsy, today—had enough food and water and remained indoors where she wouldn't wander off again and need another rescue. The kitten still failed to pay any attention to her name. Yet Gypsy was such a perfect name—she did like to roam.

When the family gathered in the parlor, Mr. Law appeared still wearing all black and with a tragic air surrounding him. Perhaps a day at the seaside would do him good, although experience had taught Isabella that little helped so soon after a loss like one he'd suffered.

Mr. Law addressed Aunt Missy. "Any luck?"

She shook her head. "Wrong name and wrong hair color."

He nodded soberly. "I didn't think it would be that easy."

"We'll keep trying," Isabella promised.

His eyes softened when they focused on her, and the first hint of a real smile touched his mouth. "I'm very grateful to you."

They all bundled into the carriage. Uncle Joseph drove them through town, taking them down the street where the prince's mistress, Mrs. Fitzherbert, resided.

Further down the road, they stopped in front of the prince's seaside retreat, known as the Royal Pavilion. Though the latest construction in this new phase of remodeling had not yet been completed, it reigned like a palace with Indian-inspired domes and towers spread out on each side in jaw-dropping splendor.

"Astounding," Mr. Law said.

Isabella sighed. "If only I could get a look at all the artwork inside. It must be wondrous."

"I'm sure it is," Mr. Law said. "Perhaps you will go inside someday."

She laughed. "I haven't the connections to gain entrance inside a royal residence."

After gawking at the opulence, they moved on. In a shop, Isabella purchased her paints and more paper. Mr. Law roamed the store in idle curiosity while Aunt Missy bought more tatting supplies.

As they paid for their purchases, two women entered. One, clearly older, strode to the display of yarn. The other, a woman of approximately thirty wearing a pelisse that was in fashion at least five years ago, admired a box of shoe-flowers with the kind of expression of someone long denied. Golden-blonde curls peeped out from around her bonnet. She removed her gloves to touch the shoe-flowers. No ring adorned her finger. Could this be Mr. Law's mysterious Ann? Isabella had pictured someone younger, but Mr. Law's elder brother might have loved someone near his age. Isabella moved toward the woman, pretending to admire boxes of goods as she moved. As she neared, the woman glanced up at her with gray eyes.

Not her, then. Isabella smiled at her in greeting, despite her disappointment. She might be overly optimistic to think they would find Ann so easily, but anything could happen.

Isabella returned to Mr. Law. "We have what we need. Do you require anything?"

He shook his head, probably reluctant to ask them to buy anything for him. It must be humbling for such a fine gentleman to find himself without funds.

Back outside, they headed toward the carriage. George and Uncle Joseph stood chatting with three ladies. As the elder lady turned her head, her face came into view. Isabella recognized Mrs. Stockton, a mother of three daughters, two of whom were out. George seemed to be in a particularly animated conversation with the elder daughter. Her laugh trilled, and she briefly touched his arm in a flirtatious gesture. After they parted, George, still smiling, and Uncle Joseph returned to the carriage.

Isabella smiled at George. "Did you have a nice conversation with Miss Stockton?"

He grinned. "I did. Funny that I never noticed how pretty she is."

Isabella put a hand over her heart. "Another young lady to succumb to the charm of George Montgomery."

He puffed out his chest. "I am rather charming, aren't I?" He grinned. "I asked Miss Stockton if I might call upon them on the morrow. She agreed—so did her mother."

Mr. Law clapped George on the shoulder in a congratulatory gesture. "Another 'port' with a girl?"

"Perhaps." His confident grin suggested a happy anticipation.

One day he'd find the right girl and give her all the love in his romantic heart. Did such a love await Isabella? She stared ahead, seeking the seascape, but her vision landed on Mr. Law. She would do well to help him and send him on his way; if her intuition was correct, he belonged to a higher class than the orphaned daughter of a ship's captain. Besides, she knew nothing about Mr. Law except that he was well-spoken and occasionally spouted flattery.

No, that wasn't fair. She also knew he'd had a falling-out of sorts with his father and he mourned his brother. Not to mention, he sought the girl his brother had loved so he might give her the news of his death. That suggested a noble heart. Besides, he'd rescued her kitten.

Still, she was not yet nineteen. Life had not entirely passed her by. She probably hadn't met her match yet. In the meantime, she had a puzzle to solve with Mr. Law and an art contest to win.

As Uncle Joseph took them through Brighton, pointing out sights of interest, Mr. Law made appropriate comments of appreciation.

After completing their tour of the area, Uncle Joseph turned their carriage toward the seashore. The seaside welcomed them with a uniquely fresh, salty tang of the ocean and warm sand. Others who came to enjoy the shore sat under parasols or portable tents reading or watching passersby or seafaring vessels sailing past. Bathing machines stretched out into the waves to dip ladies in the invigorating seawater. Boys and men cavorted in the surf. Children and ladies with their skirts tucked up waded in the waves after looking for shells or chasing seabirds. Those looking for a feast combed the sand for clams and crabs.

Isabella loved the seashore! Could it inspire her today to paint a piece that would gain the notice of the art master?

While George and Uncle Joseph set up the tent, Mr. Law helped them bring baskets, blankets, and folding chairs. Aunt Missy set out the food. After luncheon, Isabella took up her sketchbook and captured everything that caught her interest.

A familiar figure sauntered along the shore with an easel, canvas, and a box of paints. Smiling, Isabella waved. The figure changed directions and approached her. Old Pete's nearly toothless smile set in a weathered face greeted her.

He touched his cap. "Miss Isabella."

"Are you finding inspiration today?" She gestured to his painting supplies he carried.

"Not yet. Just got here. You?"

"I did, too. I'm looking for something really remarkable—something that will impress Mr. Corby."

"You don't need to impress him," Pete said. "You only need to impress your muse. Once you've done that, you'll never run out of art."

"But he could teach me so much."

Old Pete held up a hand. "Probably so, but I daresay not much more than you need to keep your heart happy. Good day to you." He touched his cap to Aunt Missy. "Ma'am." Still carrying his paint supplies, he moved off down the shoreline to find a spot to paint.

She envied his simple pleasure and confidence of his place in the world.

Mr. Law sidled up to her. "An old friend of yours?"

"He's a gifted artist. Not classically trained, but one of the most naturally talented artists I've ever met."

Miss Potter caught her vision. Isabella wandered over to where Miss Potter sat behind her easel, facing the town rather than the sea. Her masterful strokes captured the scene yet gave it a somber, tragic, dramatic slant as it revealed the paradox that was Brighton: the bright and the dark, the affluent and the impoverished, the elegance and the squalor in a shocking combination of colors and textures. Though the subject repelled Isabella, it captured an impressive depth of emotion.

She could surely never create such a piece of art. Did that mean she wasn't good enough to study with the art master? Was her work too ordinary and tame to be called true art?

Troubled, Isabella returned to her family's tent. Mr. Law stared out over the water. Closing his eyes, he drew a deep breath. As he exhaled, his shoulders lowered as if tension left him.

"I feel as if I have come to a haven of sorts," he said softly.

She nodded. "Many people feel restored after only a few minutes here."

"I wish I never had to leave."

She closed her mouth before she said the words *I wish you didn't have to leave, too.* Yes, he was handsome and in need of both cheering and completing his quest, but that did not mean she should form any sort of attachment to him.

Was she too tame and ordinary to attract a gentleman such as Rowan Law?

5

AFTER ONE OF THE most truly relaxing days of his life, Rowan lounged in the family parlor. Mr. Williams and George sat at a chessboard, Mrs. Williams took up her sewing, and Miss Isabella Montgomery worked on her newest painting.

After getting permission to mail a letter, Rowan scribbled his request and set it out to be posted. With that task complete, he wandered about the room and ended up in front of an ancient pianoforte.

He gestured to the instrument. "May I?"

Mrs. Williams glanced at him over her sewing. "Of course. Forgive us, Mr. Law. We are unaccustomed to company. Perhaps we ought to play a game?"

"Not necessary. I wouldn't want to disrupt your normal lives. I can amuse myself nicely here." He sat at the piano and began a sonata. A few of the keys played out of tune, but he immersed himself in the melody.

"I have it," Miss Montgomery announced.

Rowan stilled his fingers, his attention focused on the girl. She stood, holding a paintbrush in one hand, and made a gesture. Rowan pressed his lips together to avoid smiling at the blue smudge of paint on her cheekbone.

With her eye alight and her voice bubbling with excitement, Miss Montgomery said, "The Fosters have a blonde daughter a bit younger than I am. Her name is Anna. They are respectable, but she has no dowry—only her pretty face to attract a husband."

Hope lit inside Rowan. "She might be the one."

Miss Montgomery nodded. "I shall pay a call upon them on the morrow."

George Montgomery sighed dramatically. "And I shall pay a call upon the delectable Miss Stockton on the morrow."

"I just took your bishop, lover boy." Mr. Williams chuckled as he moved chess pieces on the board.

"Oh, no!" Mr. Montgomery said, throwing a hand over his heart. "How shall we marry without a bishop?" He grinned as if he were the most entertaining person in the room and moved a rook.

"Might I suggest a humble vicar?" Mr. Williams quipped.

"Do you wish to accompany me when I pay a call upon the Fosters?" Miss Montgomery asked Rowan.

"Yes, I would, thank you." He could see for himself whether the girl in question had the right coloring. Besides, spending time with Miss Montgomery always held appeal.

She resumed painting. Despite an overwhelming urge to be at her side, Rowan played a few more memorized pieces before succumbing. On his way to Miss Montgomery, he veered off to Mrs. Williams. It wouldn't do to make his interest so well-known, especially after the vicar's warning.

Rowan admired an intricate lace Mrs. Williams created by moving threads on colored beads in a weaving pattern. "That's pretty."

Mrs. Williams beamed. "I'm making over an old dress and thought a bit of new tatted lace might do nicely."

"Indeed." He sauntered to Miss Montgomery and gestured to her easel. "May I?"

She paused, then nodded. "It's not finished . . ."

After moving to her side so he could look at the paper

from the artist's view, he peered at her art. A watercolor of a garden in early-morning light, still wet with dew, came to life under her brush strokes.

"That's very good," he said honestly.

"Is it?" Her hopeful expression revealed a touch of vulnerability.

"Indeed. I would hang this in my house where I could look at it every day. It makes me feel peaceful. Content."

Joy and relief entered her smile. "You're too kind. I tried to paint something more dramatic, but I hated how it turned out." She gestured to an unfinished piece of art behind her of a stormy sea with alarming sky and ocean colors.

He gestured to the watercolor. "This one is much better."

"I just don't know if it's good enough for Mr. Corby."

"You must paint what is in your heart—not what others think you ought to paint."

She nodded but looked unconvinced.

He added, "I can hardly wait to see the rest of your paintings."

Apparently, emboldened by his admiration, she eagerly retrieved several other works. With her romantic, joyful, and often peaceful perspective, landscapes of cottages, gardens, seascapes, and the prince's pavilion sprang to life on paper.

"These rival any art I've seen in London," he said honestly.

"Thank you. I only hope they are good enough." The wistfulness in her voice revealed her longing. "Your playing was lovely. Was that Brahms?" she asked, clearly to change the subject.

"It was."

"Is he your favorite composer?"

"I like him, but I'm partial to Vivaldi and Chopin."

"If you can play Chopin, you are a gifted pianist."

He shrugged. "I enjoy it."

"Mr. Law," Mrs. Williams interjected. "Is there anything we can do to make your stay here more comfortable?"

He paused, taken aback by her solicitousness, motivated by pure kindness instead of the fawning he sometimes encountered—especially while traveling with his father. "Not at all, ma'am. The accommodations are quite nice."

"Difficult to sleep in a strange place, though, isn't it?"

He took a seat next to his hostess. "A bit. Do not trouble yourself. I will adapt. Perhaps my father will return soon, and you will no longer need to concern yourself over me."

"It's been a pleasure to have you with us, and you are welcome to stay as long as needed." Mrs. Williams put her hand on the back of his head, brought it in, and kissed his brow in a motherly gesture.

When was the last time he'd been the recipient of such a tender, innocent show of affection?

His own mother had patted him on the head when he was a small boy and told him to make her proud. He likely hadn't in a very long time. He cleared his throat.

The family bade goodnight, and Rowan went to his homey bedchamber more content than he'd ever remembered feeling. Perhaps his father had done him a favor in abandoning him where he could find this remarkable family.

As he lay in bed, he relived Miss Montgomery's smile, her graceful walk, the passion blazing in her eyes when she painted, her enthusiasm to help him find Ann. He spent the remainder of the night listing all the reasons why he must not give the lovely young lady with the kitten whose name she changed every day another thought: her guardian had all but forbidden him from touching or courting her, he would be gone before he knew her well enough to consider her a match, she was too free-spirited and innocent to survive the scrutiny of society matrons, she had no experience managing a sizable household, his parents would never give their blessing on such a union, on and on until finally he imagined her simply laughing in his face during his proposal and skipping away through the garden.

The following morning, as Rowan prepared to accompany Miss Montgomery to the Fosters' home, Mr. Williams stared hard at him and gave a sharp tip of his head before stepping into his study. With his hands behind his back, Rowan followed Mr. Williams.

The vicar closed the door behind him and turned. "I see how you look at her." It came out as an accusation.

Rowan put up his hands. "Sir . . ."

Before he got out another word, Mr. Williams said, "I have known Isabella and George since their births. Their mother was my wife's dearest friend. We mourned when she died and took in the children so their father could continue serving king and country as a post captain. When he was killed in battle, we grieved with them. Then, when the eldest Montgomery boy perished—also at sea—we grieved again. Isabella and George are as much in our hearts as our own children."

"She lost her parents and a brother?"

Somberly, Mr. Williams nodded. "So you can understand why I will do all in my power to protect her from further heartbreak."

Rowan had been wrong to assume that the young lady behind the perpetual cheer had not suffered her own tragedies. He looked Mr. Williams in the eye. "Sir, I vow I have not touched her nor trifled with her heart—nor will I. I give you my word."

Mr. Williams nodded, stepped back, and opened the door in clear dismissal. "I hope you find the girl you seek."

"Thank you. And sir, I appreciate you and your wife taking me in. If there is ever a way I might repay you, I vow you have only to ask."

Mr. Williams nodded.

Rowan returned to the parlor where Miss Montgomery was tying her bonnet's ribbons underneath her chin. She smiled at his approach, that ray of cheer that shone into his aching heart. Could he, too, heal from the crushing blow of losing his brother and find peace? It seemed impossible. Yet, she had. In fact, she'd lost more.

"Ready?" She beamed.

"Ready."

She put a basket on her arm and led the way outside.

Rowan reached for the basket. "May I carry that for you?"

She smiled. "It isn't heavy. I can manage."

"I'm sure you're capable of managing a great many things, but I would be no gentleman if I allowed you to carry burdens when I'm here to carry them for you."

"Then, I thank you." Smiling, she handed over her basket.

"Have you always lived in Brighton?" he asked.

"All my life. I was born only a few miles from this spot. Our family home is being let out until George reaches his majority and assumes care over the property."

"Have you ever desired to live anywhere but Brighton?"

She picked a wildflower growing along the path. "I've not thought about that. We've traveled a little—Bath, the Lake District, Dover—but it never occurred to me to really leave Brighton. I love it here by the sea. All my friends are here, and Aunt Missy and Uncle Joseph. And I cannot imagine living far from George, trial that he is." She grinned.

More reasons why he ought not consider her as a potential love interest. He'd be expected to visit the various family holdings on a regular basis.

Her voice broke into his thoughts. "You?"

"If I had a choice, I'd live here, too—or somewhere near the sea."

"You don't have a choice?"

"I will one day inherit my father's estate, so I must prepare for those responsibilities. My time is no longer my own."

Quietly, she asked, "Who are you, Mr. Law?"

He might as well tell her. She would find out one way or another. "I am the second son of the Earl of Leiderton. When my brother ... passed ... I gained the courtesy title of Viscount Hadley."

Her features flitted from one expression to another. Finally, she nodded. "That does explain rather a lot." She stopped walking and touched his arm. "I am so, so very sorry about your brother."

Of everything he'd told her, the one piece of information she commented on was how recently he'd lost his brother. Had he ever met someone as genuinely kind as she?

"Thank you," he said hoarsely. "Father immediately shifted his focus to me as if my brother had never existed. He talks constantly about managing our estate and how I am to one day inherit and that we must make up for lost time." How could he assume the role meant for his brother? He looked away until his watery vision cleared.

Gently, she said, "I'm sure your father has not simply forgotten him. He is probably trying to do the proper thing by you."

Disdainful and bitter, he said, "Proper. Yes, if there is one word to describe my father, *proper* would be it."

She looked at him with tears in her eyes. Without speaking, she touched his arm briefly, the touch of friendship and compassion. Somehow that helped. He took a deep breath and pulled himself together.

"Here we are." She gestured to a humble stone cottage with only one chimney.

The cries of a child reached them. As they walked up a lane nearly obscured with weeds and wildflowers, the front door opened, and a woman walked out with a child on her hip. She stopped short and shaded her eyes.

"Good day, Mrs. Foster," Miss Montgomery called.

"Oh, good day, Miss Montgomery." The woman dropped a curtsy and shifted the child onto the other hip.

"Are you well?" Miss Montgomery asked.

"Yes, quite. Just trying to distract the little one here. Her brother hurt her feelings."

The little girl peered at them before burying her head in her mama's shoulder.

Miss Montgomery shook her head sadly. "Boys!"

The child offered a timid smile at the display of sympathy.

Miss Montgomery gestured at the basket in Rowan's hands. "I hope you don't mind my dropping in, but we have fresh preserves and bread we wanted to bring to you."

"How kind."

"I also wanted to introduce you to a houseguest of ours."

After the introductions, Mrs. Foster said, "Won't you please come in?"

Rowan blinked in the dim interior of the house while the mother called for someone to put on the kettle.

In a moment, they seated themselves in the humble surroundings. Miss Montgomery opened the basket and pulled out jars of preserves, loaves of bread, a block of cheese, and several apples, all while asking about mutual acquaintances.

By Rowan's definition, the vicar and his family were not wealthy, but they clearly took to heart their duty to look out for those less fortunate than they.

Within minutes, two daughters in their teens hurried in, smoothing their hair and skirts. One, indeed, was blonde. In the dim lighting of the interior, Rowan could not be certain if her hair was the correct shade to match the lock nestled in his coat pocket.

"These are my daughters, Anna and Mabel," Mrs. Foster said.

Their proximity, combined with the poor lighting, made it impossible to determine the color of the blonde's eyes. Still, as Rowan sipped weak tea, he plied them with his charm and took pleasure in their reactions. Yes, he still had the power to draw blushes and titters out of girls. Even the mother seemed to enjoy him. Apparently only Miss Montgomery was immune to him.

After a respectable time had passed, Miss Montgomery stood. "This has been a most pleasant morning, Mrs. Foster."

"Indeed," Rowan said with a bow. "Thank you for your hospitality."

At the door, he turned in a last desperate hope to look at the blonde. In the light streaming in through the doorway, the blonde girl's eye color became apparent: blue. And her pale hair could not be the deep gold of Ann's lock.

Rowan's breath left in a disappointed exhale. He bade them farewell and followed Miss Montgomery out.

When they were out of earshot, Miss Montgomery sent him an apologetic smile. "I'm sorry we didn't find your Ann here."

"I appreciate your efforts on my behalf."

She laughed softly. "Are you always so charming, or did you put on a special show for those girls?"

He lifted his brows. "Aren't I always the most charming gentleman you've ever met?"

"Well, you do seem to say everything in the most

flattering way possible. One sometimes wonders if you are sincere."

"You find me insincere?"

"I'm not certain." She smiled to soften her words.

"A trusted mentor told me once that if I always speak as if I am addressing a duke or a duchess, I'll draw smiles and gladden hearts."

Her smile turned thoughtful. "We all ought to be more generous with praise. It would make us better people."

Did that mean he was exonerated? With women, it was difficult to know.

They strolled along together in a comfortable silence. Birds sang in a joyous chorus, and the trees swayed in a breeze.

After a moment, he asked, "Do you have any other ideas of who might be the Ann I seek?"

"There is the merchant I mentioned—the March family. They always come to church, so we will see them on the morrow."

He nodded. He'd failed to find Hadley's Ann today, but at least the morning had passed pleasantly.

Would he ever find Ann?

6

Isabella labored over her painting and stood back to eye her work. The proportions were good, the colors natural and varied, and the objects well-balanced. Did it lack something?

Would answers to these questions come after she began tutelage under Mr. Corby—if she ever became good enough to earn a place as a student—or did discovering the answer on her own determine whether or not he accepted Isabella?

After cleaning her brushes and removing her smock, she set the paper aside to dry and glanced at the clock. She'd painted through breakfast and now must go to church on an empty stomach. Oh, bother!

After returning to her bedchamber to don her bonnet and gloves, she stopped for a quick check in the mirror to be sure her face remained paint-free and her hair stayed in place.

"Isabella, it's time to leave." Aunt Missy's voice spurred her on.

"Coming, Aunt Missy." She raced down the stairs pell-mell and stopped short near the bottom of the staircase.

Mr. Law stood below, resplendent in his stylish black attire and poised as always. He probably thought her a country bumpkin with the manners of a barn animal.

Ever a gentleman, he bowed at her arrival. "Good morning, Miss Montgomery."

Since learning that he bore—reluctantly—the courtesy

title of viscount and was heir to an earldom, she probably ought to think of him in loftier terms. She must never forget his family lived in social circles so high above her that they might as well reside in different countries—a painful lesson his brother and Ann had learned.

Still, she could have a little fun with him. As she glided gracefully down the final two steps, she lifted her chin and said in as queenly a pose and tone as possible, "Good morning, Mr. Law. We are pleased to see you."

His mouth curved, and the expression almost reached his eyes. "Might I escort Your Highness to church this morning?"

She held out a hand and looked upward, still using the exaggeratedly formal queenly tone. "You have our permission to touch the royal hand, sir."

The expected touch came, but in a most unexpected way. At least, her reaction to his touch came unexpectedly. Despite the barrier of their gloves, heat raced through her arm like breakers on a shoreline, sending little currents all the way down to her toes.

George escorted Aunt Missy out the door, and Mr. Law followed them. As they walked to the parish church, Isabella pointed out sights along the way. Mr. Law's eyes darted about, and he appeared to listen. Once, he looked at her for a long moment with such an expression of admiration that she nearly sang out loud. Every time her feet threatened to leave the earth and send her floating, her common sense reminded her that a future earl was not for her. Besides, she might have misinterpreted his esteem; he was charming to all. She really ought to explain that to her *thumpity-thumpity* heart.

During their approach to the stone church building, heads turned and admiring gazes followed Mr. Law. Isabella followed Aunt Missy and George inside, where more glances of curiosity and clear astonishment came from every person in the room. Sitting between George and Mr. Law, Isabella looked straight at Uncle Joseph as he delivered his sermon, but she heard little over the thudding of her heart and the wild flights of fancy her imagination took. Next to her, Mr. Law shifted, and his leg brushed against hers. Heat raced outward in a growing circle from where he'd touched her, and she caught his scent. She drew a deep breath. An ache grew inside her. She dared a quick, longing glance at his profile. Even unsmiling, he was the most handsome man of her acquaintance. If he ever smiled at her, she would be lost.

The moment church ended and they went outside, the congregation descended on Aunt Missy, requesting introductions to Mr. Law. Those with eligible daughters were especially persistent. The Fosters, whom they had visited the day before, spoke with them, the girls as giggly as when Mr. Law flattered them the prior day.

George craned his neck, looking about. When the Stocktons emerged from the church's interior, George greeted the taller of the girls. She must be the one who'd stolen his heart.

The March family passed by, nodding politely but not speaking to Isabella or her family. As a merchant, and therefore a member of the working class, Mr. March and his family technically belonged in a social circle below Isabella's family, but they freely associated with one another at church. Their clothing and postures reflected an air of inflated pride common among the *nouveau riche*. Still, Isabella admired the mother and daughter's gowns. Golden-blonde curls peeped out from underneath the daughter's bonnet.

Isabella excused herself and went after them. "Mr. and Mrs. March. Good morning."

The family greeted her with open curiosity, except Mrs. March, who eyed her with disdain, as if she must endure the vicar's adopted daughter but would rather not be seen speaking with someone dressed in such inferior clothing. Isabella smoothed a hand over her favorite rose-colored pelisse. It was only a year old, for heaven's sake.

Mr. March took off his hat politely. "Good day, Miss Montgomery."

"Good morning." She smiled at them in turn.

Their daughter kept her eyes downcast. Oh, bother. How was Isabella to determine this girl's eye color?

"What a lovely bonnet, Miss March." Isabella said. "Did you get that from Madame Burchard's?"

Without looking up, the girl smiled shyly and shook her head.

"It came from London," Mrs. March said. "We went shopping when we were there for the Season, you know."

"Of course." Isabella searched for a way to address the girl so as to make eye contact.

"I don't suppose you've ever been to London?" Mrs. March sniffed.

"No, not yet," Isabella said.

"I imagine an orphan living on the charity of a vicar would not be able to afford a Season in London—such an expensive way to enter society."

Shocked at the woman's rudeness, Isabella barely managed not to gape.

Mr. March coughed into his hand. "She didn't mean it that way, Miss Montgomery."

People didn't really think she and George were impoverished orphans, did they? She'd thought it common knowledge that their father had owned Mistledown Park which George stood to inherit when he reached his majority. Perhaps, as newcomers to the area, the Marches were less informed than longtime residents.

Isabella bit back a comeback about not being so desperate for a husband that she had to put herself on the auction block called the social Season.

Instead, Isabella addressed the daughter. "Did you enjoy your Season, Miss March?"

The girl shrugged, still not looking up. How would Isabella determine her eye color if the girl refused to look her in the eye?

"Our dear Antoinette was quite the smash," Mrs. March said. "She turned down three marriage offers, you know."

Antoinette. This was promising.

"You must have broken many hearts," Isabella said to the reticent girl.

The girl—Antoinette—shrugged again, but a tiny smile played around her mouth. "Not really." She finally looked up at Isabella with soft green eyes. Not brown.

"Probably more than you know." Isabella pitied the poor men who tried to woo the girl, with her dragon of a mother lurking over her. With a kind smile, Isabella took a step back. "I wish you all a good day." After a proper curtsy, she excused herself.

Mr. Law stood encircled by a giggling herd of young ladies and waved his hand theatrically. "So I told them, 'pistols at dawn for anyone who dares interfere.'"

Squeals of laughter erupted from his herd. A sudden disliking for all those young ladies soured her tongue. None of them were worthy of an earl's son, either.

She stomped to Aunt Missy's side. "I'll walk on ahead. I'm rather tired."

Aunt Missy eyed her. "You do look a bit peaked. Or perhaps a shade green?"

Isabella frowned at the jealousy reference and searched the tree-shaded area for her brother. She found him next to his newest fascination, Miss Stockton. Isabella ignored the thought that she should greet the object of George's desire. She'd had quite enough conversation for the moment. Besides, George would probably find a new 'love' in a week or so, anyway.

With her head high and her strides long and graceful so as not to reveal her annoyance that every woman in the area under the age of fifty was enthralled with Mr. Law, and that he enjoyed their attention—curse him—she headed home. After a few moments, heavy footsteps sounded behind her.

"Miss Montgomery," Mr. Law called.

She stopped and waited for him to catch up. She must not imagine he'd left his gawking gaggle of girls because he especially cared for Isabella.

"I saw you talking to a couple with a blonde daughter," he said.

Was that the only reason he came after her, or did he do so because he preferred her company? Not that it mattered.

"Was that the merchant you told me about?"

He sounded so desperate that she finally looked at him.

His gaze searched her eyes. "It wasn't her, was it?" He waited, but without hope.

She shook her head. "She is blonde, and her name is Antoinette, but her eyes are green."

He let out a long exhale. "Thank you for trying."

"Did you enjoy your bevy of fair maidens?" The words popped out of her mouth before she could stop them.

"Not really. They are like so many I meet—too silly, too eager."

Dryly, she said, "It must be difficult to be in such demand with the ladies."

"It's nice to know some ladies still find me attractive." A wry tone touched his words.

"Still?"

"You offered me a pretty firm set down."

She stopped walking. "You mean when I refused to kiss you?" Against her will, her focus fixed on his mouth.

"You didn't even consider it." He looked either chagrined or amused; she wasn't sure which.

"It's fortunate that I did not. Otherwise, living under the same roof would be terribly awkward." She resumed her pace.

"True." He kept up with her.

If she had allowed him to kiss her, everything would have changed. At least he knew she wasn't the sort of girl who went about kissing every man who asked.

What would it be like to kiss him?

His voice broke into her thoughts. "Do you have any other ideas who might be Hadley's Ann?"

"Not yet." After a moment, she asked a question that had been nagging at her. "Did you always call your brother Hadley?"

He nodded tightly. "From the moment of his birth, he was addressed by his courtesy title. As soon as we buried my brother, Father began calling me Hadley. I know that's proper, but . . . it's too soon. Father never even speaks of my brother anymore, as if we're interchangeable—only Father's frequently displeased with *me*." He swallowed. "I don't want Hadley's name or his title or anything he stood to inherit. I just want him back." He took a shaking breath and cleared his throat.

They walked in silence while Isabella searched for the right words, but none existed to convey her sorrow and sympathy. She ached for the grieving gentleman as he grappled with a raw pain she knew well.

Isabella gave him a moment to compose himself before asking, "Is your father very old?"

"No, he's only fifty-four."

"Surely he knows you won't likely inherit for another twenty or thirty years and that there's time to teach you what you must know."

"It's as if he thinks I'll inherit in a few months rather than years."

"Perhaps that's his own way of mourning—turning his focus on you, the only son he has left. Some people find staying busy is helpful when working through grief."

Rowan considered. "Perhaps. I'd never thought of that. Father has never been one to show emotion. For that matter, nor has my mother."

"Stiff upper lip and all that—like proper Englishmen?"

He nodded.

She touched his arm briefly in sympathy but let her hand drop. Perhaps she ought not be so forward. She turned her mind to how to help him find Ann. "May I see the Lover's Eye again?"

They stood under an oak while he fished the jewelry out of his pocket and handed it to her.

Isabella studied it, noting the shape, the color of the eye, the lashes, the brow. An idea struck her. "What if instead of trying to find the girl, we try to find the artist who painted this?"

Hope lit his eyes. "How difficult would that be?"

"I imagine there are fewer artists in the area than there are blonde girls."

"Find the artist and ask if he kept a record?"

"Exactly."

He nodded. "How do we find the artist?"

"Old Pete knows everyone in the local art world. I suggest we ask him. He might recognize the artist simply by looking at this Lover's Eye. Or he may know of someone who specializes in this kind of art who could tell us."

Mr. Law nodded. "Sounds like a viable plan." His features softened. He touched her face with a finger, tracing down her cheek.

Everything inside her went quiet and still, then instantly into motion. How lovely to be touched with such tenderness! She leaned in, hungry for more. He opened his hand and cupped her cheek. His thumb caressed her. All the world grew soft and light, and a lost place inside her found its way home.

As if someone turned off a spigot, his expression and even his posture stiffened. Fisting his hand, he stepped away. "Forgive me."

Lost, confused, adrift, she stared.

"Shall we pay a call on Old Pete today?" he asked casually.

She took a moment to find her voice. "Old Pete always spends Sundays with his sister, so we'll need to wait until tomorrow." Did he notice her breathiness?

"I suppose that will have to do." He strolled along like nothing had happened. And really, nothing had happened. And yet everything was different. She'd resisted all manner of advances from all manner of gentlemen. Why did this one tempt her so?

She would not think about it. She would divide her focus between creating the work of art that would convince Mr. Corby to accept her as a student, and helping Mr. Law find Ann. Soon he would leave. And she would still have her art. It would have to be enough. Then one day, perhaps, she would find her own true love.

7

THE DAY AFTER THAT Sunday afternoon when he'd almost kissed Isabella Montgomery, Rowan drove Mr. Williams's gig through town. They stopped at Old Pete's humble home but learned he'd gone to the seashore. In the tiny carriage built for two, they sat so closely that Miss Montgomery often brushed against him when they turned or went over a bump. Could he help it if he had to turn often or if the roads were bumpy?

His senses sharpened, taking in every detail of her until even her breathing stirred a deep ache inside him. He indulged in fantasies of the slenderness of her limbs, separated from him only by a few layers of fabric. Her clean, fresh scent invoked images of a rain-drenched garden, mingled faintly with the paint she used for her artwork. He'd never wanted a woman so badly as he wanted her. Happiness lit her eyes and curved her mouth. Just being with her filled him with hope.

She let out a contented sigh as she looked about. "I do adore the ocean. I could be satisfied with the tiniest of cottages if it were atop a cliff where I could look out of a window at that great expanse."

"That's one of the few memories I have of Crestwood Manor—watching storms come in over the sea, ships sailing by, waves crashing on rocks."

She turned her face toward him and smiled so brightly that it was visible even in his peripheral vision. How could someone who'd lost so much still manage to find joy in everyday life? "Do you visit Crestwood Manor frequently?"

"Only a few times as a child. I haven't been there in years."

"I hope you enjoy it the next time you go."

He would enjoy Crestwood even more if she accompanied him. Seeing the world through her eyes made everything beautiful.

He only allowed himself a glance at her. "I hope so, too." He could have said so much more—wanted to say so much more—but kept it to himself. He refused to raise the young lady's expectations by giving into his desire for her. And her guardian had been very clear.

Would marrying such a lovely, unspoiled girl be so bad? His father had hinted at him finding a proper wife. "Proper" didn't normally describe an unsophisticated country girl. Did that really matter so much?

They reached the shore and began their search for the artist who might have answers. Rowan walked the horse and carefully maneuvered the gig around children at play, ladies strolling with their parasols, and other carriages. A brisk breeze tried to steal their hats.

As they approached the pier, Miss Montgomery touched his arm. "I think I see him." She pointed. "Just there."

A bent old man lumbered along the pier, carrying several objects, but at this distance, the exact nature of the objects remained a guess. Rowan turned the carriage toward the pier and drove it over the wooden planks. The wheels *bump-bumped* along, bouncing them both. Miss Montgomery laughed as she held onto her side of the seat.

"Oh, my, it's about to bounce me right out." She laughed again.

He caught himself smiling. Most ladies would have

complained about the rough ride. Isabella Montgomery had a love for life he'd never found in others.

As they approached the man in question, Miss Montgomery waved. "Pete!"

The man lifted his gaze and removed his hat to reveal a mostly bald head except for a few wild strays of gray that waved in the sea breeze. "Good day to you, Miss Isabella."

"Good day, Pete. How is your sister?"

"Ornery as always." He grinned.

"I'm glad to hear it."

"You've a look about you like you're on an important errand." His craggy face creased further.

Miss Montgomery nodded. "Indeed. We need your help."

"At your service." Replacing the hat, he squinted up at them.

"First, please allow me to make introductions. Mr. Law, may I present Pete Dow, a gifted artist and my friend. Pete, this is Mr. Law, who is visiting our family."

Rowan inclined his head in an abbreviated bow, which, considering their difference in station, was remarkably courteous of him.

Old Pete said, "What can I do for you?"

Rowan pulled out the Lover's Eye and handed it to him. "Miss Montgomery tells me you might know the artist who painted this."

Old Pete examined it, first up close, then at arm's length. "That's one 'o mine."

Rowan's heart tripped. "Do you happen to remember who commissioned it, or who the young lady was?"

"Lemme see. The fella was a gentleman. I can't rightly recall the name, though. But the girl, she was a real pretty little thing, with hair 'bout the color of honey."

The tripping turned into pounding. Would he truly find Ann? "You wouldn't happen to know her name, would you?"

He thought a minute. "No, don't recall. But I kept records of my commissions. I might have written down their names. I'd have to dig through some boxes."

"I would be so grateful if you would," Rowan said. He almost promised to make it worth the man's time, but he had no money in his possession. He vowed to compensate Pete when he had access to his funds. "It's very important to me that I find her."

"Most people who commission these want their love kept a secret. Why'd'ya need to know who they are?"

Rowan answered, "I know who he was—my brother, recently deceased. The girl was his love. I'm trying to find her so I can notify her of his fate." This time, loss only came as a vague reminder of pain, not the devastating storm that usually brought him to his knees.

"I see." Old Pete nodded, pressed his mouth together, and clapped him on the shoulder. The gesture comforted Rowan unexpectedly. "Good for you. Very considerate. If you'll give me a few days, I'll look through my records. If I find a name, I'll come to the vicarage."

"My thanks," Rowan said.

"Thank you, Pete," Miss Montgomery said. "This means so much."

Pete nodded. "Can't make promises, mind you, but I'll give it my best effort."

They bade him farewell and Rowan drove along the shore before pulling to a stop so they could enjoy a lingering look at the seashore.

Rowan stuffed down his disappointment that they hadn't gotten an answer today. His quest to find Hadley's Ann was filled with false hope and dead ends. If Old Pete hadn't kept detailed records, Rowan may never learn the name of the girl whose eye had been immortalized in the jewelry. He would fail her. He would fail his brother.

"We'll find her," Miss Montgomery said confidently. "This is simply a test of our determination."

Pushing back the hopelessness that gnawed at him, Rowan let out a huff of amusement. "That's one way to think of it."

"Why, Mr. Law, did you just laugh?"

He stilled. "Did I?"

"It wasn't a full belly laugh, but certainly the closest to one I've seen you do."

He sifted through possible replies. It might have been a laugh—probably should have been—but he couldn't quite reach around the sorrow that dampened every thought. "I . . ."

"I understand." She put a hand on his arm. "I found it difficult to laugh or even smile for weeks after I received news of my father's death." She paused. "And when I learned of my brother's, as well."

He nodded, too moved by her compassion to speak.

"My father was a post captain. He served for many years with distinction. His father was a sea captain as well, and his father before him. When my eldest brother chose to follow the family tradition, no one thought much of it. My grandfather and great grandfather both lived long lives so we had no true fear for him." She stopped, her expression thoughtful.

"But your grandfathers didn't serve during wartime, did they?"

"No. I know the sea can be dangerous; I've heard the stories, but I never thought it would happen to them—not even with the war."

"I know what you mean." He'd heard of the dangers of steeplechasing but never thought it would happen to his family.

"When news reached us of the Battle of Trafalgar, we waited breathlessly but still certain Father would write us to let us know he was alive and well." She paused and swallowed. "Instead, he was listed among those lives lost. Richard wrote to say he was coming home; as the heir, he understood his responsibilities. But he was on the other side of the world and unable to come home straight away due to his duties and the distance." Another pause. "We received news of his death as well."

A kinship for George crept over Rowan for a fellow "spare" who, with a father and brother gone, had inherited an unexpected responsibility. Had the passage of time made that prospect any easier? Perhaps he'd ask the young man sometime.

To Miss Montgomery, he said, "Though I haven't lost a parent, I feel for you both."

Quietly, she said, "I know. Would you like to tell me about your brother?"

"He loved Shakespeare, and lemon tarts. He was perfect in everything. My parents' pride and joy. The only thing he did that my parents didn't approve of was fall in love with Ann. But he respected their wishes regarding her." He paused. "He was mad for the steeplechase. So was I. There was an accident."

He stopped and swallowed as a tidal wave rose up in the horizon of his thoughts. He cleared his throat, but nothing prevented its forward rush. He braced for impact.

Isabella Montgomery put an arm around him and rested her head on his shoulder. Her touch soothed and comforted him. For the first time since the accident, he no longer felt alone or adrift in a sea of numbness. The tidal wave shrank, and by the time it reached him, it had only the strength of a breaker. He breathed.

"The hurts never goes away," she said. "But eventually it doesn't feel as if the pain will kill you."

He rested his head on top of hers. A growing urge to pull her into his arms tugged at him. He settled for kissing the top of her head.

"I suppose we ought to return." Clicking to the horses, he pulled onto the road leading back to the vicarage. He missed the comfort of Isabella Montgomery's head on his shoulder.

Along the way, they passed a couple strolling down the road. A feminine laugh rang out as the couple conversed together.

"Oh," Isabella said. "It's George and Miss Stockton. Do pull over, please."

Rowan pulled up alongside the couple and called, "Good morning."

The young man turned. "Good morning. Enjoying your drive?"

"Very much." Though he had failed to learn the identity of Ann, they had a good lead. And the drive had been exceptionally pleasant, thanks to Miss Montgomery.

"Mr. Law, have you met Miss Stockton?" George gestured to his companion.

"No, I haven't had the pleasure."

An uncommonly pretty girl with big brown eyes and brown curls that framed her face looked up at him.

George made the introductions. "Nancy Stockton, meet Mr. Law."

They exchanged greetings. *Hmm.* Her brown eyes looked similar to the eyes in his Lover's Eye, but her hair was brown instead of golden blonde, and her Christian name was wrong.

"A pleasure, Mr. Law," the girl said.

"And I believe you know my sister, Isabella," George continued.

"We have met." Nancy Stockton beamed at Isabella. "Are you going to the public assembly?"

"I wouldn't miss it. And we hope Mr. Law will join us as well." Isabella smiled up at Rowan with such cheer that Rowan would not have denied her anything.

He put on his best debonair smolder. "Only if you both promise to save me a dance."

Miss Stockton giggled. "Of course. But I have already promised the first one to George."

Isabella lifted her head in her playfully queenly pose when she addressed Rowan: "Perhaps I will save you a dance . . . if I am in perfect charity with you." Her impish smile broke through.

George gestured at a narrow road that cut along their path. "This is the turn off to Miss Stockton's home. I'll see you two at the vicarage."

The two groups bade each other farewell and parted ways. The couple on foot walked without touching but as closely together as propriety allowed.

"I've never seen George so enamored," Isabella said. "The way he looks at her. It's quite . . . sweet."

Rowan let out a scoff. "He was ready to duel Sir Reginald for someone else only a few days past."

"I never saw him look at anyone the way he looks at Nancy Stockton."

"I'm sure hearts are breaking all over England," he said dryly.

She laughed again. "You would know—you probably leave a trail of broken hearts everywhere you go."

"A gentleman would never tell."

In an overly serious tone that suggested her mirth, she said, "Oh, of course."

As they reached the vicarage and he handed her down

from the carriage, he looked her in the eye. "There is no one else."

She paused and, catching his meaning, went very serious. A vulnerability entered her expression. "No one?"

Earnestly, he said, "Innocent flirtations only. I am not a libertine, nor have I ever courted a young lady enough to raise her expectations. I've never given my heart away. Yet."

The softness in her eyes endeared her to him further. How could her opinion matter so much after such a short amount of time?

Could he truly find any manner of peace or joy? Was his heart whole enough to be entrusted to another? To her?

THE DAY OF THE PUBLIC assembly ball arrived. Aunt Missy eyed Isabella as she turned wearing her ball gown.

"It's lovely," Aunt Missy said. "I was beginning to wonder if we should have visited the dressmaker to purchase a new one for you, but this one we made over turned out just right. You are beautiful, my sweet."

Isabella made a graceful, overly low curtsy as if she were being presented to the queen. "Thank you, Aunt."

"Mr. Law won't be able to take his eyes off you."

If only she were right. But she mustn't allow herself to think of that. Instead, she quipped, "I think it would be dreadfully uncomfortable with someone's eyes pasted on me."

"Very amusing. You know what I mean."

"You are imagining things. Mr. Law is charming to all." Isabella sat and adjusted a garter holding up her lace stocking.

"He is indeed very charming to all. But he has special eyes for you." She nodded to emphasize her point.

Isabella stuffed down the hope that arose with Aunt Missy's words. "Well, I am the only unmarried female near his age living under this roof."

"Not just here. He was completely aware of you at the seashore and also at church, even when surrounded by young ladies. Several times he looked around for you. He seemed almost anxious and appeared relieved when he located you. And, if you recall, he ran after you the moment you left."

"Aunt, we've known each other a week. It would be premature to hope that he has formed an attachment for me. Not to mention our difference in social standing. He's heir to an earldom."

"Yes, Joseph told me, but I wasn't aware that you knew."

Isabella toyed with her earring. "He buried his brother only a week before he arrived here, and he doesn't want the title."

"I can imagine he'd rather have his brother."

"Yes, indeed. But the fact remains that he is a viscount and will one day be an earl."

"Your father was a gentleman and a revered war hero, and you have a decent dowry—not enough to attract fortune hunters, but respectable. If he's smart, he'll see what a jewel you are."

Isabella wanted to throw her arms around Aunt Missy for her unfaltering but misplaced loyalty. "I know I'm fit to marry landed gentry . . . but an earl?" She shook her head. "Their father has peculiar expectations for his heir; otherwise Mr. Law wouldn't be searching for the girl his brother was forbidden to marry."

Aunt Missy rearranged a few of Isabella's curls hanging down her back. "If all else fails, you can have the satisfaction of seeing his admiration."

"We shall see."

"Yes, we shall."

Each confident in her own prediction, they donned their gloves and went downstairs to the parlor.

Mr. Law stood talking with Uncle Joseph and George, all looking handsome in their formal evening wear. Where Mr. Law had acquired his clothing was a mystery, but he looked especially striking. How dear his face had become to her!

This did not bode well for her heart.

At her approach, he turned. For one long, satisfying moment, he looked her over as a slow, approving smile curved his mouth and lit his eyes.

Smiling, Rowan Law was, without a doubt, the most handsome man she'd ever seen. He moved to her side and took her hand into his. Holding it, he continued smiling at her. A piece of her heart split off and raced toward him.

With a soft murmur, he said, "You look exceptionally pretty tonight, Miss Montgomery."

"You look well yourself, Mr. Law."

His smile turned sheepish. "I imposed on your uncle to purchase a change of clothing."

"It was no imposition," Uncle Joseph called. "Besides, I'm charging you interest for that loan."

Laughing at the unvicar-like comment, they piled into the carriage and drove toward the public assembly. Sitting across from Rowan Law made it difficult to keep her focus on anything but him. Fortunately, conversation flowed freely, and they were a merry group by the time they arrived. Carriages lined up for blocks. Other people arrived on foot, gaining entrance sooner than those who drove. Eventually, they pulled up in front of a quaint brick building with light pouring out of the windows.

After stepping out of the carriage, they entered the public rooms. Candles burned in tall candelabras situated in every corner. A string quartet played a lively country dance that encouraged Isabella to tap her toes.

Mr. Law turned to her. "Miss Montgomery, before you are surrounded by all the bucks begging for a dance, will you do me the honor of standing up with me?"

"Of course I will." Truth be told, she had no wish to dance with anyone else. Ever. Such thinking would not serve her well. But it was too late. Her heart had already made its choice.

As the current dance ended and the dancers vacated their spots on the floor, Mr. Law took her hand and led her to the dance floor. The quartet struck up a quadrille. Soon they weaved among other dancers. Yet each time she glanced his way, he was looking at her. Oh, be still her heart! Was she a fool to believe he returned her regard? Or worse, to hope for a future with him? Yes, she was. She had only to think of Ann to know that Rowan Law—Viscount Hadley—would never be hers.

Too soon, the set ended. With Rowan escorting her to Aunt Missy, she passed a lovely blonde lady . . . with laughing brown eyes!

Her heart leaped and she grabbed Mr. Law's arm. "Look," she gasped. Still holding onto his arm, she wormed her way to Aunt Missy. "Who is that lady in the ivory gown with the lovely golden curls? She has brown eyes!"

"That's the youngest Farnsworth girl." Aunt Missy's eyes widened, and she gasped. "Oh, heavens! Her Christian name is Anissa. She might be called Ann."

Next to Isabella, Mr. Law gave a start. "Please, would you find out and introduce us?"

"I'll speak to her mother."

Aunt Missy wove through the crowd to a woman wearing a turban with ostrich feathers. The two of them spoke for several minutes while Isabella fidgeted and Rowan stood as if made of stone. Without taking his gaze off Aunt Missy, Rowan reached for Isabella's hand and gripped it. She squeezed it back. Surely, he only needed a friendly touch; he didn't intend it as a sign of affection. Did he?

Aunt Missy returned, her face wreathed in excitement. "Her name is indeed Anissa, and they do occasionally call her Ann. She is only just seventeen, though. Is that too young to be the girl you seek?"

He hesitated and looked to Isabella as if seeking her counsel. She squeezed his hand and released it, lest Aunt Missy, or anyone, notice and think it unseemly for them to hold hands.

"Possibly." Mr. Law watched the girl dance. "But we must not discount her just yet."

Aunt Missy nodded. "Come, I'll introduce you to her mother." She tugged on his arm.

Isabella watched as Aunt Missy introduced Rowan—*ahem!* Mr. Law—to the mother of the girl in question. He turned on the charm, as always, and the mother clearly fell for him, blushing and laughing and nodding until the feathers in her turban fluttered like birds in flight.

Isabella turned away. He could have anyone, of any age. He had only to ask. Why would he want a simple girl such as she?

The dance ended and Isabella remained turned away. A young gentleman asked her for a dance. She accepted—anything to keep her mind off her hopeless prospects with Rowan Law. She failed.

Moments later, Mr. Law accompanied a beaming, blonde Anissa Farnsworth to the dance floor. Isabella silently prayed that he would find Ann quickly and gain a measure of peace.

A cotillion began, and Isabella cleared her mind except to enjoy the pure delight of dancing and to make pleasant conversation with her partner.

The instant the last notes of the cotillion ended, she glanced about for Mr. Law. He stood close to the blonde, his eyes searching, his expression earnest. Had he discovered the truth?

After a few minutes, he escorted her to her mother, bowed, and returned to Isabella.

As Rowan lifted his sorrowful eyes to hers, she knew. She touched his arm in sympathy. "Not her."

"She's never heard of John Law or Viscount Hadley and has never been courted—she's only been out since the beginning of this summer."

How many times must he suffer through false hope? "I'm so sorry."

"I can only hope Old Pete has the answer."

She nodded. So much depended on an old record.

Another gentleman asked Isabella for a dance. She shot a look of apology to Rowan, but he waved her on. He had the good grace to dance every set with a different young lady. Each left the dance floor beaming and walking a little taller. He lifted everyone around him with no motives except for kindness. He cared deeply about people and had a strong code of honor. No doubt, with time and healing, he would accept the new burden placed on him and would do all required of him as a future earl with the same focus and heart he used for searching for Ann. He was gracious and thoughtful, even in the midst of his vulnerability and grief.

How could she not love him?

How would she survive when he left?

9

THE MORNING AFTER THE public ball, Rowan reread the letter a second time to be sure he had understood correctly. Then with a bounce in his step, he went in search of Isabella Montgomery.

He found her laboring over a new painting. Leaning against the doorjamb, he watched her paint, the expressions that touched her face, the halo around her dark head caused by the light pouring in through the window behind her.

She was so lovely. So kind. So genuine. And so full of life and joy. How would he ever survive the loss when it came time for him to leave?

Was this love?

She looked up and gave a start, then smiled. "I didn't see you there."

"I didn't wish to interrupt. It was too pleasant to watch you."

She huffed a disbelieving laugh. "You must be in desperate need of a diversion."

"Are *you* in need of a diversion?"

She hesitated. "I had a flash of inspiration and wanted to at least sketch it before it went away. Sometimes inspiration is like chasing a butterfly; if I take too long to go after it, it's gone."

He nodded. Having never been blessed with a creative

bent, he didn't understand fully, but many of his college friends—aspiring writers, poets, and artists—had mentioned similar thoughts.

Her gaze focused on him. "Did you need me for something?"

"I want to show something to you, but it can wait." He ought to leave her so she could create in peace. After all, this art show meant a great deal to her. To his eye, she certainly had talent. For her sake, he hoped she had enough to gain the notice of that local art master. Her expression turned focused but peaceful as she fixed her attention to her easel.

"Purrrow," said the kitten in her lap.

She petted the kitten with the back of a finger, probably in an attempt to avoid putting paint on the fur. "Do you like it, Little Muse?"

The kitten blinked up at her. "Mew."

"Muse?" Rowan pushed off the doorway and moved closer.

"Her name is Muse. I was petting her when I had an idea for a piece to enter in the art show. It's tomorrow, so this is rather last minute, but I simply had to try. Didn't I, Muse?"

"Mew." The kitten put its head down and closed its eyes.

"And she seems to respond to it, so I do believe I have finally discovered her name."

Isabella Montgomery's fresh charm captivated him. "It's a fitting name."

She smiled more brightly than ever. "Rowan Law, you have the most beautiful smile I've ever seen."

"It's because I'm looking at you."

She laughed merrily and wagged a finger at him. "Don't ply your famous charm on me, sir. You've been looking at me for a week, and you've never smiled like that before."

"Perhaps I'm finally seeing you for the delight you are."

Or perhaps he was finally healing enough to allow for a measure of cheer. Was it wrong for him to feel peace and serenity so soon after Hadley's death?

"What did you want to show me?" she asked.

"Perhaps I could show you this afternoon when you are available for an outing."

Her eyes sparkled. "I ought to be finished by then. Or, at the very least, ready to step away from my masterpiece." She laughed and indicated her unfinished work.

"May I see it?"

"Not until it's finished."

Rowan grinned. "Very well. I look forward to seeing you this afternoon."

She nodded and returned to her work. Rowan backed out so as not to miss out on watching her. As he passed the threshold, she looked up. Her smile went straight to his heart, warming it—and him—all over. He wanted to see her smile every day. For the rest of his life.

Somehow, he would find a way. In the meantime, how to while away his time waiting for her? Humming attracted his attention. He followed the cheerful sound and found Mrs. Williams in the kitchen, filling a large basket.

He greeted her and asked about her morning plans, resulting in an invitation to accompany her to pay a visit on a sick member of the parish. This woman certainly paid a great deal of time and attention to her neighbors, always arriving with basket in hand. Admirable woman.

As they walked, Rowan carried the basket and they chatted like old friends. During a lull in the conversation, she eyed him sideways.

"Forgive me if this is too personal, but may I ask, how did you come to be here in Brighton?"

Her abrupt veering off topic suggested this question had

been on her mind for quite some time. It was time for the whole truth. "My father and I were traveling to one of the family properties—Crestwood Manor. I was angry that he'd pulled me away from our family the day after my brother's funeral to attend to estate business that could have waited. In truth, I was angry about a great deal. I'm afraid I was quite disrespectful to him. We got out of the carriage. He told me that he hoped I'd learn to appreciate my heritage and my duty. Then he got in and left."

"I see." She nodded thoughtfully. "Why did you introduce yourself as Rowan Law when you are the Viscount Hadley?"

"After all you've done for me, I suppose I owe you an explanation."

"You really don't—not if it's personal."

But he did. It took all his will not to break down and sob, but he explained, all the while clenching his fists, and sometimes his teeth, as grief pounded him.

Mrs. Williams's voice hushed. "That is a terrible burden you now carry. But you are a gentleman of honor. You will bear that title in a way that would make him proud. You need time to work through your grief, but you will eventually grow into your new role until it fits. It will fit you differently than it fit him."

He nodded stiffly. As if sensing his need to compose himself, she remained silent. A moment later, she put an arm around his waist and gave him a matronly squeeze. He wanted to turn into her and accept the motherly embrace she would probably give him, but he resisted.

Mrs. Williams said gently, "We are all expected to become something slightly out of our reach, but in our attempt to strive for it, we continually become better, stronger, kinder people who look out for others—especially those less fortunate than ourselves."

As his grief receded enough for him to think, he considered her words.

She was right. He didn't need to be the Hadley that his brother was. He could be the Hadley of his own creation. It would be a work in progress.

"There is our destination," she said.

They spent the morning caring for a sick widower and his young children. Rowan rolled up his sleeves and pitched in where he could, all the time admiring the calm, caring efficiency with which Mrs. Williams interacted with them. Isabella, no doubt, performed similarly. She would make an excellent lady of the house, caring for tenants and servants alike. With Isabella at his side, he'd always be aware of who needed help.

Upon returning to the vicarage, they enjoyed a midday meal. Miss Montgomery waltzed into the dining room with her hands held high in triumph.

"It is finished! I have painted my very best one yet. This will surely impress Mr. Corby."

"Well done," Mrs. Williams said.

"I never doubted you," Rowan said. "May I see it yet?"

"Right after you show me your surprise." Isabella's excitement spilled out of her and warmed him.

"Very well," he said. "When you're ready."

After taking a few hurried bites of the repast and donning a pelisse, Isabella Montgomery declared herself unable to wait another moment. Chuckling, Rowan drove the Williams's gig to his surprise destination. He pulled in front of the prince's pavilion. Instead of stopping in front, he drove to the gate.

"What are you doing?" she asked.

He smiled at her, playing the man of mystery, and gave his name to the gatekeeper. The gates opened to admit them.

"We're going inside?" she gasped.

"Indeed we are."

"How did you do that?"

"I wrote a letter to His Highness and asked." He shrugged. "I'd met him a year ago, and since my father is a peer, I'd hoped the prince would give permission. He did. His Highness is really quite a decent chap." He was a rake in the first order, but generous and a bit of a romantic.

"Oh!" She gave a happy little bounce. "I can't believe you did this for me. Thank you so much!"

"It is very much my pleasure."

Rowan pulled up in front, handed the reins to a waiting footman, and ushered her inside, where the butler took them on a tour. Each room drew more sighs of admiration from her. Rowan puffed up his chest that he had provided a little joy for the lovely lady who'd given so much to him. After completing the tour of the opulent palace filled with equally impressive furniture and art, they returned to the gig.

Isabella hugged herself. "I have seen more beautiful art than I'd ever imagined. That was one of the best days of my life."

"I am very gratified to have provided that for you." He would make it his life's mission to give her many more "best" days of her life.

She wrapped both arms around his arm nearest her and gave it a hug. "Thank you."

"You are most welcome."

He soaked in the light in her eyes, the dazzling brightness of her smile, the beauty of her face. The edges of that hard, protective numbness encasing his heart melted, and a happiness unlike any he'd ever expected crept in like a healing salve.

He pulled his arm out of her grasp and put it around her to give her a one-sided embrace. He kissed the top of her head. Lest he be tempted to kiss much more of her, he snapped the reins and drove down the long drive.

His bliss remained during their ride home together. He wanted this feeling every day. As he helped her down from the carriage, he held onto her. He should release her. He couldn't seem to let her go. He never wanted to let her go.

She gave a tiny nervous laugh. His promise to her guardian shouted in his ear. Clearing his throat, he stepped back. His arms ached to hold her. His mouth ached to kiss her. How long could he resist?

They entered the vicarage, and she went to her bedchamber to dress for dinner. Rowan stared after her. Could he gain his father's permission to marry her?

He turned and halted in his tracks. Watching him, Mr. Williams stood in the parlor, his stance wide and combative. Rowan drew a bracing breath and strode to Miss Montgomery's guardian to hear whatever unpleasantness the man wanted to say.

"Walk with me." Mr. Williams headed to the door leading outside.

Rowan obliged him, walking next to him and matching him stride for stride rather than following after like an obedient dog. When they passed outside and walked out of earshot of the house, Rowan adopted a friendly, conversational tone.

"What is on your mind, sir?"

"You have been spending a great deal of time with my ward." His expression tight, his words clipped, the man's disapproval could not have been missed.

Rowan nodded. "I have been blessed by her presence and have enjoyed it as I've enjoyed spending time with your whole family." Not the same way, of course, but he hoped his mention of the family would deflect the man's ire. It didn't. Rowan tried one more tactic. "Thank you, again, for the use of your gig."

"If you will recall, I warned you about trifling with her heart."

Rowan took an extra-large step so as to position himself in front of Mr. Williams. "I have done nothing to raise her expectations, nor have I laid a hand on her."

"Perhaps not in the general sense, but I see how you two look at each other."

"Sir, I cannot help how I feel about her—but I'm not acting on those feelings."

"I believe it is time for you to leave."

Now? Leave now before he had a chance to learn if Isabella was the key to his happiness? No. It was too soon. He needed more time to know if he truly wanted to spend the rest of his life with her. If so, he must think of a way of convincing his father to allow the union. He refused to be robbed of happiness because he'd fallen for a girl his father pronounced unworthy based on societal expectations. And he hadn't found Ann, yet.

"Sir..."

"I know of another place where you can stay until your father comes to collect you."

"Please, sir, I beg you not to send me away. I haven't broken your trust in me, nor will I—I give you my word."

Mr. Williams looked at him for a long moment. "You are too smooth and charming by half. It is impossible to know if you're sincere. Moreover, I have met your father—on more than one occasion—and I know his ideals. In addition, I know about your search for a young lady your father forbade your brother to marry. What makes you certain that you would not find the same refusal?"

How quickly Mr. Williams dove into the heart of the matter.

Rowan searched for the words and the courage to voice

them. "I don't know all the reasons why my brother's love was denied. His girl might be illegitimate or the daughter of a member of the working class. She might be Catholic—my father has very strong opinions about our family all belonging to the Church of England. His reasons may not necessarily mean she didn't come from noble enough blood."

"Perhaps. But a peer expects a certain bloodline."

"Miss Montgomery is the daughter of a gentleman, so there is no legitimate reason why our union would be denied." He paused as determination gathered in him. "If I must, I would marry her against my father's wishes."

"Would you?" His focused gaze drilled into Rowan's.

The man's doubt in him spurred Rowan to throw out caution and speak from the heart. "She has poured healing light into my wounded soul. I feel like I'm breathing for the first time in weeks. I want to see her smile every day, to share all her disappointments and joys, and share mine with her. If I must take on this new role as heir, I want her at my side. I can't even think of facing my future without her." He huffed an amazed laugh. "I love her. Truly. Completely."

Mr. Williams folded his arms. "You've only known her a week."

"Yet we've spent as much time together as most courtships have in months." Rowan stepped forward and held out his hands. "Sir, her happiness is important to me. It is of utmost importance."

"Is it? Or does the lure of marrying a girl your father would not accept fit with your desire to rebel against him?"

The question took Rowan aback. "I would never . . . how can you even suggest that?"

"You may not consciously know that's your motive. Either way, I'm convinced it is time for you to take accommodations somewhere other than our home. There's an inn up the road. I'll put you up there until your father comes for you, as I'm certain he will—soon. Please do not call upon Isabella or engage in any sort of courtship. I do not wish for you to see her again." He left Rowan standing alone.

Never see her again? Panic ripped through him. In his fears that his father would not accept Isabella, he'd never dreamed that the vicar would reject Rowan.

10

UNDER A TENT AT the seashore, Isabella carefully displayed all the pieces of her art that she hoped to use to convince Mr. Corby to accept her as a pupil. But now that Rowan Law was gone, her eager anticipation had dimmed.

Still, he was only staying at an inn, not so very far away. And he knew of the art fair. Surely he'd come. After such a magical day at the pavilion, how could he not?

Wearing her best bonnet and pelisse, she waited under the tent where the other hopeful students stood by their art, including Miss Potter with her emotional, disturbing pieces. Looking at the other entries, Isabella's courage about her so-called masterpiece faded in the face of such competition by clearly gifted and skilled artists. Would hers be good enough?

Several townspeople strolled by, stopping at various displays. Their admiring gazes at her pieces and their questions failed to calm her thudding heart. If only Rowan were here. Just his smile would soothe her nervousness.

The art master, Mr. Corby, arrived. A diminutive man with a shock of white hair atop his head and flowing over his collar, he would never have been considered imposing, yet her future as an artist lay in his hands. She folded her fidgety hands together and tried to stand still.

Aunt Missy and Uncle Joseph waited nearby, giving her a wave of encouragement. George strolled past with Miss Stockton on his arm.

The master stopped in front of her paintings and eyed them through a pair of spectacles. "Nice coloring. Good proportions. Very restful." He nodded, then gestured at her masterpiece. "This one shows real depth of emotion." He moved on to the other paintings.

Mr. Corby hadn't stayed long. Did that mean he was quickly impressed or had deemed her unworthy of his time and expertise?

Mr. Corby studied each artist's display, pausing only a few minutes at each. He walked back along them all with his hands folded behind him. He stopped.

Facing the hopeful artists, he announced, "I have chosen my new student. I don't often accept young ladies, but this year one stands out above all the rest."

Hope bubbled up inside and nearly spilled over. Was it true? Had he chosen her? She held her breath.

Mr. Corby turned toward her. "Congratulations, Miss Potter."

Miss Potter?

With hands extended, Mr. Corby strode to the young lady standing next to Isabella. Isabella gaped. She'd thought . . .

No. Of course not. It had been too much to hope. She should have known that her sweet, ordinary paintings could never compete with such unique, passionate art as Miss Potter's.

While the onlookers applauded, the art master and his new student shook hands. The girl bubbled over with enthusiasm. All those hours, all that work . . . for nothing. Clearly Isabella was not in possession of the skills nor talent she'd always believed. All her hopes withered like flowers in a garden devoid of rain.

With all of her might going to holding her tears at bay, she stood, head high, next to her less-than-impressive art display. When she thought she could speak, Isabella congratulated the winner through her wounded heart.

Aunt Missy and Uncle Joseph waved from where they stood in the shade, both smiling in supportive sympathy.

"I'm sorry you weren't chosen," a familiar voice said.

Rowan Law stood next to her, wearing the same clothing he'd worn the day she met him. A spark of light glittered in his eyes, brightening that air of sorrow that had dimmed him for so long.

"I'm glad you came," she said. She reached out with both hands and took each of his.

He smiled apologetically and, after giving her hands the briefest squeeze, removed his hands, glancing at Uncle Joseph. "I had to be here for you today, but I'm afraid this is goodbye."

"What?" A slow, cold dread trickled into her.

"I'm leaving. And I won't see you again."

While she wrestled with his possible meaning, a newcomer strode into her line of sight.

"There you are, Hadley. I hope you enjoyed your holiday in Brighton, but it's time to leave now and resume your duties." The older man had the same strong features as Rowan. Thin streaks of gray lined his dark hair, and his clothing followed the very latest fashion. He, too, wore a black mourning band.

"Father." Rowan's eyes widened, and his mouth parted.

"It was clear to me that you needed time to contemplate your place in the world, so I asked the good vicar here to take you in while I saw to some business."

"You asked them to take me in?" He blinked and pressed a hand on his forehead. "I thought they took me in out of kindness."

"It was a kindness that we pre-arranged. I'm back now, and we must resume our journey. You have much to learn."

Rowan glanced back at Isabella but addressed his father. "I'm not—"

"You've had some time to collect yourself and"—Father glanced at Isabella dismissively—"apparently sow your oats. Now come."

Isabella gasped. Had he just implied that she was some sort of trollop who'd dallied with Rowan?

The earl gestured impatiently at Rowan. "Your mother is waiting."

Rowan's brows drew together. "We left Mother in Sussex."

"She decided to join us on our tour of the properties. Normally she dislikes this much travel, but she wanted a change of scenery. Having all those grieving relatives around her was making it worse rather than better. She's at Crestwood Manor. Come, Hadley. We're behind schedule."

Rowan Law, the Viscount Hadley and heir to an earl, turned to Isabella one final time. He looked at her for a long moment. Was he really leaving? Would he declare himself?

Did he truly care, or had she imagined it?

"I have ... enjoyed our time together. Very much." He bowed over her hand and actually kissed it. Without looking, he strode away with his father.

Bewilderment and hurt stabbed her heart. She lurched toward him, a call on her lips.

Uncle Joseph grabbed both of her arms. "Let him go."

"I can't. I have to tell him—"

"He must go with his father. The earl."

Halting, Rowan glanced over his shoulder at her, opened his mouth, looked at Uncle, then his father, and turned back around to resume walking.

She rounded on Uncle. "*You* sent him away."

He met her gaze evenly. "I did."

"Uncle! How could you?"

"To protect you. He was trifling with your heart."

"He was sincere." Wasn't he? Suddenly, she wasn't so sure. But now he was gone. She'd never know if he could one day return her love.

Uncle Joseph's normally kind face was stern. "The Earl of Leiderton would never countenance a marriage between his heir and a girl of your standing."

The truth cut through her, leaving her wounded and bleeding.

"I love him," she gasped through a sob. "We just needed more time. We could have found a way."

Tears burned her eyes, and her voice left her.

Rowan turned the corner and disappeared from her life.

Isabella's heart shattered. Every fragment vibrated in pain and loss.

11

CONFLICTED IN EVERY POSSIBLE way, Rowan numbly followed his father. Mother awaited. Responsibilities awaited. Isabella's guardian had forbidden Rowan from courting her; marriage was out of the question. He had failed to find Hadley's Ann.

He faced a future bearing a name and a title that did not fit him, one which he would try and fail all of his life to fill. He must do it without Isabella Montgomery. Alone.

A haze enveloped him like a fog blowing in off the ocean. Rowan looked back longingly at Isabella. She had turned away and stood hugging herself. She must be devastated that she hadn't been chosen as the newest student.

Could it be possible she wept for Rowan?

"Do hurry, Hadley," Father said. "I promised your mother we wouldn't be gone long. She's anxious to see you." He entered the carriage.

Rowan gritted his teeth against the scream building in his throat that Hadley was his brother's name, not his.

With a long last look at the sea, the town that had helped him find a measure of peace, and the remarkable girl who had reignited a flame of life and feeling in him, Rowan stepped into the carriage. They drove through the town, passing now-familiar storefronts and shops. Townhouses unique to Brighton streamed by, including the home of Old Pete.

"Wait!" Rowan banged on the side of the coach. "Stop the coach!"

"Hadley, what . . ."

"I need to check on one more thing." Rowan leaped out of the coach and banged on the front door. No answer.

He was probably at the art show. Since the artist had failed to contact Rowan, he had probably been unable to find the name of the girl whose eye graced the miniature in Rowan's pocket.

His failure was complete. If only he could turn to Isabella for comfort.

In the wake of her disappointment, she must be needing comfort now. Instead of giving it to her, he'd allowed others to place obstacles in his way.

What had he done? How could he leave her?

"What is the meaning of this?" His father stood beside him.

"I was trying to find a girl that Hadley loved." He turned accusing eyes onto his father. "He loved her for years, but you deemed her unworthy." A sudden truth struck him. "You know who she is, don't you?"

"The poor girl from Brighton?" Father swept her away with his hand. "She was nothing."

"Hadley loved her to his last breath. He told me the day before the accident that his biggest regret was not marrying her."

Father stiffened. "Hadley was overly sentimental."

"What is wrong with wanting to spend the rest of your life with the person you love?"

"Preserving a pure bloodline is more important than fickle emotions. I married your mother because she has good breeding and a healthy dowry. We built a relationship on mutual respect, and that grew into affection. Marrying the wrong sort based purely on passion is irresponsible. You have a duty to this family, and I expect you to uphold it. You have much to learn. We must make up for lost time."

"Why? What is the rush? You aren't on death's door, and yet you whisked us away from our grieving family to tour all the houses in the estate."

"You never know what will happen. Accidents are unpredictable." Father stopped and looked away, clenching his jaw. His first sign of grief. Perhaps Isabella had been right.

Rowan gripped his father's shoulder. "We need time to breathe. Time to grieve."

His father nodded jerkily. "That's partly why I left you here. It had become clear to me that you were not in the right frame of mind to learn what you need to know."

"You're right; I wasn't. Thank you for giving me additional time." He squeezed Father's shoulder. "I vow I will fulfill my responsibilities to the best of my ability."

Courage and determination bloomed inside him. With Isabella Montgomery next to him, he could accomplish anything. Without her cheer, her optimism, her zest for life, he might always remain a numb shell who allowed his father to push him around.

With her at his side, he was a stronger, better man. He must fight for her. He must fight for himself.

Rowan drew himself up. "I will not make the mistakes Hadley made; I won't allow you to deny me true happiness."

His father stared at him.

"I'm going back for her."

"For whom?"

"Isabella Montgomery, the remarkable young lady who was next to me. I need her." He took off at a run.

"Hadley!" A pause. "Rowan!"

At the sound of his Christian name in his father's voice, Rowan checked his step and turned back. "I won't leave without her."

Rowan raced back to the art event. She wasn't there.

Where had she gone? He searched for her, for her guardians, anyone who could tell him where she might be.

"Mr. Law, I was hoping I'd find you." Old Pete grinned at him.

"Pete!" Rowan panted. "Do you know where Isabella Montgomery is?"

"I saw her over that way, but first I have to tell you: I found the name of the girl you seek."

Rowan went still. "You found her?"

"Her name is Nancy Stockton."

Nancy Stockton. Wasn't that the name of the girl George Montgomery courted? "Nancy? But Hadley always called her Ann."

Pete shrugged. "Ann is a nickname for many names, including Nancy."

"Thank you, Pete. I'm in your debt."

He continued his search and found Isabella's brother escorting Nancy Stockton along the shoreline while breakers lapped at the sand behind them. Rowan hesitated, torn. His vow to speak with Ann—Nancy—warred with his desire to declare himself to Isabella.

He chose Isabella. He must always choose Isabella.

Searching up and down the shore, he found Isabella sitting on the sand with her back against a pile supporting the pier.

"Isabella," he called as he raced to her.

She lifted her head. Tears streaked her cheeks. She quickly wiped them away.

He ran to her and fell to his knees. "Forgive me. I abandoned you when you were most in need of a friend."

She sniffled. "You have become more than a friend to me."

Had he? That was good, right? "I'm sorry the art master didn't choose you. You must be devastated."

"I was very disappointed. But I wasn't devastated until you left."

Did she mean that? "I couldn't leave. The shock of seeing my father and learning that he had orchestrated my staying with your family impaired my reasoning. Also, I was trying to respect your uncle's wishes. But I can't. I love you, Isabella."

Isabella's sweet mouth made an *O* shape that called to him. Throwing away all caution, he leaned in and kissed those taunting lips. She responded with the kiss of an inexperienced girl but with growing confidence. So soft. So warm. So right.

He ended the kiss and drew her into his arms. "I love you. I can be anything if you are with me. Please say you'll give me the chance to prove to you how much you mean to me."

"You want to court me?"

"I want to marry you, but I'm willing to give you time."

She smoothed a hand over his cheek and hair. Every wounded place inside him opened up to her healing touch. She smiled with such tenderness that a lump arose in his throat.

"I don't need more time, Rowan. I love you, and I'd marry you today if possible."

Hope sprouted in his heart.

"But I fear that isn't possible."

He smoothed a few strands from her face. "You fear disapproval from my parents and your uncle?"

"Aunt approves. Uncle Joseph . . . well . . ." She chewed on her lip. "And I don't wish to put a wedge between you and your parents."

"You won't. Once they meet you, I'm certain they will fall in love with you."

"How can you be certain?" She held her lip between her teeth.

"Because I did in only a matter of days. Besides, we won't

live with them. We can live on any one of our properties. You'll love Crestwood Manor—the one with a view of the ocean from nearly every window—and it's close enough to Brighton that we can visit your family often."

"It does sound lovely." But doubt still colored her tone.

"And no matter what, I will always love you."

"I cannot imagine loving anyone as much as I love you." The adoration in her eyes stirred his heart. How had he ever gotten along without her?

"Isabella Montgomery, will you marry me—even if it's against everyone's wishes?"

"No. I won't begin our lives together with such adversity. We must find a way to secure our families' blessing."

"Very well, then we must speak first to my father. Then to your Uncle Joseph." He stood and helped her up. "If they give permission, will you marry me?"

An impish smile slanted her eyes and those delicious lips. "Can I bring Little Muse with us?"

He laughed and pressed her soft body against him. "Of course you may."

"Then my answer is yes."

He kissed her again. How he loved this sweet, joyous young lady!

He could have kissed her for hours, but they had a task to accomplish. They found Father moments later, standing next to the coach, gazing at the sea. With Isabella on his arm, Rowan strode to his father with purpose.

Father turned to him, looking a bit dazed. "I'd forgotten how beautiful it is at the seashore."

Rowan squared his shoulders and donned his most formal manners. "May I introduce my father, the Earl of Leiderton? Father, this is Miss Isabella Montgomery, the daughter of a famous sea captain and war hero. More importantly, she is the love of my life, and I am asking for your blessing to marry her."

Isabella sank into a formal curtsy. "My lord."

His father lost his dreamy expression. "You cannot marry a girl you met only a week ago."

"You met Mother a week before your marriage," Rowan reminded him.

Father frowned. "We were betrothed."

"Strangers. And yet you've been happily married for thirty years. I feel as if I have known Isabella forever. I love her with all of my heart." At his father's silence, he added, "I mean to marry her regardless, but I do wish for your blessing."

His father sputtered.

With Isabella holding his arm, Rowan took courage. "With her at my side, I will work diligently to learn everything to one day manage the estate so that it will be prosperous for generations to come." Quietly, he added, "Please, Father. This means everything to me."

Father studied Isabella as if measuring her worth, then stared out over the sea.

Rowan held his breath.

After a moment, Father's shoulders relaxed. "Very well. You have my blessing. And my permission." He shook Rowan's hand and said to Isabella, "Welcome to the family."

She rose up on tiptoe and kissed his cheek. "Thank you, my lord."

Father sputtered again. "Yes, well . . ." He cleared his throat.

The three of them went in search of Isabella's family and found them in the tent next to Isabella's artwork, along with several others gazing upon the pieces.

At their arrival, her guardian turned. "Oh, there you are, Isabella . . ." He trailed off as his gaze moved to Rowan.

Rowan stepped forward. "Sir, I know how you feel about me, but please understand, I love Isabella, and I mean to marry her. To her credit, she prefers not to go against your wishes. My father has given his blessing, and you are the only person standing in our way. Will you give your permission?"

Mr. Williams glanced at his wife, who clasped her hands together in front of her face, nodding. He exchanged glances with Father.

"What do you offer her?" the vicar asked Rowan.

Rowan answered without a pause. "My heart, my name, and my title. She will lack for nothing, and I will love her all of my life."

His heart drummed in his eardrums, so hard that it might have shaken the ground. Mr. Williams considered. Even the wind held its breath.

12

UNCLE JOSEPH PULLED ISABELLA off to the side so they could speak in private. "Do you want him?"

"I do. I love him so very much."

He paused, as if weighing her fervency, and searched her eyes. "Very well." He turned to the waiting gentlemen, the father looking resigned and the son looking anxious. "She says she will have you, so I give my permission for you to marry her."

Isabella threw her arms around her guardian, who had been like a father to her these past few years, then went to Rowan's side and wrapped both hands around his arm. Happiness bubbled over her and filled the world with beauty.

Aunt Missy threw her arms around them both. "I'm so happy for you!" She brought Rowan's head down so she could kiss his brow. "Welcome to the family!"

Rowan grinned. What a beautiful sight!

George walked up with Nancy Stockton on his arm. "Sorry you didn't get chosen this year, Issy. But look—all of your art sold."

She looked around. Sure enough, all of her art had sold signs on them. A few were being carefully wrapped and handed to eager hands.

"That's wonderful!" she said.

With Rowan's love secure, the sting of losing the position

of student to the art master no longer hurt. Perhaps the master artist didn't want her as a student, but clearly people appreciated her art. With a wedding to plan and her new role as a bride, she might be too busy to seriously study art—at least, for the time being.

Rowan stepped toward Nancy. "Miss Stockton, I have been searching for someone who I think might be you. Were you acquainted with John Law, the Viscount Hadley?"

A guarded expression entered her eyes. "I was. I haven't seen him in two years." She glanced apologetically at George.

Rowan reached into his pocket and pulled out the miniature. "Then I want you to have this." He held it out.

She drew in her breath and took it, fingering it reverently. "Oh..."

Gently, Rowan said, "I'm so sorry to tell you that he perished in a riding accident two weeks ago. He loved you. He was sorry he never fought for permission to marry you."

She closed her hand around it and said nothing for a long moment, simply stood with her eyes closed and head bowed. Then she looked up at Rowan. "Thank you for telling me. It means a great deal. It would have been difficult to hear it in passing or reading of it. Please accept my condolences for your loss. He was a good man."

She looked up at George to explain. "I was very young and fell in love with someone far above my station. He used to come here every summer. When he left that last time, I pined away for him. But no longer." She eyed George cautiously.

George nodded. "I understand."

"But the lock of hair is blonde," Isabella said to Nancy, "much lighter than yours."

Rowan pulled out the item in question to show Nancy.

Nancy laughed softly. "My hair was blonde when I was younger. Blondes don't often stay blonde, you know. Many darken to brown, as mine has."

All along, Isabella had expected Ann to be brokenhearted at the news. Fortunately, Nancy had recovered—perhaps after meeting someone who healed her heart. George looked at Miss Stockton with soft affection, which she clearly returned.

The earl beckoned to Rowan, and they stood apart, speaking for a few minutes. Rowan returned while his father got into the carriage and drove away.

Rowan smiled all the way to his eyes and took her hand. "He went to bring Mother here to meet you and your family."

It all seemed too good to be true. "Are you sure you want to marry a simple country girl like me?"

His smile brightened his eyes and stole her heart all over again. He touched her cheek. "You put the color into my formerly black-and-white world. I want you with me always."

Ignoring all the people around him, he cupped her face and kissed her softly, once. A kiss of promise. A kiss of love.

Donna Hatch is the award-winning author of the best-selling Rogue Hearts Series. She discovered her writing passion at the tender age of eight and has been listening to those voices ever since. A sought-after workshop presenter, she juggles her day job, freelance editing, multiple volunteer positions, not to mention her six children (seven, counting her husband), and still manages to make time to write. Yes, writing IS an obsession. A native of Arizona, she and her husband of over twenty years are living proof that there really is a happily ever after.

For sneak peeks, specials, deleted scenes, and more information, visit Donna's website: DonnaHatch.com.

Twitter: @DonnaHatch

www.ingramcontent.com/pod-product-compliance
Lightning Source LLC
LaVergne TN
LVHW021801060526
838201LV00058B/3198